MW00612504

GROUND

BOOK TWO IN THE DOYLE WITCH COZY MYSTERY
SERIES

KIRSTEN WEISS

This book is a work of fiction. Names, characters and incidents are either the product of the author's imagination or are used factiously. Any resemblance to actual persons, living or dead, is entirely coincidental and not intended by the author.

Copyright ©2016 Kirsten Weiss. All rights reserved, including the right to reproduce this book, or portions thereof, in any form. No part of this text may be reproduced, transmitted, downloaded, decompiled, reverse engineered, or stored in or introduced into any information storage and retrieval system, in any form or by any means, whether electronic or mechanical without the express written permission of the author. The scanning, uploading, and distribution of this book via the Internet or via any other means without permission of the publisher is illegal and punishable by law. Please purchase only authorized electronic editions, and do not participate in or encourage electronic piracy of copyrighted materials.

Visit the author website: www.kirstenweiss.com

Misterio Press mass market paperback edition / November, 2016
http://Misteriopress.com
Cover artist: wickedsmartdesigns.com

Thank you for ordering *Ground*, Book 2 in the Doyle Witch cozy mysteries. Show your support for the Doyle Witches by sharing *Ground* with friends in person or through social media. Post a picture of the book with your favorite cup of tea!

Instagram: @KirstenWeissAuthor
Facebook: @Kirsten.Weiss

ISBN-13: 978-1-944767-17-4
ISBN-10: 1-944767-17-7

PREFACE

Low in the Sierras, deep in a forest glade, water pure as luck bubbled through granite. The spring flowed from deep beneath the stone mountain, piercing the veil between here and there.

It had been a long time since Belle had been there.

She knelt beside the spring — her spring — and touched the surface of its chill water. Her fingers left nary a ripple. Even in the summer, the water was ice. Now, in winter, she sensed an unnatural coldness.

Frowning, she stood. Impossible as it seemed, the blight was spreading from her world to this one.

Her fist clenched. White light seeped through the gaps between her slender fingers, illuminating the bones in her hand, and died.

The sisters.

She should have strangled them in their cribs. She'd known they would be a bane to her plans from the moments of their birth. Triplets! Worse, they'd inherited magic from both their parents' lines. And unlike their forebears, they were neither of that realm nor this, but of the modern world.

A generation ago, they would have been married and mothered and dead, her magic having worked its will. But they dallied, playing at being women, and the world changed.

Last summer had been a disaster. She'd sent murder spinning the eldest sister's way. Against all sense, the middle child, the weakest of the triplets, had thwarted her efforts.

It really pissed her off.

CHAPTER 1

My wakeup call came in a pub.

Naturally.

And just as naturally, I didn't listen.

At the table, I twisted a crimson bar napkin between my fingers and hoped I hadn't made yet another mistake.

Fairy lights strung the rafters of the Bell and Thistle. A fake Christmas tree leaned, off-kilter, in a corner beside a stone fireplace.

The bar hadn't changed much since the eighteen fifties. Walls of horizontal, wood slats. An ornate bar with wooden ivy and dancing cherubs. Hanging lamps with red, glass shades. Dark corners filled with the sense of smoke, though no smoke actually existed. Smoking had been long banned in California pubs.

My back pressed into the chair's uncomfortable wooden slats. It felt wrong to be in a pub without my favorite glittery miniskirt and stiletto heels. Tonight, I wore jeans and high-heeled boots and a winter sweater. Sensible clothes, though being here was anything but.

At a nearby table, Mrs. O'Malley, a forty-something with the skin and figure of a twenty-something, shot me the evil eye. She nudged her thick-haired husband, leaned forward, and said something I couldn't hear. I could guess what she'd said. Reckless.

I smiled at her, a real smile, because how could I help it? At the bar, the man I'd loved since forever stood, his black hair coiling about his neck, ordering fresh drinks. Brayden and I were finally together.

Maybe.

Mrs. O'Malley scowled.

I wished I knew a magic spell to open her heart, but we all have our own paths to walk, and it would be wrong to interfere. Mrs. O'Malley was walking hers. Whether she reached her destination was her choice.

Biting my lip, I looked away. Our family doctor, Doc Toeller, sat at the other end of the bar, her platinum blond hair shimmering beneath the hanging lamps.

I couldn't tell who sat beside her. They both faced away from me, but he was young, with thick, brown hair, and he filled his jeans almost as well as Brayden. The mystery man leaned close to the older woman, his hand light on her arm.

I sighed. Doctor Toeller wasn't concerned about what people thought. I wasn't sure why or when I'd started caring.

Brayden, his jeans tight against his muscular thighs, ambled to our table. He set my dirty martini in front of me, and he was close enough for me to smell his cedar scent. Brayden lowered himself into the chair opposite. His forest green, cable-knit sweater set off his emerald eyes, eyes I was struggling not to get lost in.

I heated beneath his gaze, hard and assessing. But Brayden had always had that effect on me, making my skin tingle, my heart pound. It was a problem, like my yearning to lean across the table and brush the lock of wavy, black hair from his forehead. We Bonheim sisters couldn't afford to give our hearts away. That was probably why I'd fallen so hard for Brayden, married and unavailable. Now he was neither, and I had to make a decision.

I wasn't ready.

I raised my chin. This indecisiveness and insecurity wasn't me. Brayden and I were just two old friends getting together. It wasn't a date.

Or was it?

I put down the napkin and gulped the martini.

"You don't want to be here." His bronzed face creased.

"Why would you…? That's not true," I said quickly.

He cleared his throat. "If you think this is too soon—"

"I don't." It was high time to break the cool casualness that had grown between us.

"Because I'm used to waiting for you." He grinned. "You made me wait thirty minutes tonight."

"I did not." I laughed. Had I really?

"Did too."

"Fifteen minutes. Fashionably late."

"Whatever you say."

Brayden was rarely late, and he was always patient. "Look," I said, trying to break the ice, "this is stupid. We've been friends for years. What's wrong with two friends meeting for a drink?"

His green eyes darkened. "Friends?"

I caught myself reaching for the napkin and dropped my hand to the damp table. "I'm only saying, who cares what the town thinks?" It had been my motto for most of my twenty-nine years. A motto I was starting to despise.

"We're not friends," he said.

My head jerked up, my mouth going dry.

"This was supposed to be a date," he said.

"Was?"

He smiled, crooked. "Is."

So it was a date – our first. He was ready and finally free.

Was I ready? So what if I wasn't? Uncertainty had never stopped me before. I was Jayce Bonheim, dammit. Fearless party girl by night, disreputable café owner by day.

Reaching across the table, I laid my hand atop his. A jolt of heat flooded me at the touch. I would finally tell him that I loved him, had always loved him.

But he turned my hand over and ran his thumb along the inside of my wrist, and I couldn't speak a word. Ironic that I, who could tie cherry stems with my tongue, was utterly tongue tied. "Brayden—"

"Tell me about Ground."

"My coffee shop?" I drew my hand away. "Are we making small talk now?"

He raised a black brow. "Is it wrong to want to know what's happening in the most important part of your life?"

"Ground's not the most important part of my life." But it was the one part I hadn't screwed up, the one thing I'd put all of me into, finished. I'd never completed college, one quarter short of a degree in dance and debauchery. Romantic life? Disaster.

And when I'd been accused of murder earlier this year, I'd retreated into avoidance. Thanks to my inaction, my sister, Karin, had nearly been killed. Even Ground wasn't my own success. My aunt had financed the café. When she'd died last summer, my debt to her had been erased. It didn't seem right.

I fingered my gold-plated bangles.

"Then what is?" he asked.

"My family." You. "I think Nick is going to pop the question."

"Your sister's getting engaged? Good for Karin and Nick."

Why had I brought up the possible engagement? Now he'd think I was fishing for my own gold ring. I sighed. Things between Brayden and I had been so easy once. Tonight I fumbled for words.

His thumb made slow circles on my hand, and my breath quickened. "I've missed having you around," he said.

The jukebox thumped an upbeat, country song about betrayal and revenge. Couples moved to the center of the pub and made their own dance floor.

"I've missed you too. Brayden, I..." I wanted to slink out of my chair and kiss him in front of everyone. I wanted—

"Yeah?" He angled his head, his lips hinting at a smile.

"I have to find the ladies' room." I hurried down the narrow hall to the bathrooms.

Someone had opened the high window in the ladies' room, and it was cold as a morgue. Teeth chattering, I did what I needed to do, then washed my hands. The water was ice, cramping my fingers. The bathroom mirror had warped, giving my green eyes a funhouse look and putting more waves in my caramel-colored hair than my curling iron had been capable of. It wasn't just my face that was skewed. Something in the atmosphere was off, sideways, wrong. Not knowing what it might be, I grabbed for the paper towels. The dented bin was empty. I tapped the ancient hand dryer.

Broken.

Grumbling, I wiped my hands on my jeans and went to close the small window.

In the parking lot outside, a pickup's taillights flared.

My pickup.

I stared, baffled. What were my taillights doing on outside when I was in here?

My F-150 reversed from its spot.

"No!" I raced from the bathroom and through the bar's rear exit. Patches of snow dotted the dirt parking lot, and I slipped in the white stuff. My breath left a trail in the winter night air. "Stop! Get the hell out of my truck!"

The truck kept moving.

"I see you!" I shouted.

My truck paused at the parking lot entrance.

I slowed, disbelieving. Was the thief having second thoughts?

Maybe one of my sisters had needed to borrow my pickup. Maybe it wasn't being stolen.

The truck reversed toward me, its wheels skidding in the earth, its engine a whine. Faster and faster it came.

I froze, rooted in the thin snow.

"Jayce!" Brayden shouted.

My brain kicked in. I shrieked and dove, rolling between a Jeep and a red SUV and onto my back. Even in my shock, I noticed the brightness of the alpine stars, an audience watching and wondering what tiny Jayce would do next.

The truck sheered past me and skidded to a halt. It screeched forward, kicking up small stones.

Movements jerky, I stumbled to my feet and watched my pickup fly from the driveway, bounce off the curb and land in the highway. It roared down the road. Its red lights disappeared around a curve.

I brushed snow and wet earth and small stones from my palms. My hands shook. I smoothed the front of my purple knit top and jeans.

"Jayce!" Brayden raced to me, his movements smooth, athletic. "Are you all right?"

My muscles quivered with fear and fury. "Someone stole my truck!"

He grasped my shoulders and gently turned me toward him. "But are you all right?" He ran his hands over me with a practiced touch, calm and detached like the paramedic he was.

And in spite of my rage, I felt myself relaxing, comforted by his expert touch. We were both healers in our own ways, and that had drawn me to him as well. I swallowed. "I'm fine."

"You call the police," he said, grim. "I'm going after him."

For a millisecond, that sounded like a great idea. Then dread iced my stomach. "No."

"I won't do anything crazy, just follow him and let the police know where he is." He dug his keys from his jeans and made a move toward his green Jeep.

"Brayden, no!" Fear dizzied me, and I clutched his muscular arm. For once cautious, I gulped, my teeth chattering. "It's not worth it. It's only a truck. It will come back to me."

He frowned. "Is that your magical thinking talking..." He trailed off. "You're freezing. Come inside, and we'll call the police." Looping an arm over my shoulders, he pulled me close.

We walked inside, his body warm against my side. I pushed from my mind how good this closeness felt.

My truck! I've never cast a curse, and there are a whole host of reasons why it's a bad idea, but how I wanted to zap that thief tonight.

We returned to our table. Shaken, I prospected in my slouchy purse for my phone and called the sheriff's office. (It depresses me that I have that number on speed dial.) I made a report to a bored-sounding woman on the other end of the line. She told me I'd need to come to the station tomorrow.

"He was heading east," I said.

"We'll put out an alert," she said, her voice flat, uninterested.

"What are the odds I'll get my truck back?" My voice reached a crescendo, shrill.

"We'll do our best."

I knew pessimism when I heard it. "Thanks," I said. We exchanged more information, and I hung up.

"You should have told them the guy tried to run you down," Brayden said. "That might have lit a fire under their butts."

I rubbed my lips. "I'll tell them tomorrow. I'll have to go to the station then to fill out a report." Which assumed my truck wouldn't have been found by that time. My teeth clenched. Was my baby headed for a chop shop?

"I'll take you home," he said, a hopeful lilt in his voice.

"Thanks." I knew he wanted me to say everything was okay, but my mood had been ruined. As first dates had gone, this had been a disaster. Was the universe trying to tell me something? Of course it was. The universe was always speaking, my sister, Karin, insisted. I just never listened.

I let Brayden pay the bill. Speaking in short, senseless sentences, we drove west, down the mountain highway and past tall redwoods.

At a sporting goods store, he turned off the highway and into Doyle. It stood at an odd, middle place — not quite alpine, not quite foothill. Quaint, gold-rush era wooden buildings, frozen in time, lined the mining town's Main Street. Wine tasting rooms, restaurants, tourist shops had replaced dry goods stores and barns.

He turned the Jeep off Main Street and veered into an alley. We glided to a halt beside a two-story brick building. A wooden, exterior stairway switchbacked to my upstairs apartment. "Here you are."

"Yep." I made no move to unbuckle my seatbelt. I had to say something, make things normal between us. But things would never be normal.

"I'm sorry about your truck," he said. "If you need a lift anywhere, just let me know."

"Thanks. Brayden..." My speech grew rushed. "I'm sorry our date crashed and burned."

He blinked. "It didn't. You were there." Brayden stepped from the Jeep and walked around to my side, opened the door.

I unhitched my belt and stepped out. "Our first date was a disaster. I barely knew what to say to you. You probably thought I was ditching you when I ran out of the bar."

"It crossed my mind." He stood close and angled his head as if to see me better.

"And it ended early because someone stole my truck."

"Why don't you know what to say to me?"

Because a part of me thought this was too soon. Because a part of me felt guilty, that this was a betrayal of his dead wife. Because I wanted him so badly. My pulse raced. "Maybe my truck being stolen was a sign."

"A sign that you need better security. Cars get stolen. Did you even lock it?"

No, I hadn't. I rarely did, because cars didn't get stolen in Doyle. My nostrils flared. "Are you saying it's my fault my truck was stolen?"

"No. It's the car thief's fault. I'm just saying, not everything that goes wrong is a sign of doom."

Easy for him to say. Brayden wasn't a witch.

CHAPTER 2

I burrowed deeper beneath the soft, bamboo sheets. Stolen truck. Wrecked first date. Mrs. O'Malley. My eyes flashed open. Mrs. O'Malley? Why was I worrying about her?

Gray light filtered through the skylight above, reflecting off the white-painted walls. Ivy twined up the brick. I let myself sink into the illusion of being in a forest. I breathed quietly, trying to feel where this anxiety was really coming from.

My truck, okay, the theft still pissed me off. And Brayden — we'd been so careful not to admit our feelings for each other for so long. But the anxiety tangling in my chest was more than that. It reminded me of...

College. And I don't think about college a lot.

But once, after a night at a frat party, I'd awoken with my eyelids stuck together from the glue from my false lashes. I couldn't open my eyes, couldn't figure out what was happening. This morning felt a lot like that.

Squinting, I looked up through the skylight. A gray mass of clouds formed in the sky.

I shut my eyes and rolled over. It was Saturday morning. My coffee shop was closed on weekends — we catered to the local, workaday crowd — so this was my sleep-in day, and I wasn't going to waste it with worry.

The cat, Picatrix, leapt onto my bed and mewed in an annoyed tone. I say "the" cat rather than "my" cat, because no cat ever really belongs to you. Picatrix was a stray I'd taken in a few months back.

She kneaded her paws into my side.

"Five more minutes," I mumbled.

The claws came out, tiny needles piercing fabric and skin.

"Fine." I groaned. "I'll feed you."

I sat up and stroked her soft, black fur.

Someone banged on my door. The cat tensed, then leapt to the multi-colored throw rug. A striped blanket cascaded to the floor.

I checked the clock on my end table. Ten o'clock. What kind of monster would bang on my door at this hour on a Saturday?

I stumbled out of bed. Tying a silky kimono robe around my waist, I hurried to the exterior door and threw it open.

The cat bolted between my bare legs and darted outside.

My sisters, Lenore and Karin, grinned. Karin's smile was laced with repressed annoyance.

"I forgot something," I said, "didn't I?"

We were triplets, though we didn't look alike. Karin had auburn hair and a perennially serious expression. She was also an inch taller than my five-six and her features softer.

Lenore had honey-colored hair, a fair complexion, and the body and movements of a dancer. She was also an inch taller than me. I'd been gypped in the height department.

Even though we all had different noses and chins and eyes (mine were green), people pegged us for triplets. Feature-by-feature we were different, but the sum of our parts had a certain sameness.

"You forgot our brunch," Karin said, accusing. She blew into her hands then jammed them into the pockets of her thick, navy pea coat.

I opened the door wider and let them inside.

"Sorry," I said. "It will only take me a minute to get ready." I slammed the door behind them to keep out the cold.

My sisters shared a doubtful look.

"It will!" I said, defensive.

I hurried to my bedroom and pondered my closet. And all right, so maybe it did take me a while to decide if I should wear the sapphire turtleneck or the ruby-colored sweater.

I sped through dry brushing my skin. It was the single morning ritual I stuck to with any regularity, just because it felt so damned good. The brush still smelled of cinnamon oil from when I'd anointed it yesterday. The soft bristles tickled, acting as a gentle loofah and waking up my skin.

Since my sisters were waiting, I took a super-fast shower and didn't bother with my hair. My bed head didn't need much aside from a quick finger combing anyway.

I nudged shut the bedroom door to hide my unmade bed. Kicking a zebra-print throw pillow out of the way, I slipped my thick, ruby cable sweater over a babydoll dress. Applied my makeup and made a gesture, casting my morning glamour spell. Found a pair of thigh-high, suede boots to keep (most) of my legs warm.

When I emerged, Lenore was sitting cross-legged on one of my kilim throws over the distressed wood floor. My sofa was at her back and framed by the white-painted, ivy-covered brick alcove. She scribbled in her black-leather notebook — poetry, no doubt.

Karin lounged on the sofa and flipped through a fashion magazine, which meant she was bored out of her mind.

Shy Lenore, who worked in a bookstore and wrote poetry for fun, dressed like a bookish bohemian. Today she wore a long, white, flowing coat over white jeans, a pale blue knit top and matching infinity scarf. I couldn't tell what Karin had on beneath her coat aside from a pair of skinny jeans.

"I'm ready," I announced.

"You're going to freeze," Karin warned, eyeing my bare thighs critically.

"But I'll do it in style." I pirouetted, and she made a face. "Besides, it's not like it's snowing."

My cell phone rang. Anyone who knew me wouldn't call at this hour on a Saturday. Had the police found my truck? I scrambled for my purse, tripping over a discarded stiletto heel and stumbling to my couch. Brightly patterned cushions tumbled to the floor.

I answered, breathless. "Hello?"

"Ms. Jayce Bonheim?" The man's voice sounded official, and my heart jumped.

"Yes," I said, "that's me. Is this the police?"

Karin straightened on the sofa. She and Lenore shared another look. I ignored it.

"Yes, this is the sheriff's office. We've found your truck."

I squealed. "You found it! When can I get it back?" But an odd lump formed in my stomach. Suddenly apprehensive, I asked, "Is it in one piece?"

"Yes, we'd like to take you to the site. A squad car will be there in five minutes."

"Five...? But—"

The person hung up.

I stared at the phone, puzzled.

Karin rose. "What's going on? Is there a problem?"

"Someone stole my truck last night, right out of the Bell and Thistle parking lot. The police say they've found it."

"That's good news," Lenore said. "You were lucky."

"Yes," I said, uncertain. "They're sending a squad car over to take me to the site."

"Did the thief crash it?" Karin's lips pursed.

"I don't think so." I twisted the bangles on my wrists. "They said the truck was okay." But picking me up and driving me to my truck didn't track with what I knew about the Doyle Sheriff's department. Unless someone at the department was trying to make up for wrongly arresting me for murder last summer.

"What's wrong?" Lenore asked.

I shook my head. "I don't know. I've just got this feeling something's off."

My sisters shared another look.

"Oh, come on," I said. "You know how it is with my feelings. I'm totally intuitive."

"Yeah," Karin said. "It is odd that they're offering to play taxi service so you can get your truck."

"That's what I thought." I gnawed my bottom lip.

"Maybe they feel bad about arresting you earlier this year?" Lenore said.

"I thought that too." Another cool thing about being triplets is we tend to think alike, even if we aren't alike.

Heavy footsteps clumped up the stairs outside.

Twin lines appeared between Lenore's eyebrows. "That wasn't five minutes."

A heavy fist pounded on the door.

I opened it, my sisters clustering behind me.

Two uniformed sheriff's deputies stood at the top of the steps. Even though I'd known they were coming, I flinched. The hard expressions on their faces brought back bad memories. But this wasn't a murder. It was a stolen truck. My truck. I was the victim.

"Jayce Bonheim?" the gray-haired man asked. I guessed he was in his late forties, early fifties, but his face had that perfect, waxy sheen shared by all Doyle's residents.

"That's me," I said.

"We've found your truck. Will you come with us, please?"

"Let me grab my purse." I swooped to the couch and collected my bag, and then a thick, sand-colored scarf that was lying beside it. Looping it around my neck, I followed the police onto the landing outside.

The chill air stung my cheeks, and the clouds seemed to darken. I shivered. "Sorry about brunch," I said to my sisters, clustered in the open doorway. "Maybe we can do lunch instead?"

But Karin was dialing her cell phone. "I'm calling Nick."

"Maybe I should come with you." Lenore tugged on a hank of blond hair looped over her shoulder.

"Sorry, ma'am," the younger cop, his face spattered with freckles, said. "We're only allowed to bring Ms. Jayce Bonheim."

"It's cool," I said with more confidence than I felt. Something was definitely Up, but I hadn't done anything wrong. I'd called in the stolen truck right away. Brayden had witnessed everything. I'd be fine.

I followed the sheriff's deputies downstairs. The younger man opened the police car's rear door.

Stomach twisting, I slid inside. Criminals rode in the back. People under suspicion rode in the back. But it would be a tight fit if I smashed into the front with the two men, so maybe I was reading too much into seating arrangements. I tried to relax, but my skin hummed with tension.

We drove out of town and turned east, driving past the Bell and Thistle and higher into the Sierras. Patches of snow dotted the ground. The pine forest thickened.

We rounded a sharp bend, and the squad car slowed. Half a dozen sheriff's cars and a coroner's vehicle parked on the side of the road in a thin layer of snow. Too many emergency vehicles for a simple stolen truck.

The deputies stepped from the squad car.

I reached for the door, realized there were no inside handles.

The phone in my fist rang, and I checked the caller ID. It was Nick, Karin's boyfriend. "Hi, Nick."

"What's going on?" His deep voice rumbled.

"I'm not sure."

The older cop opened my door for me. "No phone calls, ma'am."

"The deputy is telling me I can't talk," I said.

"Where are you?" Nick asked.

"Just up the highway about twenty miles."

"I'm on my way," he said.

"No calls," the deputy repeated.

I hung up. "Sorry. I didn't know." I was about to see something other people weren't supposed to know about. Either that, or I was under suspicion, and the cops didn't want me tipping off any partners in crime. Restless, I turned the cheap and cheerful bangles on my wrists.

I slid from the squad car and adjusted the beigey scarf around my neck.

"Your truck is this way, ma'am." The deputy gestured toward a narrow, dirt track. Thin drifts of snow powdered the shoulders.

I knew this place. The road was short and led to a rough parking lot for a local trailhead.

In silence, we walked down the dirt road, lined by pine trees smelling faintly of vanilla — sugar pines. A chipmunk raced past us and spiraled up a tree. It glanced back at me, its beady eyes seeming to warn, "be smart and beat it, lady!"

The road sloped downward. We rounded a bend, and the track opened up to a parking area. My charcoal pickup sat parked near the trailhead, flanked by two granite boulders covered in a mantle of snow. Its front doors hung open, and Sheriff McCourt herself rummaged inside the cab.

I surged forward, but the younger deputy grasped my arm. "Wait here."

The older deputy strode to my truck and said something to the sheriff.

Sheriff McCourt backed from the cab, removed her wide brimmed hat, and clawed her hands through curly, blond hair. She clamped the hat on her head and strode toward me, her expression impassive. Her thick, greenish-brown jacket was zipped to the collar. "Ms. Bonheim. Thank you for coming."

"What's going on?" I rubbed my arms and looked around at the milling officers.

"Is that your truck?" the sheriff asked.

"Yes. I reported it stolen last night. What's wrong?"

"Why do you think something's wrong?"

"The coroner's van," I said. "Was there an accident?"

She glared at the older deputy, and his lips pressed together. "Come this way," she said to me.

Goosebumps on my thighs, I followed her to the rear of my pickup. Karin had been right about my short dress. I hated it when she was right. I hated it more that I was about to see something awful. And it didn't take a witch to foresee that ending.

"Did you leave anything inside your truck bed last night?" she asked.

"Leave anything?" I thought about it. "There was an old tire."

"Only a tire?"

"I had to change a tire last week. I hadn't gotten around to taking it in for recycling yet." Changing a tire is hard work when you don't get much practice. After I'd finished, I'd dumped everything into my truck bed and forgotten about it, ignoring the tire iron's rattling.

"Look inside the bed."

I reached to brace my hand on the tailgate.

"Don't touch anything," she said sharply.

My hand dropped to my side. Standing on my toes, I peered over the gate. A beefy, red-haired man lay curled beside the old tire. His skin was bluish. His eyes stared. Blood stained his scalp. Dizzy, I sucked in my breath. "That's Matt Zana."

"You know him?" the sheriff asked.

"He's a handyman from Doyle." My voice wobbled. Well, I'd known there'd be a body. The coroner's van had been a flashing red clue. "He installed some shelves in Ground a few months ago." And he'd been a major pain in the butt. Matt had jabbered constantly, demanding my attention. Little wonder it had taken three times longer to install the shelves than planned. In the end, I'd almost wished I'd tackled the job myself. But he was dead, and that washed away a swarm of sins.

"A few months ago?" the sheriff repeated. "When was that, exactly?"

"Um, September." Sticky sorrow weighed my chest. Matt was married. I knew, because a good bit of his conversation had been complaints about his "old lady," Melanie. The poor woman. Did she know he was dead? I didn't think they had any kids, and that now seemed like a good thing.

A steller's jay settled on a pine branch and dislodged a coating of snow, which rustled to the ground.

"When's the last time you saw him?" she asked.

"Saw him?" I parroted. "I don't know. I think he was at Antoine's Bar last week."

"What about the Bell and Thistle?"

"Where my truck was stolen?" I shook my head. "No, I didn't see him there last night, if that's what you mean." I tried to read her expression and failed. Why did you bring me here?

Her eyes narrowed. "Tell me about last night."

"I was in the ladies room. The window was open, and I looked out. It overlooks the parking lot. I saw my pickup being backed out of its spot."

"Backed out?" she asked, her tone edged with suspicion.

"Yes, that's how I parked it. Why?"

"In my experience, it's easier to back a truck of that size into a parking spot then drive in from the front."

"Well, I didn't back it in," I said. "The Bell and Thistle has a narrow lot, and there were a couple other big trucks already parked there. They stuck out, making it hard to maneuver. So I drove straight in."

"Do you remember who owned those other trucks?"

"Who else was in the bar, you mean?"

"Yes."

Weak beams of gray sunlight streamed through the pine branches. The jay shrieked, the deep-blue tuft on its head twitching.

"Mr. and Mrs. O'Malley were there." They'd been giving Brayden and me the evil eye all night. "Hank, the bartender was working that night, and Doc Toeller was there. I don't remember any of the others."

"Really?" She raised a brow. "You're quite the party girl. I'd have thought you'd have known everyone there."

I folded my arms. Normally, I might have. But last night I'd only had eyes for Brayden. And if I was telling the truth, I'd been avoiding the looks of the others — some curious, some hostile. All of Doyle knew how Brayden's wife had died, and that I'd been a suspect in her murder. "Well, I didn't. I was there with Brayden Duarte."

"Ah yes, the widower." Her lip curled. "You two didn't waste much time."

I sucked in my breath and stiffened. "That's really none of your business."

"Maybe it is, maybe it isn't. Then what happened?"

"I ran out to the parking lot and shouted for the thief to stop. The driver reversed hard, like he was going to run me down. I had to dive out of the way. Then Brayden ran outside. The truck drove off, and we called the police."

"The thief tried to run you down?" Her voice was flat, disbelieving.

"Brayden was there," I sputtered. "He saw everything. You can ask him."

"I will."

"Jayce!" a man's voice called.

We turned, and the sheriff muttered a curse.

Nick Heathcoat, flanked by two deputies, strode toward us. Tall and dark haired, and with the chiseled looks of a Greek statue, it was little wonder Karin had fallen for the man. Not only was he an awesome lawyer, he hadn't freaked out when she'd hit him with the double-barreled news that we were witches and under a curse.

I hadn't even broken the news of the curse to Brayden yet, though he was down with the witchcraft. And I knew with a sick certainty it was no accident a body had been found in my truck. Witches can't afford to believe in coincidences.

Nick flashed a grim smile. "Good morning, Jayce, Sheriff. I understand you have some questions for my client."

Sheriff McCourt's lips peeled back, shark-like. "Strange that Miss Bonheim would call a lawyer for a stolen truck."

"Strange that you'd bring out a team of crime scene investigators for a recovered truck," he said.

The sheriff turned to me. "We need to discuss this at the station."

"Discuss a stolen truck?" Nick asked.

"Discuss a murder."

He didn't say anything for a moment. "What's going on?"

"Her truck is a crime scene." The sheriff's mouth pinched. "We found a body inside."

"The truck thief?" he asked.

"Maybe," she said. "Miss Bonheim will need to come to the station to provide a statement."

A statement? I wrapped my arms around my sweater. "But I don't know anything!"

"And yet," the sheriff said, "bodies keep dropping around you. Strange that this is the third murder in Doyle you've been connected to."

"I had nothing to do with this," I choked out.

"Your truck says otherwise." She motioned to the two deputies who'd collected me from my apartment. "O'Reilley, Sully, take her to the station."

CHAPTER 3

In the end, the deputies didn't take me to the station. Nick did.

The lawyer and I were escorted to a cinderblock interview room. There, we waited.

"I hope I'm getting the friends and family discount." Muscles rigid, I paced the linoleum floor. My gaze flicked to the clock above the one-way mirrored glass. An hour had ticked past.

He grinned. "Don't—"

The metal door opened, and the sheriff strode inside. She unzipped her jacket and dropped her broad-brimmed hat on the table. "We've spoken with Brayden Duarte." She scraped a metal chair away from the table and sat.

My shoulders relaxed. "And he told you what happened."

"Your stories corroborate," she said.

"Then there's no further reason to hold Ms. Bonheim." Nick rose, his chair, rasping against the linoleum floor.

"Actually," she said, "there is. Ms. Bonheim was a suspect in the death of Mr. Duarte's wife. And now he's her only alibi, after a date at the murder site."

"What?" I cried out.

"Mr. Zana was killed at the Bell and Thistle?" Nick asked.

"In its parking lot, where both Ms. Bonheim and Mr. Duarte admit they were drinking. We only have their word for it that one of them didn't kill Mr. Zana and then call in her pickup as stolen after the body had been disposed of."

My muscles were barbed wire, wound taut. "That's ridiculous."

"Is it?" she asked. "How long have the two of you had a relationship?"

"I've known Brayden for years," I said.

"That isn't what I'm asking."

"I know what you're asking." Annoyed, I tugged on my scarf, strangling myself. "And it's none of your damn business."

Nick laid a hand on my arm.

I bit my lip and slumped in the metal chair. Dammit, dammit, dammit!

"You're fishing," the lawyer said. "You already know who killed Mrs. Duarte last summer. You have a confession and multiple witnesses. Ms. Bonheim has told you everything she knows about the theft of her truck. She won't be answering any more questions."

I took the hint and clamped my mouth shut.

Nick and the sheriff argued my fate for a good twenty minutes. I sat, nails leaving white moons in my palms. Nick was a good lawyer. He'd helped me before. I needed to trust him to do his job. But was this my future? Being blamed for every murder in Doyle now? And poor Matt – he deserved justice. If the cops focused on me, he wouldn't get it.

Finally, the sheriff rose. "You're free to go, Ms. Bonheim. But don't leave town."

She escorted us from the interview room and to the front entrance, a high atrium area dotted with potted plants. Light filtered through the steel clouds and into the skylights.

My sisters leapt from two, soft chairs.

"Jayce! Are you all right?" There was a thready, nervous jolt to Karin's voice.

"I'm fine," I said. "Nick saved the day again."

Karin smiled up at him.

He took her hand. "I didn't do much."

"He's being way too modest," I said. "How did you know I'd be here?"

"Brayden called us," Lenore said. "The police questioned and released him. He figured they'd do the same to you."

My heart jumped. "Is he here?" I scanned the atrium. Two uniformed deputies walked past, coffee mugs in their hands.

"No," Lenore said. "I think he called us from the road."

A soft, despairing noise escaped my throat. "Oh." I swallowed. Well, what had I expected? That he'd hang around the police station waiting for me?

Yes.

I should have left it alone. But automatically, my phone was in my hand, and I was calling him.

This is Brayden. Leave a message at the tone.

"Hi," I turned away from the others. "Thanks for letting Lenore and Karin know what happened. Call me when you can." I hung up, disappointed.

"Let's get out of here." Karin nudged my shoulder.

Nick checked his watch. "My parents should be at my place in Angels Camp any minute. I need to get back to town."

"Right, Angels Camp, the big city." Karin laughed and kissed his cheek. Angels Camp was the nearest "big" town to Doyle, "big" being extremely relative. "Do you mind if I—"

"Stay." He pushed a lock of her auburn hair behind her ear, and I could feel the bands of heat emanating from them both. "You three have things to discuss. Jayce? No more talking to the police without me."

I nodded and watched him stride away. Where was Brayden now? What was he thinking? Anxiety bloomed in my chest.

"Lunch?" Karin said.

Eating beat worrying about Brayden. Starving, I agreed.

We jammed into Karin's red Ford Escort, and she drove us into Doyle. She parked on the side of the road, beside a yellow cottage that had been converted into a wine tasting room. Twinkle lights twined its white bannisters and looped from its peaked roof. The garden's rose bushes had been pruned, dormant for the winter.

We walked down the uneven sidewalk to our favorite brunch spot, Alchemy. My steps were quick, and I forced myself to slow. Rushing wouldn't cool my agitation.

The hostess, Bianca, led us across the red-tiled floor to a table between an open fireplace and a blank wall. She left us with menus.

Karin didn't bother to look at hers. "Is everyone else thinking what I'm thinking?"

I laid my menu on the white tablecloth. "It's too much, isn't it?" I didn't have to think or analyze. The unease, the sense of a malevolent force watching, was growing.

"The two murders last summer and now Matt Zana?" Lenore asked. "This has to be..." she glanced around, making sure no one was nearby. "...the curse."

"Not the curse," Karin said in a low voice. "The unseelie. It's been toying with us ever since Ellen got sick and..." She blinked rapidly, her eyes growing wet.

Died. I looked away from Karin. Our aunt, a powerful witch, had protected us for years. But when her cancer had spread, all hell had broken loose.

Our family was cursed — every Bonheim woman died at the birth of her first child. The child was always a girl, who carried on our tragic tradition. As triplets, we were the first to break the pattern. This time, there wasn't just one Bonheim woman, fighting alone. There were three.

I'd been the firstborn. Then Karin, with the umbilical cord wrapped so tightly around her neck she'd turned blue. Our mother had died with Lenore still inside. The doctor had given Lenore up for dead, but a nurse had pulled her from our mother's corpse. Lenore had lived.

What we hadn't understood until recently was that someone — something — was behind it all.

A headache flared behind my temples. Not only was the fairy – or unseelie – keeping our curse alive, but it was messing with the entire town. Once every seven years, a hiker disappeared into the woods, never to be found. But there were other oddities as well. The unseelie spell caused some to be unlucky, others charmed, and everyone crazy good looking. Living in Doyle was like existing in a high-priced catalog, surrounded by ageless models. I gnawed my bottom lip. What would the three of us look like if the unseelie's influence ever broke?

Oh, well. I couldn't worry about that, and ignorance was bliss. Life had been so much easier before I'd started worrying about family curses. Now everything was weighted with meaning and dark portents. Admitting how I felt about Brayden was a trap. And a murder...

"All right." Karin tapped a slender finger on the tablecloth. "The last time this happened, a human was at fault. We only suspect the unseelie was guiding the crime to our door. Now that it's happened again, I think we can say this has moved from a hypothesis to a theory. It can't be coincidence that Jayce has been implicated in a murder again. But what does it mean?"

"It means the police will blame Jayce," Lenore said. "The fairy—"

"Unseelie," Karin corrected. She was a stickler for defining things properly, and an unseelie was a beautiful and nasty type of fairy. We weren't dealing with cutsey winged creatures.

"The unseelie," Lenore said, "will make sure of that."

"Karin," I said, "the last time this happened, you were able to see the dark connections between people." One of Karin's gifts was the ability to see the energetic connections between people. She was able to detect the dark cords of the unseelie's influence, all linking to a local fairy spring. Maybe there was another way to use Karin's talents? "If you looked at the suspects, could you see a cord connecting them to the murder?"

The waitress materialized at our table. She pulled a notepad from the pocket of her short, black apron. "Can I get you anything to drink?"

"Iced tea," Karin said.

Lenore and I ordered the same, and the waitress bustled away.

"No," Karin said. "Now that Matt Zana is dead, any energetic connection to him is gone. Besides, the darkness is all over Doyle, in nearly everyone's auras." She shuddered. "It's kind of creepy."

"Who are the suspects?" Lenore asked.

"For the murder or the fairy?" I asked.

"Let's start with the murder," Karin said.

"Matt was married," I said, thoughtful, "and the spouse is usually suspect number one." I blew out my breath in frustration. "I don't know who else. When Matt installed those shelves at Ground, all he seemed to do was talk. I wish now I could remember what he'd said." I should have listened, but I'd been busy, and Matt had talked way too much.

Karin brushed her auburn hair behind her shoulders. "This may be an opportunity."

I crossed my arms. "I might be charged with murder again, and this is a good thing?"

"You won't be charged," Karin said. "And the unseelie's been lying low for the last six months. If it's involved, then that means it's using its magic again, and that means we have a better chance of tracking it."

"How?" I asked.

Karin colored. "Magic always leaves a trail. Have either of you two sensed anything?"

"Should we… try?" Lenore asked. "Now?"

"It can't hurt," I said.

Famous last words.

We stilled, and my sisters' eyelids drooped.

It was a simple sensing ritual, beginner's play. I closed my eyes and sent my energy into the ground, imagined it extending like a root system, wrapping around the rocks, digging deep into the soil.

A burst of acrid power flooded my head in a seething rush that was both erotic and alarming. I gasped and grasped the edge of the table to keep from falling from my chair. Bands of energy snapped and roared, overwhelming. My hold on reality loosened, and I was plummeting. I wrenched myself free and opened my eyes.

"Oh." Karin's voice trembled.

Lenore, even paler than usual, blinked.

"That wasn't normal," Karin said, "was it?"

"No," Lenore said in a shaky voice. Her face had turned paper white. "It wasn't."

Lenore worked shamanically, with the spirits in Upper and Lower Worlds. I didn't want to ask what she'd experienced. Whatever it had been, it had frightened her. It took a lot to scare Lenore.

I loosened my death grip on the table. Movements uneven, I grabbed my glass and gulped water, spilling some. I wiped my chin with the back of my hand. "So. That's new." I was an earth witch. I didn't fall. I grounded. Whatever we'd brushed against wasn't playing by magical rules.

"Big magic," Lenore agreed.

"We can try this again," I said, "in the woods. If we do this closer to the fairy spring—"

"NO," my sisters said in unison.

"Why not?" My fingers drummed the tabletop. "It's the first time we've sensed her since—"

"Are you kidding?" Karin's knuckles whitened on her water glass. "That nearly knocked me out of my chair. I don't want to get closer to that power. Not until we're ready."

"But how will we know we're ready?" I asked. "Maybe we should try again. Maybe this is our chance."

Lenore shook her head, her blond hair a rippling wave. "Karin's right. It's too dangerous. Not until we've got a better plan."

"Do you think whatever's attacking us is waiting around to develop a plan?" I asked, incredulous.

Karin angled her head. "Were either of you able to get a lock on where the magic was coming from?"

"We know where it's coming from," I said. "The spring."

"Which we agreed to avoid," Lenore said.

"We know there's power in that spring," Karin said, "but the unseelie has been living among us for over a hundred years. She's somewhere here in Doyle, watching."

"We think," Lenore corrected.

"I'm connection girl," Karin said. "I think this is up to me. Why don't I—"

The smiling waitress reappeared. "Hi, are you ready to order?"

"Um, yeah," I said. We put in our orders and watched her depart, weaving through the tables and vanishing into the kitchen.

"I'll figure out the human angle while you work the unseelie side," I said. "It was my truck. This is about me." Six months ago, I'd let Karin do all the heavy lifting. I'd trusted the universe would work things out for the best, like it always had. This time would be different.

"Great," Karin said, looking pleased. "You take the mundane investigation, I'll focus on the magical."

"What am I?" Lenore asked. "Chopped liver?"

"Help Karin," I said quickly. "You've got the connection to Lower World, and that's where unseelie energy comes from, isn't it?"

Lenore ran her thumb along one of her brows. "Not exactly. Fairies have their own plane. I've never tried to find it."

"I'm not sure it matters," Karin said. "This unseelie, for whatever reason, is working in our world. That's where we need to find it. I'm assuming we'll have the best chance of taking it out on our home territory. But if we work together on this, we'll have a better shot."

I nodded. Karin was the weakest of us magically. She was the last person to lead a magical crusade. But a human had killed Matt Zana. I wanted to keep my sisters as far away from the killer as possible.

An elderly couple sat at a nearby table, and our conversation turned to mundane topics. My new spelled coffee scrub. The famous mystery writer Lenore had snagged as a speaker at the bookstore she managed. Karin's latest paranormal romance novella. You'd think she'd had enough of paranormal romance, since she basically lived one. But Karin insisted you should write what you know.

After lunch, I let my sisters think I was walking home. Instead, I turned off Main Street, striding down the short hill and past the park. Its white-painted gazebo stood forlorn and abandoned in the winter. The grass was brown, dotted by patches of sodden earth.

I rolled my shoulders, and my boot skidded on an icy patch of earth. Maybe I shouldn't have chosen spike-heeled boots for a walk to Brayden's. Or maybe I'd chosen the thigh-high suede because deep down I knew I'd be seeing him.

Twenty minutes later, I strolled through a residential neighborhood of wide lawns and snaking fences. Brayden lived in a green, ranch-style house. I crunched along its gravel driveway, passing beneath oaks. Clusters of mistletoe hung high in their branches, out of reach.

Brayden's Jeep sat in the carport. That meant he was probably home. I checked my phone. So why hadn't he returned my call?

Thighs freezing, I rang the bell. I hopped in place, blowing into my hands, trying in vain to warm myself.

After a few moments, the door opened, and Brayden's tall form stood silhouetted behind the screen. "Jayce." There was a long moment. "What are you doing here?"

I smoothed my turtleneck, and wondered yet again if I'd made a mistake. "Can I come in?"

"Right. Sure." He opened the screen door, and I followed him into the entryway. Thick parkas hung on the pegs by the door. A tumble of boots lay on the rag rug.

I waited for him to say something.

He didn't.

"Karin and Lenore told me you called them to let them know I was at the station," I said. "Thanks."

"You're welcome," he said cautiously.

"What happened?"

He turned and walked into the kitchen.

I followed the scent of coffee and bacon. A pan crusted with scrambled eggs lay at an angle in the too-small sink. But the metal counters were clean. A coffee maker perked. He didn't offer me any.

"Brayden? What did the police ask you?"

He stood at the counter, his strong back to me. "They asked me about last night, when we'd arrived, what I'd seen."

"And you told them I arrived late," I said, my stomach plummeting to the toes of my boots.

He turned and met my gaze. "I had to. I wasn't the only one at the bar who noticed. People saw me waiting."

"It doesn't matter." I rallied. "We both saw my truck being stolen."

"I'm not sure the police believe the two of us. Jayce, it was a mistake for you to come here."

"Why?"

"Because people are looking at us like we're lovers who colluded in murder."

"What people? The cops have to look at everyone with suspicion."

"Not just the cops," he said. "The murder is going to get around town soon enough, and so will our role in it."

"We didn't have a role in it!"

"Jayce, think." He rested his hands on my shoulders, and his warmth flowed through me. "We live in a small town. Our relationship doesn't look good. This can hurt you."

"Or are you afraid it will hurt you?"

He dropped his broad hands, his green eyes darkening. "You know I don't care about that."

"Maybe you should." My breath was quick, noisy.

"The closer we appear, the weaker our alibi seems."

"So what? Neither of us had any reason to kill Matt. The worst he ever did to me was talk too much and work too slow, and I'm sure he did that to all his clients. If that was a motive for murder, he would have been bumped off long ago."

"You're not wrong," he said. "But it's not about what's true. It's about what people think is true."

"Who cares what people think!"

"I care what people think about you. A bad reputation could hurt your business."

"But—"

"Stay away from me, Jayce. It's only for a little while, until things blow over."

Heat spurted from my chest to the roots of my hair. Fine. I spun on my heel and strode out the front door, letting the screen door bang. I couldn't believe Brayden was being such a... coward. But he wasn't a coward. He probably thought he was doing something noble by pushing me away.

I didn't like being pushed.

CHAPTER 4

Picatrix didn't return for dinner.

And that cat never missed a meal.

Maybe she'd picked up on my mood and decided to steer clear of the apartment.

I couldn't read magic into everything, could I? Feeling muddled, I leaned against the window frame and watched people stroll along Main Street below. Everyone had a place to go. Everyone but me.

I called Lenore. "Hey, witch. Want to come to the Bell and Thistle with me?"

Lenore sighed. "You mean you need a ride."

"We agreed I'd investigate. I can't do that without my truck, not when there's no taxi service in Doyle." There wasn't a bus service either. If it wasn't within walking distance, you'd better have a ride. Fortunately, most destinations were walkable. Unfortunately, the Bell and Thistle wasn't one of them.

There was a long pause, and I worried she'd say, no. Lenore and Karin weren't much for bars. "All right. Karin and I aren't doing anything to find the fairy tonight anyway."

"You're not?" I asked, surprised.

"Karin had to drive to Angels Camp — she's having dinner with Nick's parents."

"Meet the parents? Yikes." Things really were getting serious between Karin and the lawyer.

"They drove up from San Francisco. I don't think she could get out of it."

I doubted she'd wanted to. Karin longed for stability, and being part of Nick's family, now that ours was just the three of us, would appeal. "When can you pick me up?"

"Thirty minutes?"

"Perfect." I'd use the extra time to amp up my glamour spell. The pub was familiar territory, but a little extra flash wouldn't hurt, especially when I needed to charm information from witnesses.

We said our goodbyes, and I glanced toward the cat door. It wasn't like her to stay out this late on such a cold evening.

Frowning, I headed to my bathroom. I'd decorated it like a sultan's bath — plenty of gilt and a shimmering, cushioned footstool. I lined up a dozen essential oils on an ornate tray and, stripped to my lingerie, sat on the footstool.

I massaged lavender oil into my first chakra and visualized my roots extending into the ground. "Let me be rooted."

I selected more oils and rubbed them into my chakra points, calming. Everything would be all right. I'd get through this, maybe not quite with style, but I'd get through.

Rising, I lifted my palms and made a latticework of my fingers. I breathed my glamour incantation and parted my hands like a curtain. The top of my scalp tingled, telling me it was working. I pulled my clothes on, ran my scented fingers through my hair, touched up my makeup.

I'd just finished blotting my lipstick when Lenore knocked at my door.

I hurried to open it.

Lenore had piled her blond hair in a loose bun. Gold earrings dangled from her ears. She seemed to blaze against the night in her white, knit coat.

I squinted at the jewelry. "Are those rabbits?"

"I liked them," she said, defensive.

A gust of wind struck me, and I shivered. "They're cute." I grabbed my purse off the couch, and we clunked down the wooden exterior staircase.

On the road to the Bell and Thistle, we talked about everything but the murder and the curse. Lenore drove the slick highway at a crawl, her face puckered with concentration. "Are you sure going to the Bell and Thistle is such a good idea?"

I sighed with impatience. She and Karin were so careful. I could have walked to the pub in nearby Arcadia faster. If it hadn't been so cold and dark, I would have walked. "Someone may have seen something the night my truck was stolen."

"And it's a bar."

I grinned. "That too."

Lenore pulled into the dirt parking lot and blew out a relieved breath, her hands unclenching on the wheel. She parked between two SUVs, and we squeezed out of her Volvo. The Bell and Thistle looked nothing like an English pub. A log cabin, its peaked, green roof stretched low beneath the pines. Rock music and golden light flowed through its windows in welcome.

We crunched across the light drifts of snow to the front door. Lenore clutched her purse to her chest. I was willing to bet her notebook was inside — she took it everywhere.

Widening my strides, I grabbed the door handle and waited for Lenore to catch up. A bell the size of a man's head hung nearby. I grabbed its thin rope and clanged the bell. The sound died quickly, as if swallowed by the earth and snow.

Lenore's laugh was hollow. "You ring that bell every time, don't you?" She glanced toward the dark woods.

"It's tradition." Shaking off my unease, I opened the door, and a roar of cheerful noise greeted us.

The pub was packed, every table full. People stood shoulder-to-shoulder at the bar, but I intended to get a table, and my magic was on tonight.

Sure enough, as we squeezed through the crowd, two men abandoned their small, round table near the window. I dropped my coat over one chair and sat. A gust of wind struck the window, rattling it like bones.

As soon as Lenore was settled, I sprang up again. "Hold the table," I shouted over the noise. "I'll get our drinks." And talk to the bartender.

Lenore shouted something after me. Assuming it was her drink order (she liked hard cider), I kept moving. The same bartender, Hank, who'd been here last night was on duty again tonight. Hank knew me. He'd talk.

I scooted through the mob at the bar and ignored the looks the men gave me.

Catching the bartender's eye, I smiled and rested my elbows on the bar. Twinkle lights wound around the bottles on the mirrored shelves behind it.

Hank tossed his blond head and grinned back, mischievous. A dedicated skier, his skin had that nearly-burnt look. He spent his every spare moment higher up in the Sierras on the slopes. "So," he shouted, ambling toward me. "You've got yourself in trouble again, lady."

I rolled my eyes and leaned closer to be heard over the music. "It's not as much fun as you make it sound."

He sobered and bent toward me. "No, I guess it isn't. The police were asking about you. I told them you were here."

"It was the truth." I shrugged. "No reason not to tell them. Did you see Matt Zana here that night?"

The music stopped. A redhead ambled to the juke box and pondered the selections.

He shot me a look. "Jayce, what are you up to?"

"Nothing!" I laid my palm over my heart and winked.

"There is such a thing as interfering in a police investigation." Roughly, he polished the bar with a damp rag.

"Who's interfering? Can't I gossip with an old friend?"

He raised a brow. "So we're friends now?"

"You wound me. Come on. Did you see Matt?"

He shook his head. "Nope."

"Did you see anything, well, weird?" I asked.

"Weird like you and Brayden acting like two nervous teenagers? That was definitely not the Jayce I know and love."

I arched a brow. "Maybe you don't know me as well as you think."

An AC/DC song started up, and he barked a laugh.

Someone waved at him from the other end of the bar.

"I'd better take this order," he said. "What do you want?"

"A cider and a dirty martini."

He nodded and moved off.

The place was busy and loud and shouting another serious conversation would be tough. Maybe coming here on a Saturday night hadn't been the best idea. But Mrs. O'Malley and her husband were in their usual spot. And the same waitress was on duty as well.

I frowned, twining my finger in my bolo necklace. Now that I thought about it, the pub had been unusually empty last night. I'd been so nervicited about being with Brayden, I hadn't paid much attention before. But last night had been Friday. The pub should have been hopping. It was almost as if the place had cleared out for the murder.

I shook my head. I had to stop reading that unseelie curse into every odd thing that happened in Doyle.

"And this isn't even in Doyle," I said aloud. Technically, we were in next door Arcadia, which consisted of a general store and a handful of homes scattered in the woods.

Hank slid the drinks in front of me. "Yes, it is."

I blinked. "What?"

"The Bell and Thistle is in Doyle."

"No it isn't."

"Is too."

"The sign a hundred yards down the road says Arcadia. That's between this pub and Doyle."

His even, white teeth flashed. "Everything past our parking lot is Arcadia. But the property this bar stands on is a little island of Doyle."

"How did that happen?"

"I don't remember the whole story," he said. "It had something to do with taxes and Prohibition."

"Wait. Including the parking lot?" The skin prickled on my scalp. "That's in Doyle too?"

"Of course. That's our property. Weird, huh?"

I picked up the drinks. "Weird," I muttered. It had become my word of the day. I made my way through the crush of bodies to Lenore.

She sat stoop-shouldered, writing in her notebook, which was lying flat upon the table. Her hair shimmered golden beneath the hanging lamps.

I smiled. Typical Lenore. I loved that she did her own thing, no matter the circumstances or what people thought. We were a lot alike in that way.

I sat across from her, and she looked up.

"Learn anything?" she asked.

"Did you know this pub is in Doyle?" I rubbed the hollow of my neck.

She frowned, glancing around the crowded bar. "I'd forgotten, but now that you mention it, I do remember reading something about it. I think there's an old newspaper article with the story. It's framed, hangs on the wall."

"There is? Where?"

She pointed toward the front door.

Huh. I must have walked past that clipping hundreds of times. It figured Lenore, who was no barfly, would actually read it. "Don't you think that's odd though?"

"People do all sorts of funny things to get around the law."

"No, but..." I leaned across the table. "The curse. The fairy's connected to Doyle. We suspected the fairy can only work its mojo there. And here we are, in Doyle, where a man was killed and put in my pickup."

She set down her pen, twin lines appearing between her brows. "We don't know that the unseelie can only work its magic in Doyle."

"But we do know Doyle is where all the weirdness happens. Where the beautiful people — even the beautiful buildings — are. It's like we've been preserved beneath glass. Doyle is where the hikers disappear every seven years. Doyle is where the fairy spring is. And Doyle is where we are right now."

"But why would an unseelie care about human boundaries drawn on some map?"

"Maybe the boundaries aren't human." The words tumbled from my mouth as if someone else had said them.

Her blue-gray eyes clouded. "What do you mean?"

"I'm not sure." I turned my head. "Forget it."

A buxom waitress slid past us, her long legs tanned beneath her green miniskirt.

I waved to her. "Kelly!"

She turned, and I signaled again. Kelly had been here last night, and I wasn't just here to drink. Honestly.

The waitress leaned her hip against my chair. "Hey, girlfriend. The cops were asking about you."

"I know," I said, tingling sweeping up my neck and face. "Did you see or hear anything strange last night?"

"Nope." She shook her head. "Sorry."

"What about Matt Zana? Did you see him around?"

"Yeah, I did. I went outside for a smoke break and saw him in the parking lot."

"What was he doing?" I asked.

"Looked like he was waiting for someone."

"What time was this?"

She glanced at the beamed ceiling, stained with decades of smoke before the no-smoking laws had kicked in. "Around eight?"

I nodded. That tracked. I'd run outside at about a quarter after. So who had Matt been waiting for? And why had he waited outside, on a freezing night, instead of inside the nice, warm pub? "What about—?"

There was a crash, and Kelly swiveled toward the sound. She sighed. "Someone's knocked the tree over again. I've gotta take care of this." The waitress plunged into the crowd.

"That's interesting," Lenore said.

The O'Malleys rose from their table.

"I'll be right back." I leapt from my chair and wove through the crowd. By the time I caught up with them, the couple had reached the narrow entry. "Mrs. O'Malley?"

She turned, and a series of expressions flashed across her oval-shaped face. Disapproval. Pity. And finally, a fixed pleasantness. "Hello, Jayce. And you don't have to call me Mrs. O'Malley anymore. We're both adults." She brushed a curtain of black hair behind her ear.

Her husband turned up the collar of his thick, canvas coat and said nothing. His sideburns had begun to turn an elegant silver.

"Sorry, it's habit." I fumbled for words. "How are you?"

"Fine."

We stared at each other.

"I saw you here last night with Brayden," she said, her tone growing chill. "The police asked us about it. I don't think it's very nice."

I wondered what wasn't nice. The murder? Being questioned by the police? Brayden and I together at last? "I wanted to ask you about that too. Did you see Matt Zana or anything else strange last night?"

She zipped her black parka. "I don't think it's something we should discuss," she snapped.

"Saw him walking," her husband said.

She pressed her thin lips together. "The police won't want us talking about what we saw."

"They didn't tell us not to say anything." He ruffled his dark hair. "Saw him walking down the highway. I guess he was walking here."

"What time was this?" I asked.

"We got here around seven-thirty, so it must have been just before then. It's only a mile between here and Doyle."

"This is Doyle," his wife said, and tapped the framed newspaper clipping, yellowed with age.

"You know what I mean," he said.

"Right. Thanks." I nodded to them. Matt had walked to the pub. Had the killer come here on foot as well? That would explain why he or she had used my truck to dispose of the body — it was handy and the killer didn't have one. But why dispose of the body at all? Why not leave it in the parking lot for someone to find, or drag it into the tree line?

Mrs. O'Malley's nostrils flared. She turned on her heel and slammed out the door. Meekly, her husband followed.

I returned to our table and dropped into my chair.

Lenore looked up. "Well?"

I told her what they'd said and what I'd thought.

She closed her notebook on a poem. "Either the killer needed your truck because it was his best option for moving the body, or the killer was trying to frame you."

Snakes writhed in my gut. Matt's murder had just gotten more personal.

Thanks to Lenore, I woke up late Sunday morning without a hangover. She'd been obviously bored at the Bell and Thistle, so we'd left as soon as I was certain there weren't any more regulars to interview. Disappointment clouded my chest. Last night's investigation had not been a raging success.

Curled on my sofa between two silken pillows, I sipped my coffee. I wasn't going to slack off like last summer. I might not have cracked the case at the Bell and Thistle, but there were other leads to follow. Matt had been married. Though I didn't know his wife, Melanie, beyond saying "hello" at the grocery store, she deserved a condolence call. It was my truck that had been used to dispose of his body, and I'd known him slightly. That gave us a connection.

I dressed in jeans and my sapphire turtleneck. The clouds outside were gunmetal gray, threatening snow. I grabbed a thick, blue shawl-sweater from my closet and tossed it over my shoulders.

Blindly, I stared at the contents of my purse, fallen across the dining room table. Picatrix still hadn't returned. I'm usually philosophical about cats – they come and go when they will. But I didn't like the timing of her departure.

Cats knew things.

Shaking off my worry, I jammed my wallet into my back pocket and left.

I walked down Main, passing pristine nineteenth-century wood and stone buildings. OPEN signs hung outside the shops and tasting rooms. Like the rest of the town, they catered to tourists on their way to or from the ski resorts higher in the mountains.

I stopped in a bakery and bought a cinnamon coffee cake for Melanie Zana.

Pink box gripped in both hands, I trudged up Oak Street and tried to figure out what to say to Melanie before I arrived on her doorstep. I'm sorry for your loss seemed inadequate.

Thinking hard, I wound my way up residential streets lined with cutesy Victorian-era cottages. I'd had to mail Matt a check once, so I had his address (though it had taken me some time to find it). He lived in an updated Victorian cottage. The gate to the Zana's house stood open, and I walked into the garden, filled with lavender. The flowers had vanished for the winter, and the lavender bushes were gray spikes coated in frost.

Nervous, I walked up the steps, my feet loud on the wood. Shifting the box to my hip, I knocked on the door.

After a few moments, it opened.

Melanie clung to the door. Her eyes were red-rimmed, and the scent of vodka wafted on the stale air from the house. The widow's red hair was a tousled flame. Her peaches and cream skin had turned blotchy. She rubbed a thin hand across her cheek. "Yes?"

Sympathy slowed my heartbeat. "Hi. I just wanted to see how you're doing and how I can help."

"Oh." She turned and walked inside, leaving the door open.

Taking that as an invitation, I followed. The house was in chaos. In the green-carpeted living room, boxes were stacked on boxes and magazines stacked on top of them.

The widow wandered into the kitchen and screwed the top onto a bottle of vodka. She set it in the freezer.

I shifted a stack of unwashed plates on the green tile counter into the sink, and set my box on the counter. One of the overhead fluorescent lights was out, washing the kitchen in dull shadow.

"I brought a coffee cake," I said lamely. "I'm so sorry for your loss."

"Are you?" Melanie slouched to the counter and opened the box. She dug her hand into the cake and ripped off a slice, took a bite.

My stomach fluttered. "Of course."

"Of course," she said, her voice mocking.

"Maybe this is a bad time." And a really bad idea.

She quirked a reddish brow. "When's there going to be a good time?"

Good point. "Melanie, I—"

"I know."

"You... know?"

"I know."

I shifted my weight. "I'm sorry, I don't—"

"You were sleeping with him."

I gaped. "What?"

"You. Were. Sleeping. With him." She jammed the rest of the piece of coffee cake into her mouth, chewed a couple of times and swallowed.

Heat snuck across my cheeks. "With whom?"

"Matt."

I reared away, shocked and angry. "Your husband? No!"

No, and hell no. I had a strict no-married-men rule, and especially no to men who talked non-stop about themselves.

"I know you're lying. Why else would you be here?"

I fought my rising anger. Sure, I liked to have fun, but my reputation in Doyle had careened way out of line with my actual behavior.

And none of that mattered now. Melanie was distraught. Bereaved. She deserved to be cut some slack. Besides, she couldn't seriously think I'd been fooling around with her husband. "Matt hung shelves for me. That was all there ever was between us. I came here because I wanted to see how you were doing, and let you know I'll help in any way I can."

"Sure." Her mouth slackened, and she looked away, her pale face a careful blank.

This had been such a bad idea. "I'll get out of your hair. But the offer stands." I edged toward the kitchen door.

"He knew things."

I stopped. "What?"

"My husband knew things." She dug out another piece of coffee cake, scattering cinnamon crumbles across the tile counter.

"What sort of things?"

"He knew things about you. Your sisters."

I froze, fear scorching my gut. This wasn't the dark ages. People didn't hang witches anymore, at least not in America. But there was witchcraft and there was witchcraft, and if Matt and his wife had somehow found out... "Melanie, what do you—?"

The doorbell rang, and her head swiveled toward the sound.

"Fantastic," she said, eyes dull. "More visitors." She wove from the kitchen, her shoulder banging into the doorframe.

Matt — they — knew things? What did that mean?

The sound of the door opening. Voices. Footsteps moving towards the kitchen.

Melanie slouched into the room followed by a middle-aged couple — Eric and Rasha Gertner. Eric was a regular customer at Ground. I saw his wife less frequently.

Super-model tall and with broad shoulders, Rasha looked her elegant self in black, wide-legged black slacks and a sweater. Her trademark red scarf looped around her neck. Rasha's long ebony hair cascaded down her back, and her brown eyes glistened with sympathy.

Her husband wore jeans. A house flipper, denim was his staple, no matter the occasion. Today though, he'd put on a blue-and-white checked shirt beneath his thick, wool coat rather than his usual tee. A jagged, white scar marred his forehead, and I tried not to stare at the mark.

The kitchen's fluorescent light buzzed in a last ditch attempt at life. It flickered, went gray.

Eric stopped short in the entry. "Hi, Jayce. What are you doing here?"

Rasha shot her husband a look. "She's paying condolences, like a good neighbor."

He scraped a hand through his thin, blond hair. "Sorry. It's just strange to see you outside your natural habitat."

"Matt did work for her," Rasha said. "Of course Jayce would come."

"You heard about that?" I asked, surprised. The shelf installation hadn't been a big job, even though it had seemed to go on forever.

One corner of her mouth edged upward. "It's a small town. Matt worked for everyone." She hugged Melanie. "What a terrible, terrible thing. What do you need us to do?"

The widow sagged in her arms. "It's all so unreal," she whispered. "I can't believe he's gone, that someone murdered..." Her voice hitched.

"We don't know he was murdered," Eric said.

"He was hit in the head and left in the back of a stranger's truck," the widow said.

Crossing my arms, I gazed at the tips of my narrow-toed boots. So the police hadn't told her about my truck's role in the murder. Should I? Melanie would learn the truth eventually. Not telling her would make things weird. I glanced up.

Eric shifted his weight, his arms crossed in unconscious imitation of me.

I cleared my throat. "It wasn't a stranger's truck. It was mine."

Silent, they stared at me.

"Someone stole my truck," I said. "The police found it the next morning with Matt inside the bed. They called me out to see."

Melanie straightened, pulling away from Rasha. "You? They called you? He was my husband!"

"I don't know why—"

She blanched. "Get out! Just get out!"

"Melanie," Rasha said, "it isn't her fault."

I edged backwards, into the open doorway. "Melanie, I'm sorry—"

"You were always around my husband," she shrieked. "I always suspected you two. And now you've killed him. Get out!"

I fled, stopping only when I was on the uneven sidewalk. Heart pounding in my ears, I stopped beside Eric's red Porsche. Heavy footsteps clomped down Melanie's porch steps, and I turned.

"Hey." Eric walked down the wooden steps. His face reddened. "She didn't mean it."

But I was pretty sure she had. "It's okay," I choked out. "She's upset."

His shoulders slumped. "Yeah. But she didn't mean it." He shuffled his feet. "So the police called you to view the body?"

"Yeah."

A frigid gust of wind rustled the dry lavender spears.

"Did they say anything?"

I shook my head. "Not really." Not aside from don't leave town.

His smile was sympathetic. "Violent death is rough on everyone."

I nodded. Eric would know. His first wife had died driving drunk fifteen years ago. The crash had nearly killed him too. All Doyle knew the story, a story that I imagined played out in his mind every morning and night when he saw that scar in his bathroom mirror.

"Look," he said, "don't worry about Melanie. Matt was a player. Everyone knew it, even her. But we know you two weren't involved."

Slovenly Matt was a player? It didn't seem possible. "Thanks," I said, uncertain. "I didn't know he was..." I fumbled for the right words. A cheater? That didn't seem right to say out loud.

Eric smiled, wry. "Good with the ladies?"

"Plural?" My brows rose.

"Hey, everyone knows you were way out of his league. Everyone except for maybe Melanie. I wouldn't worry about it."

"But who was he seeing?"

"Ah, I really couldn't say."

"Do the police know?"

He shrugged. "I'm not sticking my nose into their business. If you know what's good for you, you won't either."

"But who—?"

He turned and strode up the steps. The door banged shut behind him.

Matt? A player? I tried to reconcile that with the Matt I barely knew. He'd told me some salacious stories. They'd been inappropriate, but I'd put up with them. But if he'd cheated on his wife, that opened up an entire minefield of motives. Had Melanie killed him in revenge? Had one of his girlfriends gotten fed up when he wouldn't leave his wife?

My fists clenched. If the police believed Melanie's accusation, they might have real reason to suspect I'd killed the man.

CHAPTER 5

I stalked down the road. I'd never been accused of cheating with another woman's husband before, and it stung.

Sunlight glinted off a windshield, blinding me. I winced, slowing.

Who cares what anyone thinks?

But...

I slowed for an SUV backing from its driveway on the steep hill. But if the police believed I'd been involved with Matt, would they think that gave Brayden a motive for murder? How had this happened? I'd done the right thing, dammit! Brayden and I both had.

How many times had I taken the light, the easy, the wrong path? But the no-married-men rule was inviolate, and Brayden had been out of bounds.

My nostrils flared. Okay. Think. Not everyone believed I'd been involved with Matt. His wife, who'd just lost her husband, had accused me, and she'd been drinking. But she'd seemed so certain. Had Matt said something about me to make her think...?

I adjusted the blue shawl across my shoulders. I shouldn't have gone to Melanie's house. I wasn't a private investigator. I'd told Karin last summer I wasn't a detective, and I should stay out of the investigation then. So I should stay out of it now. I had a lawyer. Things had worked out before. They'd work out again. And my real problem wasn't the murder. The root of the problem was that damned curse and that damned unseelie, whoever it was.

I turned down a looping road. Homes sat far from the street, their windows dead eyes. Skeletal oaks rustled, their branches bare in the winter's chill. A dirty red Honda sat in a rough parking lot beside the trailhead. I climbed over the fence's rungs to the trail, and my skin tingled. This was the official forest boundary, and the woods knew it. I paused, mastering myself.

"Hello," I whispered to the spirits of the place. "I mean no harm. May I enter?"

A breeze rippled the tops of the oaks.

Taking that for approval, I stepped onto the narrow forest trail. Its beginnings paralleled a wooden fence that marked the boundary between woods and humans. I passed Karin's shingled, craftsman-style bungalow, its backyard dotted with sage. A single-path, lavender labyrinth spread across the center of her backyard.

For a moment, I hesitated. The labyrinth was our power spot and would be a good place to meditate. But I needed to work off my energy first.

I turned onto the trail weaving up the hill, toward the fairy spring.

Frost laced the tips of the tall, dried grasses. A granite stone, covered in pumpkin-colored lichen, pointed like a finger to the soot-colored sky.

I hiked onward, my anger dissipating. The forest was my place. Since last summer, my sisters and I had been avoiding it, and I'd resented our banishment.

A squirrel loped past and vanished into the roots of a twisted oak. I scanned the ground with an eye for foraging, then remembered that I hadn't brought any containers or knives and grimaced. My self-imposed restriction from the forest ended today.

I climbed higher, into the redwoods. The shadows deepened, and I pulled my shawl more tightly about me. In a gully to my left, a stream splashed. I passed a redwood stump, damp and broken and lined with moss. Chunks of bark littered the path. I continued up the hill. Patches of snow whitened the forest floor.

A broken branch from a douglas fir lay across the path. I shifted it, noting its location. I'd grab it on my return trip so I could harvest its needles for tea.

Pausing to catch my breath, I imagined roots flowing from my feet and into the earth, grounding me. I visualized branches flowing from the top of my head, reaching high above the forest canopy. Energy, white from the sky, red from the earth flowed into me, steadying, and my heart unfolded like a spring flower. Why had I kept myself away from this place?

I ran my hands across the bark of a sugar pine. Its vanilla scent coiled around me.

"Hello again, old friend."

I pressed my palm to its bark, feeling for the thrum of its energy and struck a sickening wall of ice.

I blinked.

Frowning, I studied the tree. The needles on the lower branches had gone yellow.

"What's happening to you?" I muttered, running my hands over the rough bark.

Uneasy, I studied the surrounding trees. They all looked okay, but a cold stone weighted my stomach. Maybe I was misreading the symptoms. I wrapped my arms around the pine, hoping no hiker would see and think I was nuts. Pressing my ear to its trunk, I asked permission for my energy to mingle with its own.

There was no resistance. I extended my aura, gently probing inside the tree.

The vanilla scent turned bitter, sugar burnt black. My gorge rose.

Stepping away, I muttered an incantation, a request for healing, and laid one palm against the tree. I visualized dark energy being sucked from the tree through my palm and then into a violet flame.

I let my arm drift down the trunk, feeling for other spots of heaviness. Whenever my arm stopped, I repeated the magical clearing, until I found no more blocks. Then I laid my right hand on the trunk again, my left palm up, and asked my helping guides to send healing energy into the tree. Warmth flowed through me, and I sensed the tree warming as well.

Unhooking a clear quartz pendant from my necklace, I buried it near the tree's roots. I patted the tree's side. "I'll come back later to see how you're doing."

The wind whispered in its branches, a soft sigh.

Healing work always pumped me up before it drained me, and my heart lifted. I trotted down the narrow, earthen steps cut into the hillside and to the fairy spring. I'd reached it before I remembered I wasn't supposed to be here. But I was only looking. No big deal.

Water poured steadily through a break in the granite and into a crystalline pool. I averted my gaze. Karin had nearly drowned by magic after looking too close. I might be reckless but I could learn from others' mistakes.

Barren branches arced above the spring. Browning ferns, coiled like snails, clustered about the pond. A creek tripped over stones and rambled along the valley floor.

The spring had to be the source of our problems. Karin had told me when she'd been pulled inside the spring, she'd had a vision of another world. This spring might not be the fairy's home, but maybe it was where it had come from or come through. If so, the nearby trees might be able to tell me something about our enemy. Trees had a long memory.

So what if we'd agreed Karin and Lenore would take charge of the magical investigation? I was here, and what my sisters didn't know wouldn't hurt them.

I knelt between the roots of a redwood, moss and damp earth cushioning my knees. "Greetings, old one. I'm Jayce."

Above, the branches whispered their approval.

Laying my palms on two thick roots, I extended my senses. I felt the rustling of the leaves. The footsteps of two hikers, a mile away, trembled through the root system. Down the valley, a crow landed heavily on a branch, setting it swaying. A far-off pinecone thudded to the ground, its seeds scattering. Heat and life and green flowed through my veins, and for a moment, I was unsure where I ended and the forest began.

Something came through this spring. I asked the trees. Something powerful, something magic, walked into this world. Do you remember?

Power flowed through me like a river, sweet and sensual, and I gasped, aching with desire. My lips parted, warmth radiating throughout my body. It was close to what I'd felt at the restaurant, and that should have frightened me. But I hadn't tasted magic then. I'd never tasted magic before this. The energy now was like warm honey, carnal and decadent. I wanted more.

In that instant, I was the forest. I was the stones and water. I was the earth and could sense its turning.

This was true magic. Why had I been playing with spells and incantations and charms? My witchcraft was a pale shadow of this earth magic, and I half rose, excited, feverish, thinking to tell my sisters.

But they wouldn't understand. How could they? Everything they'd been taught by our aunt — and how misguided she'd been — was child's play. And I certainly couldn't explain this power to Brayden. Not that it mattered. Nothing mattered. Not our silly attempts at magic. Not...

Why did you come here? The voice in my head was a masculine growl.

Startled, I swayed.

There was something... A reason... It had to do with my sisters — not that they mattered.

Don't they?

And Brayden — not that he mattered.

Doesn't he?

I shook my head. The energy flow was electrifying, lifting the hair on my arms. Lifting me. But I was in control—

You are not.

— and Brayden could...

My sisters...

Reality flooded in, and I remembered.

I wasn't supposed to be here.

Nausea choked my throat, and I was on my hands and knees retching, my fingers digging into the soft earth. My back arched, painful. I rolled to my side, panting, my muscles limp.

Disoriented, I flopped onto my back and stared up at the canopy of branches. The spring had brought me here, and I'd let it happen. It had tried to exert control and almost succeeded.

I clenched my fist. I had beaten it.

A murder of crows roosted in the branches above me. The branches swayed, as if the birds had just landed. The branches crackled, brown and dead. An old saying popped into my head on counting crows:

One's bad,

Two's luck,

Three's health,

Four's wealth,

Five's sickness,

Six is death.

I sat up on my elbows and blinked. There were a lot more than six crows, so they weren't a death omen. A desiccated branch plummeted to the ground and landed with a thud beside me.

Scalp prickling, I picked it up, looked around. The branch was completely dead. All the plants surrounding the spring were withered. The redwood needles were yellow. How had I not noticed before?

A crow croaked above me.

The others joined in, cawing and making their odd clicking noises.

I stumbled to my feet and braced my hand on the nearby redwood for balance. The reddish bark was cold. Frowning, I laid both palms against it. Then, still dizzy, I pressed my body to its trunk, extending my aura to feel its energy.

There wasn't any.

I stepped backwards and away, craning my neck and now seeing the pattern in the foliage. A ring of dead and brown plants encircled the spring. Fear spun inside me like a torturer's wheel.

"What the hell?"

The crows above fell silent.

Slowly, I gazed up and into the branches. The ebony birds watched, their beaks glistening.

Trying not to make any noise, I backed up the first few earthen steps away from the spring. My heel caught on the hillside, and I stumbled, turned, ran, taking the steps two at a time.

The crows burst from the redwoods. Dead leaves and twigs and needles rained down on me. I brushed them away. The back of my hand struck feathers, and there was an angry squawk.

Terror thundered in my ears. I reached the top of the steps and pelted down the trail.

Something sharp and solid hit the back of my head, and I cried out.

A crow skimmed above me. And another. The crows zipped past. One snatched at my hair, and I swatted it away.

A beak stabbed at my hand.

I ran faster, letting gravity assist in the downhill, ignoring the stitch in my side whenever I reached an uphill slope.

The birds swirled around me, striking, cawing, and I shrieked, flailing my arms. This was an Alfred Hitchcock nightmare, and I tried to blot the image of the eyeless corpse from The Birds. This wasn't happening. It wouldn't happen. I was a witch, dammit. I was one with nature, and—

"Ow!"

Another crow had dive-bombed me, striking the top of my head.

I crested the final hill and pelted down the trail. Karin's shingled cottage — safety — lay on the other side of the low, wooden fence. I vaulted the stile into her garden. The lavender labyrinth lay between me and her rear door.

I hurtled the first clump of lavender bushes. The crows soared high into the air, shrieking.

I jumped the second row, the third, the fourth and glanced up.

The crows circled, a swirling cauldron, flying higher above the labyrinth. I jumped the fifth row, the sixth, and stumbled to a halt in its center.

The birds were a midnight wall of confetti, their wingbeats percussive. None penetrated the airspace above the labyrinth.

Yet.

Afraid to move, I stood in the center of the labyrinth. It was a sacred place, and I'd violated it's magic by jumping its lavender "walls" rather than walking its single path to the center. But the crows weren't entering.

I gulped down painful breaths. How long would the labyrinth's magic hold them at bay?

A breeze kicked up, tossing dried grass and leaves and mingling with the beat of the crows' wings. The sound grew to a roar, and I clapped my hands over my ears. Words formed in the beating of wings, the whistle of wind.

Rose rabbit.

The rear door to the cottage flew open, and Karin raced into the backyard, her auburn hair streaming behind her. "Go away!"

The birds soared high into the air and vanished over the hill.

Shocked, I stared at my sister.

"Come inside." She smoothed the front of her blue, v-neck sweater. Her chest heaved. She was breathing almost as hard as I was.

Movements stiff, I clambered over the lavender bushes. At the entrance, I backed out. That last bit of ritual, at least, I could manage. "So the labyrinth works." My voice trembled. I climbed the three wooden steps to her door.

"What happened?" She shut the door behind us and locked it.

I beelined for her kitchen, hoping there was something stronger than coffee inside. "I went to the fairy spring."

"Alone?" She slammed shut one of the blue cupboard doors. "What were you thinking?"

I hadn't been thinking. That scared me. I'd been fairy struck, in a daze, but I couldn't admit that to her. She'd freak out. "I've been to that spring hundreds of times on my own. I thought the trees might tell me something about whatever had crawled out of it. And now I'm thinking I could use a drink."

Her lips flattened, and for a minute she didn't speak. "I've got wine." She moved to the white-tile counter and uncorked the half-empty bottle of zinfandel atop it.

I leaned against the counter and tried to relax.

"It's a bit early for drinking." But she poured a goblet of the red wine and handed it to me.

"It's five o'clock somewhere." I gulped it down. The wine was full bodied and peppery on my tongue.

She frowned, disapproving. "It's not even lunch time."

I clasped the goblet to my chest.

"So," Karin said. "The crows. You did magic to find the unseelie, and you promised you wouldn't."

"I didn't exactly promise."

She glared at me.

"Look," I said, "something new is happening. There's a blight. I noticed it in one of the redwoods over the fairy spring, and I cast a healing spell. I thought I'd succeeded. So I went down to the spring and worked through the roots to learn if the fair... unseelie had used the spring as a portal to our world."

"What did you see?"

"I didn't see anything," I said. "I felt."

"Felt what?"

"Power."

She angled her head. "What kind of power?"

How to describe it? I gazed into the wine glass, unable to meet her eyes. The power had been almost erotic. I didn't mind that so much, but the disdain I'd had about my sisters and Brayden shamed me. "Something dark and bigger than me. I couldn't control it. It had me."

"Had you?" She turned from me and grabbed a sponge from the sink. She wiped the counter with hard, jerky motions. "How did you break free?"

Frustrated, I rubbed the back of my neck. "I'm not sure. I kept hearing this voice, reminding me of what was important."

"One of your spirit guides?"

"No. This was new. Different. And it said..." I bit my bottom lip.

"Said what?"

"I thought I heard the words, rose rabbit."

She turned to me. Water dripped from her sponge onto the wood floor. "The rose rabbit again. What the hell is it? I've researched and researched, but I can't find a rose rabbit in any literature or anywhere else for that matter."

Morose, I studied my empty glass. "It would make a good name for a wine."

"But what is it? Is the rose rabbit the name of the unseelie? Or is it something else? Was it involved in the crows' attack on you?"

Since I didn't have any answers, I poured another half glass of wine.

"Forget the rabbit for now," she said. "So you broke the link, and the crows attacked?"

"They chased me all the way from the spring to the labyrinth."

"You must have provoked the attack somehow."

I stiffened. "Thanks a lot!"

"You know what I mean."

Someone rang the doorbell. Karin left to answer it.

I examined my hand. Blood trickled from a scratch on its back. Setting the glass down, I stepped to the sink and washed my hand with lemon soap and water.

Karin returned with Lenore, her long, cream-colored duster flowing about her slim form.

"What happened?" Lenore edged into the cramped kitchen.

I didn't ask how she'd known something had happened. Lenore always knew. I explained.

"Were you hurt?" Lenore leaned against the fridge and folded her arms.

I probed my scalp. No blood stained my fingers. "Doesn't look that way."

"They chased you all the way from the spring?" Lenore asked. "That's nearly two miles, and there's lots of open spaces for them to attack. I'm surprised all you got were a few scratches."

"Weren't they enough?" I grabbed my goblet and took another swig of the zinfandel. Bad enough someone had used my truck in a murder and an evil fairy was out to get us. Now, even the local fauna wanted me dead.

Lenore shook her head. "I thought we were going to tackle the fair…"

Karin shot her a look.

"…unseelie problem together," Lenore said, her blue-gray eyes accusing.

Karin shrugged. "I said the same thing."

"Well," I said, "I'm kind of stuck on the question of who stole my truck and killed Matt Zana. I had to do something."

"You could have asked us for help before running into the forest," Lenore said.

"I wasn't planning…" I stopped myself. If they knew I'd been drawn to the spring, they'd really go nuts. "Have you done any better?"

Lenore pinked. "Maybe."

"Oh?" I asked.

"Matt may have been having an affair with the new realtor," she said, "Phoebe England."

I straightened off the counter. "Where did you hear that?"

Her flush deepened. "The bookstore."

"Really?" Who'd of thought a bookstore could be a hub of gossip?

"The owner, Mike, told me she and Matt were giggling over the Kama Sutra," Lenore said. "She bought it, and they walked out together."

Not definitive, but definitely worth following up on. "Thanks, Lenore. That's good intel."

"Intel?" Karin grabbed the wine bottle and jammed the cork in, not noticing it was empty. "Maybe we shouldn't be sticking our noses in this at all. Last time—"

"Last time you did all the work and nearly got killed," I said sharply. "I'm not letting that happen again."

"Exactly," Karin said. "I nearly got myself killed. Doesn't that tell you anything?"

"This is my problem, my responsibility." Coming from me, the words sounded false. But this mattered, and I was damned if I was going to let a killer push me around.

CHAPTER 6

Frustrated, I stared at the ingredients lined up on my kitchen counter. Dried rose petals in a mortar. Epson salts in a box. Glittering blue bottles of essential oils and dried herbs.

The attack at the fairy spring that morning had left me rattled. Worse, Brayden hadn't returned my call today. And my sisters and I hadn't come up with any better answers for what had happened at the spring. So I'd spent the afternoon online, searching for rose rabbit references. I don't know why I bothered. Karin was a master researcher, and if she said nothing was there, nothing was there.

Nothing was there.

I glanced out the kitchen window overlooking Main Street. The light from the street lamps cast beer-colored triangles across the road. Its pavement glittered black, damp from a sudden shower. A harvest moon – burnt orange and pendulous – rode low over the Sierra peaks. On the sidewalks, people stopped outside restaurants to chat.

And Picatrix still hadn't returned. I'd called the pound, but no black cat had been brought in. I was starting to worry, even if she wasn't my cat.

I lit a cluster of candles, turned off the lights, and centered myself, setting my intention.

It was the hour of Venus, and the moon was in Taurus — an excellent time for the magic I planned. I returned to the kitchen and ground the rose petals.

I was making bath bombs spelled with love and confidence to sell in Ground. It wasn't usual café fare, but the bath bombs made a pretty display in their wooden bowl. And lots of people bought my used coffee grounds scrub, so the bath bombs were a natural, complementary product.

In my aunt's favorite cast iron cauldron, I stirred herbs and dried roses and other, more mundane ingredients. I muttered blessings over each.

Carefully, I added drops of lavender essential oil, and then water. The citric acid in the mix fizzed, and I winced, stirring fast. The fizz was a natural reaction to the liquid, but I didn't want to activate the citric acid too soon.

When it looked right, I grabbed a fistful of the salt mixture and squeezed, opened my palm. Like damp sand, it molded to the shape of my clenched palm.

The candles flickered.

I added a pinch of crushed rose petals to the bottom of my metal forms — globes cut in half — and filled the rest of them with the mixture. I pressed two forms together, squeezing hard, and set the ball aside, filled another form.

Something creaked downstairs.

I stilled, my heart thumping.

The clock ticked on my fireplace mantel.

My grip on the metal form relaxed. The building was old and the walls were constantly settling, shifting. The sound was probably nothing.

I scooped the salt mixture into the bottom of a form.

Downstairs, something scraped.

My head jerked up. That wasn't the building settling.

Setting the form down on the counter, I tiptoed from the kitchen. I was light as a feather, praying my footsteps were soundless. At the top of the staircase, I edged open the door.

The stairwell was dark, its base in the coffee shop lost in inky blackness. I extended my senses and sensed... nothing.

No one was there.

Was I going crazy? I'd swear I heard someone in my coffee shop. Could an animal have somehow gotten inside? Maybe one of my employees had let Picatrix in earlier, and I hadn't noticed?

Right, just the cat.

Barely breathing, my ears straining, I crept down the steps, cold beneath my bare feet.

At the bottom, I paused, listening. I stood in a narrow passage between the Ground kitchen and the alleyway door. The candlelight upstairs had adjusted my vision to their dim light, but this was a different level of darkness.

I widened my eyes, straining to see more. And then I realized how ridiculous this all was. If it was Picatrix, there was no reason not to just turn on the light.

I reached for the switch.

A dark shape rushed toward me. There was a metallic clank.

I cried out, flinging my hands up in a warding gesture.

Something pummeled into me, knocking me to the linoleum floor. The door slammed open, and frigid air rushed inside.

I rolled, pressing myself against the wall as if I could make myself smaller, squeeze through a crack like a mouse and vanish. Chest heaving, I stared, open mouthed, at the open, metal door, swaying in the breeze.

I stumbled to my feet and closed it, flipped the deadbolt. Panic filled my lungs. My magical sensing had failed me. What if someone else was in here with me?

I raced up the steps to my apartment and slammed the door, locking myself inside. Enough playing Nancy Drew.

Hands shaking, I scrambled in my purse for my cell phone, couldn't find it. I turned my macramé bag upside down and dumped the contents onto the soft couch.

No phone.

I shook my purse. The phone plopped onto a cushion and bounced to the rug. Swearing, I grabbed it, called nine-one-one.

"Nine-one-one, what is your emergency?"

"This is Jayce Bonheim. Someone broke into my coffee shop, Ground. It's at three-thirty-three Main Street."

"Are you there now?"

"Yes. I'm in my apartment over the store." Hurry, hurry, hurry.

"Is the person still there, in your coffee shop?"

"No," I said, "he ran out. I think he was alone, but I'm not sure."

You must have provoked the attack. Karin's words echoed in my head, mocking.

"I've dispatched units to your location. They should be there in five minutes. Stay on the line with me."

"Thank you," I whispered. I paced, glancing at the clock.

Five minutes passed. I strode to the front window.

A police car sped up Main Street, siren off, lights flashing. "There's a police car here," I told the dispatcher and sagged against one of the white-brick walls. "I'll go downstairs and let them in."

Hanging up, I hurried down the steps, flipping on lights as I jogged through the narrow hallway, into the tiny kitchen. I brushed through the brown and grey-streaked ikat curtains and flipped the light switch.

Pendant lights illuminated natural brick walls lined with paintings and wall hangings. Ferns twined with white twinkle lights hung above the long wooden counter. More white lights hung draped from the rafters. Someone banged on the red-painted front door, rattling the mistletoe and berry wreath. "Sheriff's department!"

"It's me, Jayce! I called you!" I shouted and trotted to the red-paned door, unlocked it.

Two grim-faced deputies stared down at me, and I relaxed. I knew these men. Good natured and not much older than me, they were regulars in Ground. Denton, the blond, had a baby face. I suspected they'd both grown stubbly beards to make them appear older and tougher.

"What happened?" Officer Hernandez asked, his hair tousled and nearly black.

Officer Denton walked through the coffee shop, his expression wary.

"I was upstairs and heard a noise in Ground," I said. "I thought it might be an animal, so I came downstairs to check. Someone knocked me down and ran out the alleyway door."

Hernandez's jaw tightened. "Did you get a look at him?"

"It was too dark," I said. "I can't even say for sure if it was a him." I hugged my arms against the cold and wished the deputies would close the door.

Two more sheriff's SUVs cruised to a stop on the street outside. Uniformed men and women stepped from the cars.

"Any idea how he or she got in?" Hernandez knelt beside the front door and examined the locks. The paned windows on top weren't smashed out. There were no scuffs around the lock. No broken wood.

"No," I said. "I'm guessing he came in the rear door, because he got through it pretty quickly when he left." But the locks there had been working as well. I knew, because I'd relocked them... and left my fingerprints all over. I swallowed. "I shut and locked the back door after him. Do you think I ruined any prints?"

Sheriff McCourt strode inside Ground, and my neck tensed. She removed her hat and tossed it on one of the small, wooden tables. "You seem to be the center of excitement this week." She then ruffled her short, curly blond hair.

My pulse grew loud in my ears. "I didn't ask for it." I curled my toes, wishing I'd put shoes on.

"I'm sure you didn't," she said, gruff. "What happened?"

I repeated my story, and the sheriff nodded.

"Could you have left the door unlocked?" she asked.

"I don't think so."

"Sheriff?" one of the deputies called from behind the curtains to the kitchen. "You might want to take a look at this."

"Officer Hernandez will finish taking your statement." She strode past the long, metal counter, and through the curtains.

"What else can you tell me about this intruder?" Hernandez asked. "Was he bigger than you?"

"I think so." I edged toward the polished counter, away from the open door. A chill breeze blew through it, lifting my hair.

"Bigger than me?"

"I..." My cheeks warmed. I didn't know. With everything that had happened last summer and in the last few days, how could I have been so unobservant? "I don't know. It was dark," I finished lamely.

The sheriff brushed through the curtains. She wore blue, plastic gloves now and carried a tire iron inside a clear, plastic bag. The bag was marked in big red letters: EVIDENCE. "Do you recognize this?" she asked me.

My mouth flopped open, snapped shut. What the hell?

"It's a tire iron," I choked out.

"Is it your tire iron?" she asked.

"They all pretty much look alike, but I don't keep mine in my coffee shop." I kept my tire iron where it belonged, in my truck. My mouth made an O. Silently, I cursed.

"What's wrong?" she asked.

I swallowed. "Remember when I told you how I changed a tire last week and hadn't had a chance to take the tire in for recycling?"

She nodded.

I grimaced. "I might have left the tire iron in the truck bed as well."

She lowered her head, skewering me with her stare. "You left a tire iron to rattle around in the bed of your truck?"

"Once I'd replaced the spare with a new tire and got everything back in, it was late. By the time I realized the tire iron hadn't been put away, I was tired, so I left it." And then I'd managed to forget about it, even if it had rattled around the truck bed. Stupid, stupid, stupid!

The sheriff tilted her head, considering. "Earlier, you said you'd changed that tire around a week ago."

My cheeks warmed. "Yeah?"

"You left the tire iron in your truck bed for an entire week?" Her blue eyes narrowed.

"Out of sight, out of mind." I mustered a weak smile. "I forgot about the tire iron."

"That was careless."

I couldn't argue the point. The room grew hot, and a ribbon of sweat trickled between my breasts. "I don't know how that tire iron got inside Ground." My voice quavered, and I hated myself for the weakness. "But I didn't put it here."

She examined one end of the tire iron. "Looks like there's blood on it. A bit of hair too."

I closed my eyes. No, no, no. This wasn't happening. Not again. I met her gaze. "Whoever stole my truck, must have been the same person who broke in here. The burglar planted that."

"Maybe," she said, her tone disinterested.

"Maybe?" I gesticulated wildly. "Who else could it be? Why would I call you to Ground, knowing you'd search it, and leave a bloody tire iron for you to find?"

"I don't know," she said. "Why would you?"

"I wouldn't!"

"There's no evidence of a break-in," the sheriff said.

"Someone was in here," I said. She had to believe me.

"But there's no sign of a forced entry," she said. "So how could someone have gotten inside Ground?"

I laughed. I couldn't help it. Last summer, when I'd been suspected of murdering Brayden's wife, I'd been asked the same question. Karin had figured out the answer then, and I couldn't believe this was happening all over again.

"Ms. Bonheim?" the sheriff prompted.

"You know as well as I where all the keys are," I said.

"Is the spare key still in the drawer in the back room?"

"It had better be." I should have put it somewhere safer, but I'd figured the odds of lightning striking twice were too low, and I'd let it slide. Now my stomach felt like it was on the wrong end of a pub crawl. I pulled the keys from my pocket and tossed them to her.

"Stay here." She marched into the kitchen. A few minutes later, she returned. "The key was in the drawer. We're taking it into evidence. Maybe there will be some prints."

My muscles let go, and I sagged against the metal counter. She believed me.

"My officers are taking prints of the alley door," she said. "We still have yours on file, so we won't need them tonight for comparison purposes. But don't leave town."

She exited, the tire iron in its bag clenched in her fist.

I shut the front door behind her and glanced at Officer Hernandez. "Will you be printing the front door too?"

He nodded. "We know your prints will be all over it. But like the sheriff said, we've got them on file."

I watched the deputies work and twisted the charm on my necklace. Matt's killer had gotten inside Ground, and he'd had a key.

I'd change the locks tomorrow, but the decision didn't make me feel less vulnerable.

CHAPTER 7

Upstairs in my kitchen, I could hear the deputies' movements below. The grind of shifting furniture. The clank of a kitchen utensil falling to the floor. A soft curse. I fidgeted, wishing they'd go.

Undone, I stared at the iron cauldron filled with bath salts and the two forms I'd completed. I knocked the side of one metal globe with a spoon and pulled it apart.

The bath bomb collapsed, crumbling to glittery pink and white dust. I'd left it too long.

My cell phone rang, and I fished it from the pocket of my jeans, answering without looking at the caller I.D. "Hello?"

"Jayce, it's Brayden. Are you all right?"

"I suppose you saw the sheriff's cars," I said hollowly.

"What sheriff's cars? What's going on?"

I straightened. "Nothing. Forget it."

"It's not nothing if the sheriff's involved. What happened?"

"It's no big deal. Someone broke into Ground."

"Are you okay? Did they hurt you?"

The rumble of his voice made my heart swell, and all I wanted was for him to be here, to bury my head on his chest. But that would be a very bad idea. The sheriff was already suspicious of us. "I'm fine." I brushed my palm clean on the thigh of my jeans. Salt bomb crumbles drifted to the rag rug. "Someone broke in, and I called the police. They're here now."

"I'm coming over."

"No!" I shook my head. "Sorry. It's..." Complicated. "If you didn't see the sheriff's cars, why did you call?"

"I'm not sure," he said. "I just had this... feeling that something was wrong. It kept getting stronger, so I called."

"You must be psychic," I said lightly and dumped the remains of my bath bombs into the cauldron. If I put them in a jar and added a muslin soaking bag, I could call them bath salts.

"Psychic only when it comes to you. Why do I know you're not telling me everything?"

Because I couldn't tell him about finding the tire iron in Ground. It was too close to what had happened to his wife last summer. They say history repeats itself, but the similarities between his wife's murder and now were eerie. The police had caught his wife's killer. So if the deaths were suspiciously alike, it wasn't because Alyce's killer was still at large. It was because of someone else.

Something else.

My hand squeezed the cell phone. The curse.

"Everyone knows that curse story is B.S.," he said.

My head jerked up. Had I spoken aloud? "You know about our family curse?"

"The whole town knows."

"What have you heard?" I asked, curious.

"Only that business about your family being cursed. All the women dying in childbirth. But there's got to be something hereditary going on, right? And modern medicine has changed things."

"Right," I said faintly. So logical. So simple. So wrong. "You know, the men in our family die within months of their wives."

"Who'd want to live without one of you?" His voice, strong and sensual, sent a ripple of anguish through me.

My vision blurred. He wasn't ready to believe, and that changed everything. I couldn't do this.

"I don't like that someone got inside Ground," he said. "Is your apartment secure?"

"The locks to Ground and my apartment are different. They're different keys." That, at least, I'd fixed last summer.

"Still—"

"I'm going to stay with Lenore tonight." She wouldn't mind, and she had that big house with all those spare rooms. I didn't like the idea of someone chasing me out of my home. But I needed a sister to talk things over with, and it was late, and I was rattled.

He gusted a breath. "Good. Do you need a lift over there?"

"Lenore's coming to get me," I lied. I knew she'd collect me, even if I hadn't asked her yet. If I saw Brayden, I'd lose it. I didn't want to lose it.

"Good," he said. "If you need anything, let me know."

"I will. Thanks."

We said our goodbyes and hung up.

I bent over the counter and braced my hands on either side of the cauldron, inhaling the mixture's lavender scent. Brayden had always been okay with my witchcraft. Interested, even. He'd never joked about it, never acted like it was weird or silly. But he didn't believe in the curse, and that hurt. A lot. Had he ever believed in my magic?

It shouldn't have mattered to me one way or another. People had different beliefs, and not everyone needed to share mine. As long as those close to me accepted it, that would be enough.

But our curse didn't affect only the Bonheim women. It killed the men as well. For the last hundred and fifty years, every Bonheim mother had died at the birth of her first child. Every first child had been a daughter. And every husband had died within a few months before or after the birth. It wasn't a myth. It was fact. We had the family Bible and genealogy records to prove it.

Karin's boyfriend, Nick, knew the score and believed. He'd chosen to be with Karin anyway. Could I be with Brayden if he didn't understand the risk?

My breath caught. The answer to that was easy: no.

So why was it so hard to set him free?

Straightening off the counter, I called Lenore.

"Jayce. What's happened?"

"Can I stay at your place tonight?"

"Sure. What's going on? Something has happened, hasn't it?"

"Someone broke into Ground tonight. It's no big deal, but I don't feel like staying here."

There was a long pause, then, "I'll be there in fifteen minutes."

"Thanks. Bye."

We hung up.

I shoved clothing and makeup, hair products and devices into a leather travel bag. On impulse, I grabbed my favorite Tarot deck as well and dropped that on top of the clothing.

Someone knocked at the interior entrance to my apartment, and I opened the door.

Officer Hernandez stood at the top of the steps. "We're finished here."

"Thanks. I'll see you out."

I followed him downstairs and walked him to the front door.

"Take care of yourself, Jayce." He clapped my shoulder, and I suddenly felt lighter. I had friends in this town, even if they were duty-bound to arrest me should the evidence demand it.

"Thanks," I said. "You too."

He hesitated on the doorstep. "How's Lenore?"

"Same as she always is." I angled my head. "Why?"

"No reason." He strode, whistling, to his SUV.

Puzzled, I locked the door after him and hurried upstairs in time to hear Lenore pounding on the apartment's exterior door.

I locked up and followed her, her long white coat fluttering like a specter. In the alley, I tossed my bag into the back seat of her Volvo. We drove to her house — our aunt's old house. I wriggled from the gray car, struggling to extract my bag, and dropped it on the gravel driveway.

Light streamed through the windows of the gabled house. It had a fairytale look to it — shingled on the top, stone on the bottom, and curling beams beneath the eaves.

I followed my sister up the porch steps. She unlocked the door, and I trailed inside.

Wiping my feet on the rag rug in the entry, I inhaled the scent of home. Though Ellen had died months ago, the house still smelled like her. A stab of pain caught me behind the heart and squeezed.

"Which room do you want?" Lenore asked.

"I'll take my old bedroom."

"You know where the sheets are."

I nodded and trudged upstairs to my childhood room. Ellen had redecorated it when I'd left for college, converting it into a chic guest room with a sisal carpet. Vintage travel postcards in a stand lined one shelf. Antique women's hats rested on forms on another. The full-sized bed was covered in a simple, bamboo-colored spread.

I dumped my leather satchel and went to the linen closet in the hallway, grabbed a set of sheets and pillowcases. When I returned to my room, Lenore had already stripped the mattress. Together, we remade the bed.

"What happened?" She tucked the sheet beneath the mattress.

I told her about the break-in. "It had to have been Matt's killer. He must have left the tire iron in my kitchen intentionally, to frame me."

"But the sheriff didn't arrest you." She shook a pillow into its case, propped it against the wooden headboard.

I collapsed onto the half-made bed. "No. Not yet."

"Why would you call to report a break-in, knowing you had a murder weapon stashed in Ground?" She braced her fists on her slim hips. "Of course you're being framed. She'd have to be an idiot not to see it, and no matter what you think of Sheriff McCourt, she's no idiot."

"But she was suspicious."

"She's paid to be suspicious. That's her job."

"It was more than that." I couldn't figure out why she hadn't arrested me, and I wished Lenore wasn't so determined to explain it away.

"How could someone have gotten inside Ground again?"

Determinedly, I stared at the wood-beamed ceiling. "Do you have to ask?"

I heard the creak of a chair — Lenore sitting. "We've been through all this before, haven't we?"

"There are no keys to Ground lying around for people to steal."

"But you said there was no sign of a break-in."

"Right. So the burglar had to have had a key, because I did not leave the doors unlocked."

"What about the spare key in the drawer in that little back room?"

"It was still in the drawer."

"What if the burglar replaced the key after he or she ditched the tire iron?"

A spider worked in a corner of the ceiling, its spindly legs spinning a web.

"Maybe," I said. "But how would they have gotten the key in the first place? I know you and Karin think I'm reckless. But after Alyce's murder, I've been careful about the keys."

"Your assistant manager has one, right?"

"Darla?" I asked. "She wouldn't kill Matt."

"How do you know that?"

I raised my head. "Because it's Darla!" She loved her job, largely because I refused to fire her no matter how many mugs she broke. Poor Darla was the unluckiest person ever. If she really had been cursed by the fairy, I couldn't fire her over that. It wouldn't be fair.

"You don't know what goes on in her head," Lenore said. "What do you know about Darla's private life?"

Not as much as I should. My natural inclination was to be friends with everyone, but sometimes you had to be the boss. So I'd found myself creeping around the edges of friendship, not getting too close to my employees. I didn't like it. "I just know her, okay? Maybe I don't know every detail of her personal life, but I know what kind of person she is. And Darla's no killer."

"But your other employees would have had access to that key."

"No, they wouldn't have, because I keep that desk locked now. Only Darla and I have the key to that drawer."

"Could someone have forced the lock?" she asked.

I rolled onto my side. "I'm no expert at lock picking. I doubt anyone who works for Ground is either. I'm telling you, no one had access to that spare key."

Graceful as a dancer, she stretched out her long legs. "Matt did some work for you. Did you give him a key? Maybe the killer took it off his body?"

"I've been careful! I'm telling you, I was always there when he was installing those damned shelves. I let him in and locked up after he left. There was no reason..." I trailed off. Kuh-rap.

"What?" She unraveled her chignon, and her hair shimmered across her white blouse.

I groaned. "The shelf installation took longer than we expected. There was a day I wasn't there. Darla had to deal with Matt."

"And?"

"And I don't know! I don't know what happened. I assumed everything went okay, and I didn't ask."

"But Darla might have given him a key," she said.

"Maybe. I don't know. I'll ask her tomorrow." I stood, suddenly desperate to end this conversation. "And if I'm going to wake up in time to open, I'd better get some sleep."

She rose from the chair. "You'll be up before I am. Lock the door when you leave."

I nodded. Our aunt had rarely locked the door, but life was different now.

I stripped and slipped into my chemise. The sheets were cool, and I shivered in the darkness and curled into a semi-fetal position. The air crackled with static electricity, and tiny bursts of lightning flickered in the waves of my sheets. Ellen may have redecorated my old room, but the moonlight cast familiar shadows, and I felt small.

CHAPTER 8

Lenore was a late riser. I doubted I'd be able to wake my sister if I tried, but I tiptoed as I left her house that morning. The sky was dark and would remain so for another two hours. Winter in the foothills was long.

Enjoying the morning quiet, I strolled into town. A night bird swooped above me, the only sign of its passing the flap of its wings.

I shivered. The crows hadn't hurt me, but they had shaken me. No animal had ever turned on me before. And I liked crows, clever and elegant. Their attack felt like a betrayal.

The walk and the chill air snapped me into wakefulness. By the time I arrived home, I was humming.

In my upstairs apartment, I took a leaf of dried white sage from my magic cupboard and lit it with a match. The flame rose, flickering, and steadied. I blew it out. The tip glowed, the leaf smoldering. I opened the bathroom window that faced over the alley.

This was my home, dammit, and I wasn't going to let some creep taint it with his bad mojo.

I saged the coffee shop, visualizing any dark energies that had been left behind pushed into a violet flame.

Upstairs, I repeated the process. The intruder hadn't made it into my apartment, but negative energy trails might have slipped inside. When the leaf had been reduced to a smoldering fragment pinched between my finger and thumb, I ran water over it from the tap. I tossed the stem in the waist bin beside my sink and shut the bathroom window.

Closing my eyes, I extended my aura, probing. All I sensed was my own magic, green and bright. My space was clear. But I'd thought it was clear last night, and I'd been wrong. How had that happened? Were we wrong? Was Matt's killer magical? It would take a practitioner – or something paranormal – to hide from my probing. Either that, or I was really losing it.

Downstairs, a key rattled in a lock, and I started. I hurried down the steps to Ground.

Darla let herself in through the alley door and wrinkled her freckled nose. "Sage?" Her blond hair was tied in a neat bun. She pulled a delicate net from her pocket and pulled it over her hair.

My assistant manager might be the unluckiest person I knew, but she was conscientious.

"Someone broke in last night," I admitted.

Her toffee eyes widened. "What? How?"

"It looks like they had a key."

"Another one?" Her broad face fell. "Did they take anything?"

"No. I scared the guy off."

"You're so brave. I would never have gone after an intruder." Shaking her head, she walked to the closet and leaned inside.

"Do you remember when Matt Zana was doing some work for us?" I asked. "That day I couldn't be here to oversee the shelving installation?"

She pulled out an apron. There was a crash, and cardboard cylinders of cleanser rolled into the hallway. A plastic bottle was hooked inside the loop of her apron. Her fair skin colored, and she knelt, scooping up the containers. "Sorry."

"No damage done." I helped her return the cleanser to the closet shelf, one that Matt had installed. "About Matt. Do you remember that day?"

"Vaguely. Why?"

"Did you ever give him a key?"

She stiffened. "No! I unlocked for him and locked up afterward. I remember, because I'd just found my own key that day." Darla pinked.

"You mean you'd lost your key?"

"Not really." She sucked in her cheeks. "I mean, I found it again, at the bottom of the washing machine that morning. It didn't seem like a big deal."

"How did you get inside the day before?"

"When I realized I'd misplaced it, I'd borrowed the spare key," she said, talking fast. "You know, the one in the drawer." She nodded to the small, distressed wood desk, wedged against the wall. "If I hadn't found my key, I would have told you and asked to make a copy. But like I said, I found it the next day."

"The day you let Matt Zana into Ground." I twisted the bangles on my wrists.

"Right."

"And then you replaced the spare key?"

"Right away! I felt terrible that I'd borrowed it and worse that I'd misplaced the original key. I'm sorry I didn't say anything sooner."

I skimmed my hand over my ponytail. "It's okay. You're the assistant manager. I trust you, and like you said, no harm done. You found the lost key."

She broke into a relieved smile. "Right."

"Where was Matt when you replaced the key?"

"Matt?" Her forehead wrinkled. "I guess he must have been near the closet. Oh! I remember. I was worried about forgetting to replace the spare. So I returned the spare key to the drawer as soon as I walked inside. So Matt must have been right behind me."

And he'd seen where the spare key had been kept. I turned from her, wiping an already sparkling counter with a cloth. "Did you lock the drawer?"

"Yes. No. I don't... Were we locking it then?"

My lips pressed tight. I wasn't sure when we'd instituted that policy. "I can't remember either." If Matt had seen where the spare key had gone, he could have taken it. But why would he? Someone was always here on weekdays to let him inside. There was no reason for him to have his own key.

"I'm really sorry," she said.

"It's all right. You have nothing to be sorry for."

"But if I hadn't misplaced that key—"

"You think I've never run something through the wash I'd forgotten about in my pockets? It happens."

"But another break-in." Her forehead creased. "You're sure nothing was taken?"

Something had been added. "Like I said, I scared the guy off." But had it been a guy? My memories jumbled.

"You're lucky you weren't hurt."

If being here had been good luck, I could take a bit of Darla's bad.

The alley door opened, a breeze ruffling the streaky ikat curtains at the other end of the narrow room. Sal, another of my staff, walked into the corridor. She grabbed an apron – red for the holidays – off a wall peg. "What's up?"

"Opening," I said, knotting my ponytail into a bun. "Let's go."

We got busy prepping the coffee shop, and I turned the CLOSED sign to OPEN at six. My morning regulars trickled in, lining up at the counter for pick-ups on their way to work.

Ground buzzed with Matt's death. This was the first work day since his murder, the first chance for gossip. We didn't have many murders or handymen in Doyle, and he'd done work for many Doyle residents.

Wynter Swanstrom pressed his trim stomach against the counter and waited for his double espresso. His head nearly brushed one of the ferns, glittering with white twinkle lights, above the counter. The city manager's hair was white with a yellowish tinge – its natural color since he was in is mid-forties. His ruddy face was handsome in a just-off-the-ski-slopes kind of way.

I passed the paper cup across the dark-wood counter and sniffed ginger. It was one of our holiday brews. "Here you go."

"Thanks. I hear your truck was used in the murder of that jackass, Matt Zana."

My brows rocketed upward. Jackass? "He installed some shelves in one of my closets."

"You let him in your closet? I thought you had more sense."

He was joking, but for some reason the comment stung. "Here in Ground."

He snorted. "That's better."

"Did he ever do work for you?"

"Unfortunately."

I snapped a dead branch from one of the ferns hanging above the counter. "What happened?"

"You know what he was like." He turned to go.

A seed of suspicion sprouted tentacles inside me. "How did you hear about my truck?" I asked.

He glanced over his shoulder. "I shouldn't have, but you know how it is in small towns." He strode out the red-painted door.

It hadn't been much of an answer, and the tentacles grew. I was being paranoid. Maybe he'd learned about it through his position as city manager. Though "city manager" seemed an odd title in a town with an official population of 4,502.

I returned to my coffee-making duties, and Darla took orders and made change. She passed me a cup labeled simply Doc, and I smiled. I didn't need to know the order – Doc Toeller was another regular. I made the caramel macchiato and handed it across the counter into the doctor's waiting hand.

She smiled sympathetically, her blue eyes crinkling. "Jayce, how are you doing?" Her cap of silver-gold hair glinted beneath the overhead lights. Her ice-blue turtleneck hugged her slim figure. Doc Toeller had to be at least fifty — she'd delivered my sisters and I. But like so many in Doyle, she could have been any age.

I blew the bangs out of my eyes. "I suppose you heard about the truck too?"

"What truck?"

"The police impounded my pickup."

She raised her paper coffee cup in a mock toast. "I told you to slow down on those roads."

"Someone stole it and put Matt Zana's body inside."

Her eyes widened. "No. And then you were burgled?"

"You heard about that?"

"It's a small town."

My mouth compressed. "So everyone keeps telling me."

She laughed. "It's impossible to keep secrets in Doyle. But keep your chin up." She strolled out the door, and every man in the room turned to watch.

By nine, the worker bees had departed, and the retirees wandered in. They shoved tables together for their regular coffee klatsch. It would last for hours, but they were good customers, so I was happy to have them filling my seats.

I was lucky. I loved my coffee shop — not just the scent of the coffee beans or the satisfaction of having my own place, but the diverse energy of the customers.

At ten, our first wave of work-from-homers poured into Ground. The café had become their office away from home. Younger, these clients tended not to spend on expensive brews. Still, they kept the chairs filled, and I'd installed wi-fi for a reason.

I pulled my apron over my head. "Darla, can you take over for thirty minutes?" According to my sister, Matt might have had something going with the new realtor, Phoebe England. It was time I followed up on that lead.

She glanced over the crowd, heads bent over their computers. This crew wouldn't be ordering much more coffee today. "Sure."

"Thanks." I bolted upstairs and grabbed my denim-blue shawl, then left.

The crisp air snapped at my cheeks. I inhaled deeply. A vintage pickup drifted past, and I admired its curving lines. The sky above was cloudless, the soft morning sunlight sparkling off the shop windows that lined the street.

I stepped from beneath an overhang. Tilting my head toward the sun, I briefly reveled in its warmth on my face. I walked down an informal, dirt path that meandered between the sidewalk and the road. The earth was soft, damp.

My shawl snagged on a rose bush, pruned seemingly to nothing. I disentangled myself, pulling out a loop of blue thread. "Darn it." Maybe Karin could fix it. And maybe I shouldn't be running to her for help so much. Adjusting the shawl over my shoulders, I walked on.

A red Porche parked in the dirt across the street, in front of an old barn that had been converted to a wine tasting room. Eric Gertner stepped from the car and glanced my way.

I gnawed the inside of one cheek. He'd heard Melanie Zana's accusation, that I'd been sleeping with her husband, but he'd also seemed not to believe it. Hopeful, I smiled and waved.

He stared for a moment, as if he couldn't remember who I was. Returning a half-hearted wave, he strode towards the tasting room. I'd been dissed.

I stopped in front of Phoebe England's realty office and pretended to examine the flyers papering the inside of the window. She was new in town, and I only knew her to say "hello." Accusing her of an affair didn't seem a good starting point for our relationship.

Homes for sale. Vacation rentals. I studied the flyers. Most of the real estate on offer wasn't in Doyle.

Behind the glass, Phoebe glanced up from her desk, smiled and waved.

I opened the door. Smiling brightly, I walked inside. "Hi, Phoebe."

She smoothed her lustrous blond-streaked hair, and the gold charm bracelet around her wrist tinkled. "Jayce Bonheim! What brings you here?" Phoebe was close to my age — maybe a few years older. Her white blouse and navy skirt might have looked schoolgirl, but the skirt was longer than any self-respecting teenager's.

"We're still in the process of settling my aunt's estate," I said, "and we're not sure if we're going to sell her house or not." I sent a silent apology to Lenore. We'd already decided to keep the house. It was too big a part of our childhood, and Lenore needed a place to live. Poetry and bookstore management weren't the most lucrative careers. "I thought you might be able to help us figure out its value."

She rose and motioned to a business-like chair, and her charm bracelet jingled. "Grab a seat. Can I get you some coffee?"

"No, thanks." I sat.

"I guess offering you coffee is like bringing tea to China." She smiled, but it didn't reach her eyes. They were red-rimmed, as if she'd been crying. Maybe the rumor about Phoebe and Matt Zana was true.

"I probably drink too much." Coffee, and other beverages. I stuffed my hands in the pockets of my jeans. "Are you all right?"

Phoebe blinked, sniffed. "Yes, of course."

"Matt's death has shaken a lot of people. I heard you two were close."

"Where did you hear that?" She moved a stack of paper from one side of the desk to the other. "I wouldn't say we were close, but I did work with him. He'd do quick fix-ups for my clients before I sold a house. You'd be surprised how little details can wreck a home sale. Most buyers have so little imagination. You have to make it easy for them to see themselves inside your house. I'd need to see the inside of your aunt's house to know whether staging makes sense, or what we'd have to do to get you and your sisters the best price."

Wait. Staging? "Right now we're more interested in getting a valuation."

"You'd need an appraiser for that, and I can certainly recommend one."

"At this point, we were hoping for something more informal. My aunt kept up her house, though I don't think she ever used Matt's services. It's a pity he's not around now. I'm sure there are things that need fixing or touching up in there that he could have done. He helped me install some shelves in Ground once."

"I think he mentioned that."

I angled my head. "Oh?"

Her olive skin darkened. "You were one of his references."

And if someone had asked, I would have given Matt an okay reference. I'd only become more critical since he'd been killed. "I'm surprised he mentioned me. It was a small project — a simple shelf installation."

"Most of the work he did for my clients was small too."

"He was a fun guy. I'm sorry he's gone." I smiled reminiscently. "He had quite a reputation with the ladies."

She stiffened. "I wouldn't know. We were only business associates."

She was lying. But I didn't know how to break past the falsehood, and I didn't know if it even mattered.

"When would be a good time for me to stop by your aunt's house and give you my opinion?" she asked.

I blanked. "My aunt's house?"

"About a sales price, what needs to be done?"

"Oh! Right!" I fumbled in my macramé purse. "Sorry, my phone is vibrating," I lied. I pretended to check the messages. "Urgh, I forgot I've got another appointment. Sorry, let's talk later, okay?" I hurried to the glass, front door.

"I could stop by tomorrow? When would it be convenient?"

"Right, sure." Nearly running, I sped onto the sidewalk. What had I agreed to? If the fairy or Matt's murderer didn't kill me, Lenore surely would.

CHAPTER 9

I returned to the café. A second wave of thirsty customers poured in, packing Ground's tables. Heads bent over laptops, they sipped holiday confections piled with whipped cream and garnished with cinnamon sticks. Darla went home for the day, leaving just me and Sal.

I took a rack of steaming mugs from the industrial dishwasher and set them on the counter in the tiny kitchen to cool. Leaning over the clean mugs, I enjoyed the rising heat, warming my face and neck.

Brayden, in his usual jeans and flannel shirt, brushed through the ikat curtains.

I couldn't help it. I grinned at the sight of him, my heart flying skyward. But he'd told me we should stay apart. What was he doing here?

He shoved his sleeves to his elbows. "We have to talk."

"What's wrong?"

"Why didn't you tell me the burglar knocked you down? What were you thinking, confronting him?"

"Because I didn't know there was a burglar." I wiped my hands on my apron. "I hear noises all the time, and they're usually just the building shifting or an animal outside."

"Why didn't you tell me?"

"What would it have changed? Nothing happened. It was all over."

His hands fisted. "How did he get inside?"

I rolled my eyes. "I don't know! Do you think I haven't been trying to figure that out?"

"This is serious, Jayce."

"Oh, really?" I snapped. "I had no idea."

"That's mature."

"Right, because I'm such a child compared to you. You're a whole ten years older than me, another great excuse for us never to..." I hung my head. I wasn't angry about his appearance here or his critique of my self-defense skills. We couldn't be together, and he didn't know it yet.

I hadn't told him we were going nowhere. But that had always been our direction, hadn't it? And that's the way it would always be. A piece of me seemed to fragment deep in my chest.

Behind me, something splintered, cracked, and I whipped around.

In the plastic carrying tray, a crack traveled up the side of one of the mugs, still hot from the dishwasher. The white mug split in two, the pieces seeming to leap away from each other.

"Weird," Brayden said. "The heat must have expanded a hairline fracture."

I pressed a hand to my chest. "That's probably it." Because he'd never believe it was magic, my unconscious magic acting out through metaphors and symbols.

"Look, Jayce—"

"No, Brayden. I'm working. This isn't a good time."

"Oh." His expression turned... not blank exactly, but unreadable.

"Brayden—"

The sheriff strode through the brown-and-gray streaked curtains and stopped short. Her gaze flicked upward. "I thought you might be here."

Two deputies crowded in behind her.

"It's mid-day," I said. "Of course I'm here."

But she was glaring at Brayden. "This makes things convenient," she said. "I need you both to come to the station for more questioning."

I felt the blood drain from my face. "More questioning?"

"Why?" Brayden asked. "We've already told you everything we know."

"The deputies will escort you to the station," she said. "Ms. Bonheim, you can come with me."

"But..."

She gave me a hard stare, and I stopped arguing.

"May I tell Sal that I'm leaving?" I asked. "She'll need to call someone in to help close up if I'm going to be long."

The sheriff nodded.

Two deputies escorted Brayden outside. He wasn't in handcuffs, but he wore the hunted look of someone who'd been rounded up.

I spoke briefly to Sal then followed the sheriff. To my surprise, she opened the front, passenger-side door of the SUV and nodded to it, before walking around to the driver's side.

Fractionally, I relaxed. Riding in the front seat had to be a good sign.

The sheriff dropped her hat on the seat between us and started the SUV. "Since we've still got your truck, I figured you could use a ride."

And she'd come to collect me herself? My stomach hardened with suspicion. I buckled up, one hand resting on the metal seat lock. "Thanks."

She pulled onto Main Street. "Did you see Mr. Zana earlier on the day he died?"

"If you mean the day my truck was stolen, no. I didn't see him in the pub."

"He wasn't in the Bell and Thistle, earlier?" She rumpled her curly, blond hair where the hat had pressed into it, leaving a dent.

"No," I said, confused. "Why?"

"We're trying to figure out Mr. Zana's movements that day," she said conversationally.

My breath quickened. Liar. "I should call my lawyer."

"Do you need him to tell you where you were?"

I clamped my mouth shut.

"This isn't official," she continued. "I want to find the person who killed Matt Zana. I think you want that too."

"Of course I do. But I don't know anything."

"You didn't know that your boyfriend was seen arguing with Matt earlier that day?"

I sucked in my breath. What?

She turned onto the highway, lined with pines, and glanced at me. One corner of her mouth angled down. "From your reaction, I'm guessing you didn't."

"Why would Brayden argue with Matt?"

"We'll ask him that at the station." She slowed behind a truck piled with redwood logs. "Strange that he didn't mention the argument to either of us. Or maybe it isn't."

"What do you mean?"

A muscle jumped beneath her skin. "Sometimes, the people we care about aren't honest for fear of disappointing us."

"Or maybe he didn't say anything, because it didn't happen. Maybe whoever told you Brayden and Matt argued was wrong."

"Maybe," she said, noncommittal.

"Why are you telling me this?"

"Your boyfriend's last wife died under suspicious circumstances."

"You caught the killer. The murderer confessed."

"Mm. Still, it makes you wonder, doesn't it? A lot of death seems to follow him."

She was trying to split Brayden and me, make us doubt each other. Maybe she thought I knew something and was covering for him. But Brayden hadn't killed his wife. We knew who'd committed that crime. And Brayden sure hadn't stolen my truck and dumped Matt Zana's body inside the bed.

"We were together when my truck was stolen," I said. "He couldn't have stolen it to dump Matt's body."

"So you say."

"What's that supposed to mean?"

"Lovers have been known to cover for each other." Her face tightened. "It isn't worth it."

"We're not lovers."

She raised a blond brow. "Oh?"

"We're friends. We've always been friends."

"Hm."

"I get that it's your job not to believe me—"

"And I don't. But what's important is what the D.A. believes. And then, maybe a jury."

"A jury!" I turned to the window and pressed the back of my hand to my mouth. Beside the highway, pines flashed past. "You're arresting me?"

"Did I say I was arresting you?"

She pulled into the Sheriff's Department parking lot. The sleek, glass building rose before us. She parked in a spot marked SHERIFF, beside the front steps, then turned to me. "Try and look at it from my perspective. Your boyfriend was seen arguing with the victim the morning before he died. That evening, you say your truck was stolen, but we only have you and Brayden's word for that."

"People saw us at the bar."

"They saw you in the bar. They didn't see what happened when you went outside. And Brayden conveniently left his argument with Matt out of his statement when we first pulled him in for questioning."

I unbuckled my seat belt. "If you think I'm covering for anyone, you're wrong. Brayden didn't kill anyone. And if I thought he had, I'd tell you." Because if he'd killed someone — and I knew he hadn't — then he wouldn't have been a man I could love. Terror washed through me, and I steadied myself, clutching the door handle. I still loved him, and the sheriff thought he was a murderer.

The sheriff led me inside.

"I want to call my lawyer," I said.

"You've got your cell phone?" she asked.

I nodded.

"Then call." She stuck me in a small, cinderblock room. I'd been in rooms like this before. A video camera angled in a high corner. A mirror, which everyone who ever watched TV knew had detectives behind it, flashed dully in one wall. A metal table with two brackets to chain a prisoner squatted in the center of the room. There were three plastic chairs. I knew which one was for me, and I sat opposite the door. Above it, a clock ticked.

I pulled my cell phone from my purse and called Nick Heathcoat.

"What's happened?" he asked, brusque.

My gaze darted around the cinderblock room. "I'm at the sheriff's station, in an interrogation room. They've brought Brayden and me in for questioning."

"How do you know they have Brayden?"

I winced. "He was in Ground when the sheriff came to get me."

"You're calling from your cell phone," he said.

"Yes." And then I understood. Last summer when I'd been brought into the station, the sheriff had always confiscated my phone. She'd made sure the only calls I made were on her payphone. Sure, someone might be listening to this conversation from the other side of that mirror now. But letting me keep my phone was unusual. Could she actually believe me?

"I'll be there in twenty minutes," he said. "Don't say anything more."

"Thanks."

I sat and waited, watching the red, second hand of the wall clock tick forward.

Twenty-three minutes and eighteen seconds later, Nick in his sleek business suit strode through the door. "Let's go."

I rose and pressed my fingertips into the cold, metal table. "We can go? What about Brayden?"

"He's not my client."

"But—"

"He has his own lawyer," he said. "I ran into her in the atrium. Brayden's well represented, don't worry."

Feet dragging, I left the station with Nick and got into his black SUV.

He twisted in the seat to face me, his left arm draped over the wheel. "What happened?"

"Not much. The sheriff drove me here—"

"The sheriff herself?"

"Yeah," I said. "She even let me sit in the front seat."

"And she asked you questions, didn't she? Tell me you didn't answer."

I winced, feeling foolish. "Maybe a little."

"What did you tell her?"

"She asked if I'd known that Brayden had argued with Matt Zana the morning he died."

"Did you?"

"No. And I don't believe it. She implied we might have been colluding — that my truck hadn't really been stolen. How did you get me out?"

"I asked," he said. "The deputy told me you were free to go."

I flexed my fingers on the seat belt. She'd been trying to shake me. "This was all a game."

"Not a game. You need to watch yourself, Jayce. The sheriff is deadly serious."

CHAPTER 10

I paced my darkened apartment and stared at the phone in my hand. Candles flickered on the low table before the fire. A log snapped, sparks shooting up the chimney. A program on the Civil War played silently on the TV. I liked history – the stories were dramatic and real – but I hadn't been able to sit still and watch.

I'd left half a dozen messages for Brayden, and he hadn't returned a single one. Was he avoiding me or still in custody? In either case, I was starting to embarrass myself with all the voicemails.

My blood hummed, electric. I needed to get out, to do something. My options were limited without wheels, but Doyle was a small town, and I lived downtown, such as it was.

I shrugged into a burgundy sweater-coat that hung to my knees. Looping my beigey scarf around my neck, I trotted down the exterior steps to the alley.

Main Street's old-fashioned hotels and B&Bs were darkly quiet, emptied of their weekend tourist hordes. A lone pickup cruised past, its tires swishing on the damp pavement.

I walked beneath iron street lamps and past blackened windows. Across the street, a pink neon sign in the shape of a cocktail shaker blinked, calling to me. Antoine's.

The interior of the bar was rough, unpolished wood and dim lighting. A jukebox sat unlit and unplayed in one corner. Framed, old-timey photos littered the walls, and three brass chandeliers hung the length of the narrow bar. The owner and bartender, Antoine, stood behind the empty counter.

I scanned the bar, Monday-night dead. A man's white hair bobbed behind one of the smooth, wood booths, as if in time to music only he could hear. I discovered I was holding my breath. Feeling sick, jittery, I released it. A small, insane part of me had hoped to find Brayden.

I slid onto a cracked barstool.

Polishing a beer mug, Antoine ambled along the bar to me and grinned. "Haven't seen you here for a while. Where you been?" His curly white hair was tight against his head. There was something almost boyish about the older, African American man and his easy smile, trim figure, and soft skin. Boyish, until you looked into his deep, brown eyes, which spoke of wisdom and experience and sympathy. Antoine had been married to the same woman for fifty years, and I'd given up trying to keep track of their grandkids.

"The police questioned me again." I looped my purse on one of the hooks beneath the bar. "I'm starting to think the sheriff doesn't like me."

"Don't take it personally. I reckon she doesn't like anybody these days, not with her husband up for early parole."

I blinked. That put a different complexion on our interview. "Do you think he'll get it?" Her husband had been caught embezzling from the county. The sheriff had been a witness for the prosecution.

"Who can say? I doubt he's given the prison guards much trouble." His face creased. "I heard they commandeered your truck."

"Word gets around fast. Hear anything else?"

"Want a drink?"

I nodded. "The usual." Antoine would say what he needed to say in his own good time.

The older man turned his back on me, grabbed a bottle of vodka.

A floorboard creaked behind me, and I glanced over my shoulder.

Wynter Swanstrom, Doyle's city manager, sauntered to the bar. He set his empty mug by my elbow. "Hi, Jayce. Drinking alone?"

I smiled. "Not anymore." I wasn't flirting. And so what if I was? Neither of us were married, and Brayden hadn't called.

Antoine slid the martini down the bar, and it stopped precisely in front of me. He was the only bartender I knew who could do that with pretty much any type of glass. "Another?" he asked Wynter.

"Yep," Wynter said.

I studied the two men, with their white shocks of hair. Antoine, with that smooth, well-tended sheen that all Doyle citizens had, his white hair lit with silver. Wynter, younger, more muscular, his white hair tinged with gold.

The city manager was at least thirty years younger than Antoine. But I knew that because I knew it, not because the age difference was obvious. They both had that plastic, ageless appearance, a look I'd managed not to see, until Karin had forced me to notice.

Growing up in Doyle, everything had seemed normal. Nothing was.

I wondered what would happen to us all if the unseelie's spell ever broke, and I worried for my sisters if it didn't. None of us were pregnant, but I suspected none of us were long for this world. Another good reason not to start something with Brayden.

"Something wrong?" Wynter asked. "You've got a funny look on your face."

"I'm thinking about Matt," I said.

Wynter scowled, his ruddy face twisting. "Leave it to Matt to make things as inconvenient as possible for everyone, even in death."

"You mentioned he did some work for you," I said.

The bartender replaced Wynter's beer and moved a few feet down the bar. He polished its shiny surface, his head cocked.

"I hired him to re-tile my bathrooms," Wynter said. "He said the project would take two weeks. It took three months. Matt kept finding better places to be."

One corner of my mouth curled upward. "Sounds familiar." I sipped my drink, the green olives rolling at the bottom of the cocktail glass. "But I can't imagine someone killing Matt because of a delayed project."

"No, but..." Wynter's white brows slashed downward. He took another swig of beer.

Antoine polished the bar more vigorously.

"But what?" I asked.

"I swear I caught him snooping," Wynter said.

"Snooping?" I asked.

"At the time, I was sure of it. Then I started to think I'd imagined things. But now that someone's killed him, I wonder."

I set down my glass. "What happened?"

"It was a weekday. I came home from work early — not to check on him – okay, maybe a part of me was checking on him. But I'd forgotten my lunch, left it in the refrigerator. His truck was in the driveway, but when I went into the house, he wasn't in the bathrooms. I found him in my home office, leaning over my desk. He said he'd just come in from the backyard — which was possible, because there's a door to the yard from my office. But there was no reason for him to be near my desk, and he had this look on his face."

"What sort of look?"

"Half smug, half like a kid who'd been caught with his hand in the cookie jar. When I looked at my desk later, it seemed like some of the things had been moved."

Uneasy, I shifted in my chair. "What sort of things?"

"Only work stuff — some zoning docs, that sort of thing. Nothing super private, but I told him to stay the hell out of my office from then on. He didn't mess with any of your things, did he?"

"There was nothing to mess with in Ground," I said, thinking hard. If Matt Zana had been a snoop, was that why he and Brayden had argued? He'd worked for Brayden, and Brayden liked his privacy. It wasn't hard to imagine him blowing up if he'd caught the handyman skulking through his things. But if that had happened, the argument would have happened immediately, at Brayden's house. They wouldn't have fought in public, where others could see and tell the police.

My heel bounced on the rung of my bar stool. Had something happened between them? "The police called me in for questioning again today," I said.

"Did they?" Wynter asked. "But I see they let you go. I'm sure they're questioning everyone."

"Have you said anything to the sheriff about Matt's spying?"

"No, but I guess I should. I will. I don't know why I didn't say anything to her before." He finished his drink and laid some bills in a neat row on the bar. "I'm sure you've got nothing to worry about, Jayce. Take care of yourself."

"Thanks."

I watched him go.

Antoine sauntered down the bar and counted the money Wynter had left.

"Did Matt ever do any work for you?" I asked.

The older man grunted, which I took for a yes.

"Anything odd happen?" I asked. "Go missing?"

"Nothing went missing." Antoine tucked the money in the breast pocket of his shirt and picked up the abandoned beer mug.

"And no snooping around, I guess."

Ignoring my question, Antoine walked to the other end of the bar.

I waited. The bartender liked his drama. But to my surprise, he didn't return to drop tidbits of gossip into my eager ears. I finished my drink.

Instead of offering me another, he stayed put at the opposite end of the bar and washed mugs.

"Thanks, Antoine," I called.

Another grunt.

He really wasn't talking to me. Weird. Antoine loved to gossip. So why wasn't he now?

I retrieved my glass and sidled down the counter. "Are you all right?" I asked.

He didn't look at me. "I'm fine."

"Because it seems like you're avoiding me. We've been friends for ages, and the bar's not exactly packed."

He met my gaze, his brown eyes somber. "I guess I was. The thing is, I did know Matt. Know his wife too. And I don't like what's been happening in Doyle. We don't get murders here. At least we didn't used to."

"But Doyle does have a history of disappearances," I said.

"Disappearances?"

"In the woods. Haven't you noticed? A hiker disappears every seven years." The seven-year cycle was another bit of Doyle weirdness Karin had made me aware of.

"Every seven?" he frowned. "Seems more often than that. People get lost in those woods all the time."

"Lost, yes," I said, "but every seven years, a hiker is never found again."

"People don't respect the mountains." He flipped a drying cloth over his shoulder. "They think if people are allowed somewhere, it must be safe. That none of the happy forest animals will bother 'em. That a sudden storm will be a romantic adventure and not a death sentence. Respect. You've got to respect nature, because nature's got no respect for you."

I shifted on the barstool. "I'm worried about Matt's murder. The police have pulled me in for questioning twice now. They still have my truck. I knew the man, but not well enough to kill him. But after what happened earlier this year..." Earlier this year, when I'd been accused of killing Brayden's wife. Of course the police suspected me now. Why wouldn't they? I looked away, studying the unlit jukebox.

"No one who knows you would think you capable of killing Matt Zana." His expression softened. "And why would you? You were cleared of Alyce's death last summer. The real killer confessed to killing Brayden's wife."

"So why did this one use my truck to move Matt's body? Do you think someone chose it intentionally? That I'd make a good pastsy?"

He smiled, rueful. "I'll bet they picked it because it was convenient. You never lock that truck. I've told you and told you to lock your doors, but you never listen."

I sighed. And I'd gotten so diligent about locking the doors to Ground and my apartment.

He patted my hand. "You've got nothing to do with this business. Put it out of your mind."

Like that was possible. "Thanks, Antoine. And from now on, I'll listen to you."

He laughed. "Sure you will."

Grinning, I paid and left.

I walked down the wood plank sidewalk, my footsteps clunking hollowly. The phone in my purse buzzed. I scrabbled for it, pulled it out. Brayden! Thank God. "Hi," I said, breathless.

"Sorry I missed your calls." His voice was flat, impersonal, and disappointment ripped through my veins.

"Are you okay? You're out, right? This isn't your one phone call?"

"The police released me an hour ago. I'm at home."

"I'm on Main Street. I can be there—"

"No, Jayce. If someone sees you—"

"Who's going to see me?"

"It will look bad for us both."

"That didn't stop you from coming by Ground today."

"You were in danger!"

"Was, past tense. Brayden—"

"Coming by Ground was a mistake. I'm sorry."

I stopped beneath an iron street lamp and clawed my hand across my scalp. My breath misted the night air. "This is ridiculous. We're friends. We're in this together. Wouldn't it be suspicious if we didn't talk to each other?"

"Maybe, but it's too late."

Too late? What was that supposed to mean? My stomach twisted, and I hunched. "The police told me someone heard you arguing with Matt Zana. Is it true?"

"It was nothing. A misunderstanding."

"You mean you didn't argue with him?"

"Jayce, drop it."

"What the hell's going on? I spent hours in the police station today. Did you or did you not get into a fight with Matt Zana?" A light went on above the Karate studio across the street. I lowered my voice. "Brayden, after everything that's happened between us, why can't you tell me what's going on?"

"Because nothing's going on."

I could hear the lie in his voice, and wet heat burned my eyes. "Matt is dead. The killer used my pickup. I know you didn't kill him, because you were with me—"

He laughed, harsh. "You need evidence?"

"You're not being honest with me. I don't know why, but I do know that."

"Jayce." His voice deepened. "I care about you. That's the only reason I'm staying away and asking you to keep your distance. And if I had any idea who killed Matt, I wouldn't let us both twist in the wind, waiting for the police to figure things out on their own."

"But—"

"Go home, Jayce. We'll talk later." He hung up.

I stared at my phone.

I went home.

CHAPTER 11

Karin typed inside Ground's front window, her long legs crossed. She could have been in a holiday card, holly swagged above her, her legs sheathed in forest-green tights beneath her plaid mini-skirt.

Two men walked past outside, slowing to stare at her through the window.

Intent on whatever she was working on, my sister didn't notice. She could have been working on a romance novel or a client's will. Her expression was the same whether composing love scenes or legalese. I suspected her presence here this morning had a dual purpose — get some work done and keep an eye on me.

It worried me that she felt she needed to.

Absently, she sipped from an empty coffee cup and set it down.

I walked to her table, removed her cup, filled it, returned it.

Karin didn't respond.

She had to be working on a romance novel. There was no way a will could be that riveting.

"Hey witch, how's it going?" I tugged down the sleeve of my low-cut sapphire sweater.

Her shoulders twitched, and she shot me a look. "I wish you wouldn't say that in public Someday, people are going to figure out you're not joking."

I grinned. "I'll take that chance."

She glanced at the clock on the natural brick wall and swore. "Is it after lunch already?"

"Yep. The rush has come and gone."

She shut the lid of her laptop. "I've got an appointment in twenty minutes, and I wanted to talk to you."

"So talk."

She jammed her computer into her ginormous purse — half briefcase, half knitting bag. "Nick said you were at the police station yesterday. What happened?"

"Nick didn't tell you?"

She scowled. "Attorney-client privilege. Did the police find any new information?"

I opened my mouth, shut it. Karin liked Brayden, but she'd blamed him for getting me into trouble before. And I knew how she'd respond if she learned he'd gotten into a dust-up with the murder victim. "The sheriff is digging," I said. "Brayden and I alibi each other, and she doesn't like it. I think she wants me to be guilty, like that could make up for her accusing me of Alyce's murder last summer."

Her brow puckered. "Nick has made me swear I'll stay out of it and let him handle your legal case."

"Not investigate like you did last summer, you mean? It's not a bad idea."

Her expression turned fierce. "You can't expect these problems to just disappear. Not when..." She glanced about the coffee shop.

A hipster wearing glasses and a ragged beard stared vacantly at his computer.

"Not when there's something more behind this," Karin whispered. "We need to do something."

"I am. This isn't last summer. I won't let you or anyone else get hurt on my behalf."

A look of uncertainty crossed her face. "Lenore and I have an idea about the unseelie problem. Let's talk more later." She checked her watch.

"Get out of here," I said. "I promise not to cast any unseelie-finding spells until the three of us come up with a real plan."

Her shoulders relaxed. "Thanks. See you soon." She rushed out the red front door, the bell jangling in her wake.

I shook my head, not trusting my sister's pledge not to play detective. I couldn't let her get hurt on my behalf again, but I wasn't sure how to convince her I was handling it.

The front door opened, and Darla bustled into the coffee shop. She peeled off her coat and hung it on the hook near the door. Her fair skin was pink, and her chest heaved. "Sorry I'm late. I got a flat tire on the way to the gas station, and—"

"It's okay." I hadn't even noticed my assistant manager was late. "The lunch crowd has gone." We only had a few regulars left in the café. The work-from-home crowd typed away on their computers. Mr. Carlyle, an elegant, elderly man sat in a far corner and read the Wall Street Journal.

Darla tugged on the horseshoe charm around her neck. "I don't why I bother wearing this thing. It doesn't help. I got another flat tire. Bad luck follows wherever I go."

"The more you believe in bad luck, the more power you give it," I warned, unable to meet her plaintive gaze. Darla's problems were real, but not even she would believe in a fairy curse.

She shook her blond head. "I'll get to work. Have you taken a lunch break? You must be starving."

My stomach rumbled. "I guess I am." I laughed. "I'll be back in an hour."

"Take your time."

I trotted upstairs to my apartment, grabbed my blue, wool shawl from off the couch, and arranged it over my shoulders. Eating at home would have made more sense, but something seemed to be driving me outdoors.

Outside my window, the sky was iron gray, threatening rain. I glanced at the umbrella in its stand by the door. Deciding to risk it, I left it there, hurrying downstairs and outside.

I walked quickly. Main Street was quiet (too quiet?), the macadam dark from last night's rain. I stayed close to the old buildings, imagining they had to be radiating some heat. But the shop doors were all closed, trapping the warm air inside.

A shiver raced through me, and I wished I'd brought my coat instead of the shawl. I stopped in a deli and stood in line, pondering my next step. An avocado and sprouts sandwich was in my future. Beyond that, the outlook was murky.

I picked up the sandwich and a bag of chips coated in thick, spicy powder. They were a color orange that could never be found in nature, but I loved the damn things. At a window table overlooking Main, I ripped open the chips and paused, a movement across the street catching my attention.

Rasha Gertner strode into the yarn shop across the street, a red scarf draped over the shoulders of her elegant, black coat. She was friends with Matt's widow. Maybe she knew something.

Hastily, I dropped the chips into my sandwich bag and hurried outside, stepped into the street.

A horn blared. Crushing the sandwich in my grip, I lurched onto the sidewalk.

A battered red pickup belonging to Malcolm Malone roared past. The middle-aged pharmacist would probably yell at me later. I guess I deserved it.

Grimacing, I checked the road this time before crossing. It was totally, completely empty. I hurried to the yarn shop. Knit gnomes and Christmas trees lined the front window. I stepped inside, and a blast of hot air raised the loose strands of hair around my neck.

Rasha stood before a wooden shelf filled with fat, jewel-colored yarns. She picked up a skein of ruby wool, and cocked her head in thought. Her lustrous ebony hair cascaded over her shoulder.

I grabbed the emerald wool nearby. "Oh, hi Rasha," I said. "I didn't know you knit."

Her full lips curved. "Only in the winter. I'm not as dedicated as your sister. Is that for Karin?"

"I thought some yarns might make a nice Christmas gift," I ad-libbed, loosening my shawl.

"Then I'd suggest getting at least two skeins of the color you choose, or all she'll be able to make are mittens. And that yarn you're holding is too thick for mittens."

"Thanks. I didn't know that." Knitting was part of Karin's magic — knots, connections, the ties that bind.

"You're welcome." Rasha started to turn toward the register, then pivoted back to me. "By the way, I was so sorry about your aunt. You did a good thing keeping her at home. I know how hard it was."

"Thanks," I said shortly. To talk about my aunt was to risk getting misty eyed.

"I cared for my mother when she was ill. I was by myself, and it wasn't easy – having to be on call constantly, and the little things like moving her from her bed. You were lucky to have your sisters' help."

"I know. I'm sorry you had to go through that."

Nodding, she strode to the register.

Watching Rasha's straight back, I tried to think of something to say that would pry clues to Matt Zana's murder from her head.

Not a damned thing came to me. What did I know about Rasha? Like me, she and Eric had lived in Doyle their entire lives. But they were a generation older than me – distant enough in age that I hadn't paid much attention to them growing up. Their wedding had been big news. They'd married late in life, after Eric had become a widower, a happy ending for a sad tale.

Abruptly, she turned to me, her long coat flaring about her knees. Twin lines appeared between her dark brows. "About the other day..."

"The other day?" I remembered Melanie's accusation, and my stomach bunched.

She glanced around the shop, as if making certain we were alone. A trio of sleek, silver-haired grandmothers sat knitting in one corner. They murmured to each other, inaudible. The shop's owner, a woman with carrot-orange hair, stacked a new shipment of yarn at the opposite side of the shop.

"Melanie wasn't herself," Rasha said. "She didn't mean what she said."

"I hope she still doesn't think Matt and I had something going on. He installed shelves. That was it."

"I know, I know. Try not to think about it. My husband and I certainly haven't."

"With everything that's happened, it's impossible not to think about it," I said in a low voice. "Someone stole my truck and put Matt's body inside. And Melanie — I can't blame her losing it when I showed up at her door. How do you deal with your husband being murdered?"

"I don't know," she whispered. "I can't imagine it."

"Who could have wanted to kill Matt?"

"I don't know that either. Matt liked to keep to himself. He was a private person."

Chatty Matt? "Private?" I asked, incredulous. "He sure talked a lot when he was installing my shelves."

Spots of color appeared in her dusky cheeks. "About certain things," she said in a rush, and I knew she wasn't telling the whole truth.

"What sorts of things?"

She bit her lip.

"Wait, do you mean he kept things from his wife?" I asked. And then I understood – the affairs. No wonder Rasha looked so uncomfortable. But that implied she'd known. I cleared my throat. "That's not so unusual, is it? I read that Paul Newman and Joanne Woodward made a point of not sharing everything. They kept some parts of their lives secret to keep their marriage fresh."

She nodded eagerly. "Right. Matt was just a secretive person. Eric is — was — his best friend, and even he didn't know all that was going on. I don't think Matt meant to keep things from Melanie, but she learned to live with it."

"But she thought her husband was having an affair."

She drew breath.

The front door opened, and Eric walked inside in a gray fisherman's sweater and jeans. "You ready?" he asked his wife.

"Just about." She turned again to the register.

Dammit. What had she been about to say?

The owner bustled behind the counter. "Do you want that yarn wound?"

"Yes," Rasha said. "Please."

The owner strung the yarn on a wooden contraption and turned it on. The yarn whirled, spooling.

"Hi, Eric," I said.

He shifted his weight, his almond-shaped eyes guarded. "Jayce. Nice to see you again, after..."

"Yeah," I said. After Melanie Zana had accused me of sleeping with her husband. I grabbed another skein of green yarn. Actually, it wouldn't make such a bad Christmas gift for Karin.

"I heard the police called you in for questioning again," he said.

Crap-ola. Did the whole town know? "They think I might have witnessed something."

His handsome face creased. "Like what?"

"Like Matt at the Bell and Thistle on the night he died."

"Did you?"

"Not a glimpse."

"Do the police have any idea who was responsible?"

"If they do," I said, "they're not telling me."

"Huh. I guess they wouldn't."

"Have they spoken to you?"

He nodded, grim. "They wanted to know where I was that night."

Rasha joined us, a paper bag clutched in her hand. "Fortunately, Eric was with me. Not that he had any reason to kill Matt."

Eric's eyes clouded, and he rubbed the scar on his forehead. "Yeah."

"I'm sure they only wanted to talk to you because you were friends." My stomach quivered, heavy, a sure sign something was off. "You flip houses. Did you ever use Matt to help with the remodeling?"

"Everyone used Matt," he said, "He knew his stuff. Matt was meticulous."

"And you never had any problems," I said.

"Did someone say there were problems?" he asked.

"No." My gaze lost focus. Who was Matt, really? The careful contractor or the seedy snoop? Both?

Rasha squared her shoulders, her expression less friendly. "Why?"

"I'm just trying to get a better picture of Matt," I said. "I know it sounds stupid, but after my truck was used to move his body, well, I feel like I should."

"Right," Eric said. "He did some work for you too. You know his quality."

"Mm hmm." And Matt had done quality work on those shelves, even if the project had taken longer than expected.

Rasha's nostrils flared. "So what—"

The front door jingled open, and Doc Toeller strode inside. She sported an ice-blue trench coat, belted at her slim waist. The doctor shut the door, and the overhead lights glinted off her cap of silver-gold hair. "Hello, Jayce. Buying a Christmas gift for Karin?"

"That obvious?" I asked.

Eric's face shuttered. Rasha tucked her arm in his and pulled herself close.

"Hello, Eric," the doctor said. "I know you're not here to buy yarn."

"No," he said, stiffening.

"I didn't know you knit, Doctor," I said, glancing between the two. Doc Toeller's expression was cool, but Eric's was arctic.

"Needlepoint," she said. "I know it's old fashioned and impractical, but I find it soothing."

Eric flashed a smile at me. "Nice seeing you again, Jayce." He nodded. "Doctor." He marched his wife from the store.

"How strange," the doctor said. "Eric seemed upset about something." She stared at the slowly closing door.

"We were talking about Matt's murder," I said. "I think he and Matt were close."

"Everybody knew Matt. He even did some repair work for me." She leaned closer. "A terrible snoop. I caught him going through my lingerie drawer." She winked. "Fortunately, that's not where I keep my incriminating photos."

"Do you think that's why someone killed him?"

She pursed her lips, thoughtful. "It's possible. But I suppose that depends on what secret he uncovered. If any. And I'm ashamed of myself for speculating."

"I'm not. The police invited me to the station yesterday for more questioning."

"Invited?" The doctor laughed. "You can be so droll."

"They're not happy about Matt's body being found in my truck."

Her blue eyes widened. "It's hardly your fault your truck was stolen by a murderer. You reported the theft to the police, didn't you?"

"Not five minutes after it had been stolen. Unfortunately, the police have a different point of view when it comes to potential suspects."

"They can't help but do their jobs." She shrugged. "I wouldn't take it personally."

"It's impossible not to."

"Impossible? I don't think so. Difficult, perhaps."

"Who could have a secret worth killing over?" I asked.

"I really couldn't speculate."

"But you must have heard something." I wasn't learning anything of value, and if the doctor didn't have a clue—

"I hear lots of things," she said. "But if I gossiped, no one would trust me again. Doctor-patient confidentiality exists for a good reason."

"I know." My face tightened. Doctor-patient confidentiality. Attorney-client privilege. They were great concepts until you had to know something.

Leaving Doc Toeller to peruse the thread section, I bought the yarn and walked up the hill. There was one person who might know something, and she wasn't bound by any confidentiality rules.

Bags of lunch and yarn in hand, I hiked upward, past cutesy cottages, and crossed the snowline. A tingle buzzed through me, alerting me to this natural boundary, and I slowed. The sidewalks were clear, and the snow light on the ground in people's gardens. But the roads could be deceptively slick.

I approached Melanie Zana's cottage of wood and stone. Lights glowed through the curtains in the front window.

Walking up the porch steps, I knocked on the door.

It swung open beneath my fist. Instinctively, the top half of my body angled away. I forced myself to lean inside. "Hello?"

No one answered, and a chill rippled my flesh.

I stepped inside, scanning the narrow foyer. Clutching the paper bags to my chest, I crept past the green-carpeted living room filled with its jumble of boxes. "Hello? Melanie? Are you all right?"

"What are you doing here?" a voice behind me growled.

I jumped, dropping my bags, and whirled around.

Melanie stood between me and the front door. Her red hair was a tangle. Her striped blouse was rumpled, stained.

"Melanie!" I pressed my palm to my chest. "The door was half-open. When no one answered, I... Are you okay?"

"Get out."

"I'm sorry," I stammered. Kneeling, I grabbed my bags.

"You're all the same. Wanting things. Taking. Lying."

"I didn't mean—"

"Out!"

I fled.

CHAPTER 12

"And then she slammed the door behind me." I groaned, prodding my spaghetti with a fork.

My sisters and I sat around the dining table at our aunt's – now Lenore's – house. The windows reflected black against the night. A cheerful blue-and-white checked cloth covered the table. Garlands of holly and pine branches twined with twinkle lights swagged the windows. A Christmas tree decorated with white lights and rustic, wooden ornaments stood in one corner. For our house, this was minimalist decorating, but with Ellen gone, none of us were really in the mood for the holidays. I wondered where our aunt's old holiday tablecloth was, and my throat closed. This would be our first Christmas without Aunt Ellen.

Karin tucked a strand of auburn hair behind one ear. "You're lucky Melanie didn't shoot you." She'd changed out of her miniskirt and into a blue cashmere cardigan over a t-shirt and jeans.

"Do you think she's got a gun?" I asked.

"This is Doyle," Karin said. "Everyone's got a gun."

"You don't," I said.

"Yes, I do," she said.

"What?" I yelped. "When?"

"I've had it for years." Karin filled her empty water glass from the pitcher on the table. "I practice at the range in Angels Camp."

"Good to know," I said.

"I don't plan on shooting anyone with it," Karin said, wry. "Unless they break into my house. Like I said, you were lucky."

"Her front door was practically open," I said. "It was like one of those cheesy horror movies."

"And so you walked inside like one of those cheesy movie heroines," Karin said.

I turned to Lenore. "Help me."

Pale in her gray turtleneck and slacks, Lenore grimaced. "Don't look at me. And I've got a shotgun."

"When did my sisters turn into Annie Oakleys?" I asked.

"A shotgun is excellent for home defense," Lenore said. "And I got it last summer."

Last summer had thrown us all. "The point is, I got nowhere," I said. "Rasha couldn't tell me anything. The doctor told me she caught Matt snooping, but... I didn't even get a chance to ask Melanie about her husband."

Lenore braced her elbows on the table, her pale forehead wrinkling. "It sounds like she's not doing too well. Maybe I should talk to her."

"Don't you dare." I didn't want Lenore anywhere near this mess. "She might accuse you of having an affair with her husband too."

"Why did you go over there?" Karin pushed aside her plate. "You knew she had the wrong idea about you and Matt."

"Isn't it obvious?" I asked. "She's the wife of the murder victim, suspect numero uno."

Karin's mouth compressed. "I don't think you're being strategic."

"Strategic?" I gaped at her. "How am I supposed to be strategic when my whole life is in chaos? Again!" Was this my fault? Had I somehow invited it?

"I think we should focus on the curse." Lenore collected the plates and carried them to the kitchen. She returned with a pot of coffee, and I inhaled, recognizing one of my own blends. "Let the police deal with gathering evidence about the murderer. That's a concrete, mundane world problem."

"Agreed," Karin said. "We should play to our strengths." She shot me a look. "Which are definitely not detecting."

"You're a fine one to talk," I said. "You played detective last summer, even though I asked you not to."

"And nearly got Nick and myself killed," she said. "I've learned my lesson."

Lenore poured cups of coffee and handed them to me and Karin. "The curse," she said gently. "A human may have murdered Matt Zana, but the darkness growing over this town is magical. It's influencing everyone. That's where the troubles began."

My skin prickled. "What have you felt?"

"The spirits are agitated." Lenore sat and stared into her mug. "And my journeys to Lower and Upper Worlds are becoming more difficult."

Karin knit her fingers beneath her chin. "Difficult? How?"

Lenore lifted the sleeve of her nubby gray sweater. Three, angry red lines marked her forearm, and I sucked in a quick breath. The lines were raised, as if infected.

"Why didn't you come to me?" I demanded. "I could have given you something for that." She knew I made my own magical salves and healing potions, and they worked too.

Lenore shook her head. "I've put your four thieves ointment on it—"

"Which clearly isn't enough." I rose, pacing the wooden floor. "When did it happen?"

"Last night," she said.

"But it's not supposed to happen at all," Karin said. "Your journeys aren't on the physical plane. Nothing there should be able to harm you like that."

Lenore shook her head. "That's not quite true. Shamanic healings take place in Lower World and affect the physical body. The opposite can happen."

"And has happened," I said. "Is this the first time?"

"It's the first time I've been left with an actual mark," she said.

Karin leaned back in her wooden chair. Folding her arms, she lowered her chin. "I've been seeing things. Something's changed. It's like a stained film has been laid over Doyle. Everything's grown murky. What about you?" she asked me.

"The only change I saw was the tree blight I told you about," I said. The memory stirred my disquiet. "I don't think it was natural. It's infected the trees near the spring." I didn't need to say which spring.

"But why would an unseelie cause a tree blight?" Karin asked

I rumpled my hair. "Why would an unseelie come to Doyle and curse my assistant manager with bad luck and our family line with dying in childbirth?"

"It's more than that," Karin said. "You were square in the middle of a murder last summer. Now you're bang in the middle of another. It can't be a coincidence. A human may have killed Matt, but your connection to these deaths has got to be connected to our family curse."

"Or the unseelie really doesn't like you," Lenore chimed in.

My foot bounced. "Thanks. How and why should the fair... unseelie change its modus operandi from killing us in childbirth to getting me in trouble with the law?" I asked.

"Because we should all be dead by now," Lenore said.

Karin and I stared.

"Think about it," Lenore said. "Yes, all the women in our family died in childbirth, but they also died young. In the past, women were having children much earlier. We've just turned twenty-nine and have already outlived every woman listed in our family Bible."

"You think the unseelie's lost her patience?" I stopped in front of the paned window and gazed at my reflection in the black glass. My face wavered, distorted. "I thought immortals took the long view. If we're right, this unseelie has been haunting Doyle for over a century. Why freak out if we're a few years behind schedule?"

None of us had an answer.

"It's a stupid curse anyway," I burst out. "None of us have to have children. We can adopt. And I'm having way too much fun to settle down now." Except... Brayden. I'd allowed myself to believe he was the one man worth giving up my single life for. A sudden longing struck me, so intense I smothered a gasp. Where was Brayden now? I squeezed my eyes shut, glad my back was to my sisters.

"But the curse was effective in the past," Karin said. "I think you're both right. The world has changed, and so has the unseelie's tactics."

"This is all guesswork," I muttered.

Lenore rose and walked to a high shelf. A thick, worn, leather-bound tome lay sideways atop it.

We watched in silence as she pulled down the book and opened it on the table. I knew which page she'd turn to. In spite of the fact I'd read the passage before — I nearly had the damn thing memorized – I stood behind her and read over her shoulder.

"Nathaniel hied away to the fae spring
To gather herbs and flowers for his bride.
Belle, mischief mad, behold anon the man.
Oh Moon, she raved, smit dreadfulle to her heart,
She wove her magic spelle and bound him close.
Away to me, she called, forget your love,
Forget your mortal pledge, a haunting cry.
Three days he tarried in the unseelie bower.
His home and hearth forgotten in her couch.
Then fire more fierce than fae's blew through his soul,
And waking, stumbled to his mountain home.
Return! She cried. I bind you with my charms,
I call the Morrigan, tie fast his fate,
If he resists, its Uffern's gate he'll knock on."

"Belle, the unseelie," Karin said. "Maybe it's time we named our enemy."

"Maybe it's time we find our enemy," I said. "Aunt Ellen thought the unseelie was living in Doyle."

"There aren't any Belle's living in Doyle," Karin said. "Do we interview every woman in town and try to figure out if she's really a supernatural being? We need to be smart about this. And every time we've tried to use magic to find Belle, something bad has happened."

"We can scry," I said.

My sisters looked at each other, consternation written across their faces.

"What?" I asked. "Scrying is baby magic. There's hardly any power involved at all. The unseelie won't even notice."

"I don't know." Lenore knotted her blue cloth napkin.

"The other times we've tried to find her, we've been in the forest, on her territory," I said. "We can do this here, in our house."

"If Aunt Ellen was right," Karin said, "the entire town is Belle's territory. And that's not true. We tried at brunch—"

"In a restaurant," I said. "We hadn't prepared. This house is warded like nobody's business. Between our aunt's old enchantments and Lenore's recent protection work on the house, we'll be fine."

"Famous last words," Karin muttered.

"You can't have it both ways." I paced in front of the dark window, my movements jerky. "You were the ones who said we should tackle the curse. We can't do that without going after the unseelie behind it. That means we use magic."

"I just don't think we should rush into anything," Karin said.

"Okay," I said. "In that case, I'm off to investigate Matt Zana's murder."

Karin rolled her eyes and growled. "Fine. We'll try scrying." She stood and braced her fists on her hips. "Anyone got a pendulum?"

"Duh." I lifted the necklace from around my neck. A narrow quartz crystal topped by a gold band hung from the chain. Wrapping a couple inches of chain around my two fingers, I let the crystal dangle. "Anyone got a map of Doyle?"

Lenore sprang to her feet and hurried from the room. She returned with a tattered winery map. "It's not super detailed," she said, "but if this works, it should get us closer." She unfolded it on the checked tablecloth.

I whisked my cupped hand over the crystal, clearing it. My energy is mine, I thought. It will not mingle with any other energy besides the Divine as I scry tonight.

Taking three slow, deep breaths, I quieted my mind. I imagined a white, sparkly light flowing down from the above, flowing through my body and filling my aura.

Karin and Lenore came to stand on either side of me. Energy leapt between us.

My skin tingling with magic, I dangled the pendant over the map. "Is the unseelie, Belle, in Doyle?"

The pendant twitched.

We waited, and I caught myself holding my breath.

The pendant began to swing, back and forth — a yes.

"Where is the unseelie now?" I asked.

The crystal's motion stopped.

I waited for a tug, for something that would pull my hand towards the spot on the map representing the unseelie.

Nothing happened.

I frowned. "Where is the unseelie now?"

The quartz crystal bounced.

Once.

Twice.

Stopped.

A bead of sweat trickled down my temple.

"Where is the unseelie, Belle, now?" I asked, impatient, waiting for the pull.

A tremor ran up the gold chain, and the room grew cold. The sweat on my brow turned clammy.

The overhead light dimmed, and I glanced up.

"Jayce," Karin murmured. "It's not working."

"No," I said, "wait." The crystal swung in a small, slow arc. Its circle widened, quickening. I gripped the chain more tightly, feeling the crystal's centrifugal tug.

The crystal flew, nearly parallel to the table. My stomach clenched. This wasn't right. I should have felt the crystal pull my hand somewhere. It wasn't supposed to merry-go-round around. But I'd never scryed for a magical creature before, and someone had once told me patience was a virtue.

Closing my eyes, I focused on the energy sizzling between my body, my hand, and down the chain.

"Jayce," Karin said more urgently.

I shook my head. I was getting somewhere.

Heat flared beneath my hand.

"Jayce!" Karin shouted.

I opened my eyes.

The map was on fire.

"Crap!" I snatched my hand away, pulling the pendulum to my chest.

Karin grabbed the water pitcher and dumped it on the flames. A pool of water darkened the checked tablecloth, dripped off the ends of the fabric, plopped onto the hardwood floor.

Ashen faced, Lenore peeled the soaked map from the table and stared through the burnt hole in its center. "Does that mean the unseelie is somewhere in the center?"

"It means the unseelie noticed what we were up to and got through all the wards around this house," Karin snapped. "I told you—"

"Well, we had to try something," I said.

"Every time we go off using magic half-cocked," Karin said, "there's a disaster."

"You mean every time you use magic half-cocked," I said. "I've never had a problem with it before."

Karin paled, and she looked away.

Shame scorched my cheeks. It had been a low blow. Karin had only really come into her magic this past year, and she'd had a rocky beginning. I opened my mouth to apologize.

"We need to re-set the wards," Lenore said.

"Right," Karin said, gruff. "I'll check the ones outside." Avoiding my gaze, she strode from the dining room.

I hurried after her. "Karin, I didn't mean it—"

"It's fine." She stalked down the short hall. She paused beside the front door and slipped into her sensible shoes, lying beside the rag rug. "You're right. Just because my magic works a certain way, it doesn't mean I should try to make you do the same."

"Stop being so reasonable and let me apologize."

"You don't need to." She wrenched open the front door and took a quick step backward. "Oh!"

Phoebe England stood on the porch, her hand raised to knock. The realtor's smile wavered, her teeth white against her olive skin. She dropped her fist, encased in a woolly, gold-brown glove that exactly matched the color of her hair. "Hi, Jayce, Karin. Is the whole family here?"

"Oh." I said. Crap. I'd forgotten I'd sort of told her Lenore was selling our aunt's house. "Uh..."

And of course, Lenore chose exactly that moment to wander to the front door. "What's going on?" she asked.

I whirled to face her and mouthed, Go with it!

Lenore's brow wrinkled.

"Hi, Lenore!" Phoebe waved. "Jayce told me you were thinking of selling."

Lenore's eyes narrowed. "Did she?" she asked, her voice flat.

Lenore was so gonna to kill me.

"I was in the neighborhood and saw your lights were on," Phoebe said. "I could see the three of you through the front window. I had some materials in my car on local property values, so I thought I'd drop them by. I'm assuming all three of you have an ownership stake in the house?"

"Yes," I said quickly. "Thanks so much, but now's not—"

"Come on in," Lenore said. "What else did Jayce tell you?" she asked in a honeyed voice.

Aghast, I watched Lenore lead Phoebe into the dining room.

Karin shrugged and followed.

Phoebe sniffed. "Do I smell smoke?"

"We had a small accident with a candle," I said, fidgeting.

"I'm sure the odor will go away soon." Phoebe set her big leather purse on the table, noticed the soaked cloth, and shifted the purse to a dry spot. "Did you know that the scent of baking bread can help sell a house? Oh, here they are." From her bag, she pulled out a red-and-white folder with her realty's logo on the cover. She handed it to Lenore. "This house really is lovely. I can imagine how hard it must be to think about selling. You must have so many memories."

"I hope Jayce told you we haven't made any decisions yet," Lenore said.

"She did," the realtor said. "And if I seem overeager, I apologize. There just isn't any new construction going on in Doyle, so if you do sell, I know I'll be able to get you top dollar. If the rest of the house is like this room, you won't have to make any improvements to hook a buyer."

"So we won't need Eric's house flipping services," I said.

She grinned. "I bet he'd love to get his hands on this place. There's always some crazy thing that people want to add. Sauna showers are hot right now, no pun intended."

"We don't have one of those." Lenore opened the folder, and her eyes widened. "The house down the road sold for over a million?"

"Um, thanks, Phoebe," I said, steering the realtor from the room. "We'll look that stuff over."

"No problem and no pressure. Let me know if you've got any questions."

"Actually, I do have one question," I said in a low voice. I followed her onto the porch and shut the door behind us. "It's about Matt Zana."

Phoebe stilled. "Matt?"

"I know you two were having an affair." I didn't know it, but I was getting desperate.

Phoebe went white. She grasped my wrist. "How—? Jayce, for God's sake don't say anything. He's gone now, and it will kill his wife."

So the rumor was true. The affair might have killed Melanie if she'd found out while Matt was alive. But had it killed Matt? Because it made a strong motive for his wife to murder the handyman. The wind rustled in the browning oak leaves, and I shivered.

"Please," she whispered.

"I won't say anything to Melanie." I couldn't imagine an uglier conversation.

Beneath her fawn-colored coat, her shoulders relaxed. "Thank you."

"But she may already suspect. She thinks he's been having an affair with someone."

"That doesn't entirely surprise me." She lowered her head. "He was filing for a divorce."

"Really?" That made another motive. "And Melanie knew about it?"

"I don't know. No. I don't think so. I don't know." The color rushed into her face. "Matt was more than a simple handyman. He had bigger plans."

"What sort of plans?"

She flushed again. "It's not important anymore. You and your sisters are fishing around for answers, aren't you?"

"Not my sisters." Keep them out of this. "But I am."

"I heard about what happened last summer, about you and Karin and that woman's murder. Do you really think the police need your help?"

"Probably not, but they did use my pickup to dump Matt's body. It feels personal."

"Well. Thanks for not saying anything." She adjusted the shoulder strap of her purse. "I heard the police brought you in for questioning again. Have they said anything to you about his murder?"

"Not a thing."

An odd expression crossed her face, one I couldn't read. "Well. Thanks again." She hurried down the porch steps and vanished between the cars parked in the driveway. I backed into the house and shut the door. On the street, an engine revved, drove off.

So Matt had plans. I was certain they hadn't included dying.

CHAPTER 13

Karin offered to drive me home, and I suspected it was to lecture me. But it was late, and my muscles were so taut I thought they might snap from beneath my skin. So I agreed to the ride and braced myself for well-meaning advice.

It didn't come.

My sister was quiet as we piled into her Ford Fusion. She was quiet as we wound down Doyle's darkened streets, the stars glittering above us. She was quiet when she slowed to turn into the alley behind Ground and parked beside the exterior, wooden stairwell. And her quiet rattled my marrow with alarm.

I glanced through the rear window, the skin between my shoulder blades prickling. But no lights followed behind us. Shaking off my paranoia, I followed Karin out of the small car.

I dug my keys from my macramé purse, my breath frosting the air. Beneath the cheap, metal lamp nailed to the stairs, I fumbled with the lock on the metal door to Ground.

"Nick and I are getting married," she blurted.

I dropped the keys. They jangled, striking the pavement.

"Married?" A warm bubble of happiness radiated from my chest, and I threw my arms around her. "That's wonderful! Congratulations!" I pulled away, releasing her. "Why didn't you say anything sooner? Does Lenore know?"

Her cheeks flushed flamingo pink, and she tugged down her soft, blue knit cap. "With everything that was going on, it didn't seem right to tell anyone. But then not telling anyone didn't seem right either."

"We need to call Lenore! You need to call Lenore. She'll kill me if she finds out I heard about this first." I knelt and picked up the fallen keys.

"It's just..." Her hazel eyes widened, anxious. "Am I doing the right thing?"

"What are you talking about? You two love each other. You were made for each other! Besides, who else but another lawyer is going to put up with all your systems and policies?" Karin organized the things in her dishwasher by size, shape and usage.

"I'm serious," she said. "He knows what the curse means. But... Am I being fair to him?"

"By letting him make his own decisions?" I raised a brow. "It would be unfair to make the call for him." The words came easily, but did I really believe them? But it was different with Brayden. Unlike Nick, Brayden didn't believe. He couldn't make an informed decision.

"It's not only about Nick."

"You're worried about yourself."

"No! Well, yes, but that's not why..." She bit her lip. "I'm being stupid, aren't I?"

"Only a little." I pinched my thumb and forefinger together.

She punched me lightly on the arm. "Thanks."

"Don't thank me." I unlocked the door and pulled it open. "Lenore and I are taking you out to celebrate and getting you totally drunk. So call her quick."

She grinned.

On impulse, I darted forward and squeezed her in another bear hug. My little sis was getting married!

A crack shattered the alley's stillness.

Karin cried out and sagged against me, her weight driving me down. My knees folded. We tumbled into the coffee shop. I hit the linoleum hard.

Karin rolled onto her back. The light from outside cut a diagonal line across her face, laced with pain and surprise.

"What?" I stared. "Karin?"

A crimson pool spread from beneath her.

"Karin?" I shook her.

Her eyelids fluttered closed.

"Karin!"

Icicles of fear speared my throat and chest. Instinctively, I kicked shut the door, but it caught on Karin's legs. Half-sobbing, I pushed her limbs aside and slammed the door, bathing us in darkness.

Lurching to my feet, I flicked on the light, illuminating the narrow hallway. My cell phone lay on the floor beside Karin. I grabbed it, called nine-one-one.

"Nine-one-one, what is your emergency?"

"I need an ambulance! I'm at Ground, at three thirty-three Main Street. My sister's been shot." My legs gave out. I stumbled against the wall, slid down it. "Hurry," I whispered. "This is Jayce Bonheim. I'm at three thirty-three Main. I need an ambulance."

"Are you in a safe place?"

I crawled to Karin. My knowledge of first aid was rudimentary. Pressure on the wound.

She lay on her back, and I didn't see any blood on her front, so her bodyweight was providing her own pressure. If I turned her over, the blood might gush free, killing her.

A gunshot. She'd been hit by a gunshot. My breath came in quick, painful gasps. I grasped Karin's hand and felt (or imagined?) a faint squeeze. She was alive. She had to be.

"Hello?" the dispatcher asked.

"Three thirty-three Main Street! Hurry! She's been shot!" I dropped the phone.

Ignoring the blood seeping into the knees of my jeans, I held one hand, palm down, over her torso and the other hand palm up. I closed my eyes and connected to the earth and sky, felt the energy run through me, and I prayed. I called every angel I could think of, begged for divine healing.

Hot energy flowed through the crown of my head, down my arm and into Karin's body.

She lay unmoving.

My magic wasn't enough. "Please," I whispered, I didn't know to whom. "Please."

Someone pounded on the front door.

I tore myself from my sister and raced through the dark coffee shop. Blue lights flashed through the windows, a dizzying strobe.

My thigh banged into a table, and a bolt of pain shot up my leg. Cursing, I stumbled to the front door and threw it open.

Two sheriff's deputies — Hernandez and Denton — stood on the sidewalk.

"Jayce?" Hernandez asked, his handsome face grim. "What's going on?"

Police? I didn't need police! "I need an ambulance! Paramedics!" I moved to shut the door.

Denton stepped forward, grasping the door. "Someone's been shot? Where?"

Hand shaking, I pointed to the kitchen. "Karin."

The deputy brushed past me. I turned to follow.

"Jayce," Hernandez said. "Denton was an army medic. He'll take care of her. What happened?"

A siren wailed. The ambulance. Please, let it be the ambulance and not a freaking fire truck or another sheriff's deputy.

"I don't know," I said, my words a sob. "We were standing at the back door. There was a shot. Karin was shot."

"Are you sure?"

Dazed, I shook my head. Was I wrong? Had I misinterpreted that crack? I didn't know anymore. I believed in fairies, but I was having a hard time believing in a gunshot. But something had hurt my sister, and it hadn't been me. Or had it? A strangled laugh escaped my throat.

"Come on." Gently, Hernandez led me to a chair. "Where are the lights?"

"By the kitchen curtains."

He strode to the curtains and flicked the switch. The overhead lights came on, glinting off the counter, the polished wooden tables. I looked at the red-paned windows. Karin had sat at that table yesterday, banging on her computer. I couldn't breathe.

A paramedic in a thick, blue parka hurried inside. "Where?"

Hernandez pointed to the kitchen.

A second paramedic, one I didn't know, strode into the café and followed the first at a trot.

I moved to go with them. They'd know how she was. They'd tell me she'd be all right.

"No." Hernandez laid gentle hands on my shoulders. "It's a small space back there. They'll need room to work."

Things were happening too quickly. I had to fix this. I couldn't fix this. I raised my hand to claw my hair and realized I was still holding my phone. "Lenore. I need to call our sister."

"You sit. I'll call her."

Confused, I stared at him.

"I'm a book lover," he said, prying the phone from my hand. "I've got her number. Sit." He guided me to an out-of-the-way table. Not Karin's, thank God. I closed my eyes and told myself she'd be okay. She had to be.

More people in uniform arrived, filling the café. This was my fault. She'd been shot here, at Ground. Someone had been waiting. Waiting for me? An ache pierced the back of my throat.

The sheriff strode inside. She wore an ugly red holiday sweater, jeans, and a pinched expression. I guessed I'd caught her off duty. "What happened?" she barked.

Hernandez spoke to her in a low voice. She nodded, came to me.

"My sister." I leapt to my feet. "They won't tell me—"

Someone brushed the kitchen curtain aside and a paramedic backed out, carrying one end of a stretcher.

I gasped.

He angled past the counter.

I braced my hand on the table. Karin on a stretcher. Not a black body bag. Karin. She was alive. I wound through the tables, banging my hip on a chair. "Is my sister going to be all right?" I asked the paramedic facing me.

"She's in serious condition. You should notify any other family members."

I swayed. Notify. Karin was dying.

"Miss Bonheim," the sheriff asked. "What happened?"

"We were outside the back door." I tracked the movements of the paramedics. "My sister was shot."

"How'd she get inside?"

"The door was open. I pulled her through."

"Did you see the person who shot her?" she asked.

"No," I said. "I didn't see anyone. I have to go to the hospital." And I didn't have my truck. I wanted to shriek, to punch someone. Karin wouldn't have even been here if I hadn't needed a ride. "I need my truck!"

"You'll get it back tomorrow," the sheriff said. "Hernandez, drive Miss Bonheim to the hospital."

"Yes, ma'am."

I raced out the door and hurried to the waiting police car, its blue lights blinding. I yanked open the passenger door and jumped in.

Hernandez slid inside more slowly.

"Hurry," I said.

He pointed to the ambulance, and my sister being loaded into the back. "We'll follow them. It won't do any good if we reach the hospital before they do."

"What's taking them so long?" My hands fisted in my lap.

"I got ahold of your sister, Lenore." A muscle jumped in his jaw. "She said she'd meet us at the hospital."

One of the paramedics leapt inside the ambulance. The other closed the doors and hurried to the front.

"Buckle up," Hernandez said and turned on the siren.

We raced to the hospital, the seatbelt pinching every time I leaned forward to make us go faster. Which yes, was totally irrational, but my sister was shot, dying, and the roads weren't that slick. I drove faster on these roads than that stupid ambulance did. "Is he a new driver?" I muttered.

"She'll be all right," Hernandez said.

"How do you know?" I asked.

"Just a feeling. Cops get feelings."

Nausea spiraled inside me, and I struggled to stay calm. Witches got feelings too, and I had no idea if my sister would live or die.

The ultra-modern, five-story hospital rose behind the redwoods, and Hernandez killed the siren. We followed the ambulance, then peeled off and parked in the red zone in front of the emergency room.

He stepped from the car. "This way."

At a run, I followed him through the silent, sliding glass doors.

Families sat in clusters on the soft, blue lounge chairs. Ten years ago, Karin wouldn't have gotten treatment so fast. Somehow Doctor Toeller had managed to fundraise and finagle this palace to modern medicine for our county. I prayed it saved Karin.

Lenore flew across the sleek, tiled waiting area, her long, cream-colored sweater coat flying behind her. "What happened? How is she?"

"I'll find a doctor," Hernandez said and strode to a nurse's station.

"What happened?" Lenore demanded.

"I don't know," I said. "We were in the alley. I'd just unlocked the door, and she was shot. I didn't see who did it."

Head bowed, Lenore lurched to an empty chair and grasped its arm. "This can't be happening. How bad was it? Is she conscious?"

"She wasn't, when..." I choked, my throat sticky, my chest heavy and clotted with pain.

Hernandez approached us with a nurse in pale blue scrubs. She glanced at her clipboard. "Ms. Bonheim?"

"Yes," Lenore and I said in unison.

"We have some forms for you to fill out."

"How is she?" I asked.

"Your sister is in surgery. We'll know more later."

"Is Doctor Toeller there?" Lenore asked.

The nurse referred to the clipboard. "The operating surgeon is Doctor Menendez." She smiled briefly. "She's excellent. We're lucky to have her, and your sister is lucky to be operated on by her. She's one of the top surgeons in the Sierras."

Which wasn't saying much. I would have preferred a top surgeon from San Francisco or New York. I would have almost preferred Doc Toeller – at least she knew our family.

"Thanks," Lenore said faintly.

The glass doors glided open, and Nick strode inside the waiting area, his expression dark and wild. "How is she?" His jeans and thin, white t-shirt were hardly enough protection against the winter night.

I stepped backward. Nick. I hadn't even thought to call him. Fortunately, Lenore had.

"She's in surgery," Lenore said.

"But how is she?" he demanded. "What's the prognosis?"

"We don't know yet." She took his hand and guided him to a chair.

Wordlessly, he sank into it and braced his head in his broad hands.

"These things can take a while," Officer Hernandez said. "I'll round up some coffee." He strode away, his booted feet quiet on the ceramic tiles.

"What happened?" Nick asked. "How did this happen?"

"I don't know," Lenore said. "We're lucky Jayce was there. She was able to get help right away."

He turned to me, his eyes a Texas storm. "You were there? What happened?"

I ran him through it. When I finished, he didn't say anything. He didn't have to. We both knew whose fault this was.

Hernandez returned carrying a plastic tray and three paper coffee cups. "It's not as good as Ground's, but it'll keep you going."

And it did. We paced. Spoke in low voices. Hernandez got a call on his radio and left. We worried. The clock above the help desk ticked. Its bronze-colored second hands ground forward more and more slowly.

Hours passed. Finally, a lanky doctor emerged from the swinging double doors. Her olive skin looked papery, lines carved beneath her eye sockets. She looked around, spotted Lenore, and walked toward us. "Are you relatives of—"

"Karin Bonheim," I leapt from the chair. "How is she? Will she be all right?" My nails bit into my palms. Karin would survive. She had to.

CHAPTER 14

The doctor's elegant face split into a smile, and my shoulders sagged, boneless. "The surgery was successful," she said. "Your sister's recovering now."

Lenore collapsed into the soft, blue chair. Nick's dark head sank to his chest, and he blew out his breath.

I grasped Lenore's slender hand, cool in my own. My sister was even more pale than usual beneath the waiting room lights. "When can we see her?" I asked.

"It will be several hours," she said. "Why don't you go home, get some rest, and return in the morning?" She glanced at the clock above the nurse's station. "When it's light out."

Nick rubbed the back of his neck. "I'll wait."

"There's no law against it." The doctor glanced at Nick as if she wished there was. "But you'll be more comfortable at home."

"Jayce, Lenore," a woman called from behind us.

Doctor Toeller strode toward us, her lab coat rustling, her short, silver-gold hair sleek. "I heard the news." She turned to the operating surgeon. "How is Karin Bonheim?"

The two doctors conferred, their medical jargon flying past me, uncomprehending. But Nick nodded as if he understood.

"I should have been here." Toeller tugged on the stethoscope looped around her neck, and her brows drew together.

"Why?" the operating doctor asked. "You're not a surgeon, and you're here now."

She shot her an exasperated look and turned to Jayce. "Your sister's prognosis is good. She was lucky."

No, Karin had been unlucky. Unlucky for driving me home. Unlucky for lingering to tell me the good news. Unlucky for taking the bullet meant for me. The shooter hadn't been aiming at Karin.

"If you'd like to wait," Doc Toeller said, "there are better places than this waiting room. At this time of night, nothing's open in the cafeteria. But the waiting room in the main wing is more comfortable than this one."

"I remember," Lenore said. "Thanks."

"Of course." Toeller made a moue of regret, and she gave a short shake of her head. "This isn't your first visit to this hospital. Don't worry about Karin. She's in good hands."

Nick wrung their hands, and the two doctors departed through the swinging doors.

"We should get some rest." Lightly, Lenore touched Nick's arm. "Karin will recover."

I realized I was still squeezing her hand, and I let go. Lenore, with her connection to the otherworld, knew when people were dying. I put more faith in her prognosis than the doctors'.

Nick paced, his expression haggard. "I can't go."

I laid a hand on his shoulder, and he stiffened. I let my arm fall to my side.

"Toeller was right," I said. "There are better places to wait — the cafeteria has got tables and vending machines, even if it's not serving food. And there's the library lounge she mentioned."

"This hospital has a library?" he asked dully.

"All donated books," Lenore said. "The lounge there is more quiet and more comfortable, and it surrounds an atrium."

"I don't want to be comfortable," he growled. "I need to do something. We know who was behind this."

"We do?" Lenore asked.

The glass, front doors slid open and Officers Denton and Hernandez walked inside, looked about. Catching sight of me, they beelined for us.

"How is she?" Hernandez asked Lenore gently.

"She's in recovery," she said in a low voice. "The doctors say she'll be okay."

"Thank God." Hernandez jerked his head toward the doors. "Jayce, we've got to ask you some more questions."

"At the station?" I asked.

"No." Denton's baby face scrunched with discomfort. "Here will do. But it's best if we talk in private."

"I'm her lawyer." Nick clenched his fists, and I could feel his impotent anger rolling off him in hot waves. "I'll be there too."

"She's not a suspect," Denton said.

Nick glared. "I'll be there. Come on, Jayce." He strode through the front doors.

I glanced at the cops, and the three of us followed him outside, leaving Lenore behind.

Greedily, I inhaled the scent of redwoods and fresh earth and realized how deadened my body had become inside the hospital. As hospitals went, this one was practically a spa. But I was glad to escape, especially now that I knew Karin would be okay. The sky was clear, the stars going on forever, and I felt small, insignificant.

Nick stopped beneath a lamppost. If the night air chilled him in his thin t-shirt, he didn't show it.

Hernandez stopped beside him and touched a plastic device clipped to the front of his thick, black sheriff's jacket. "We'll be recording this, just to make sure I've got everything right," he said. "Now, where exactly were you two standing when your sister was shot?"

I ran him through the attack, this time in more detail. Now I understood why they'd wanted a second interview. The first time he'd interviewed me, I'd been so panicked by the thought of losing Karin that I'd been vague, confused.

Hernandez probed, asking more questions, and I realized he was being careful not to guide me to answers he wanted. Hernandez and Denton were good cops. The sheriff was too. I couldn't blame her for considering me a suspect. I'd looked guilty last summer, and I looked guilty now. But even she had to realize I wouldn't shoot my own sister.

When the deputies finished, Hernandez clicked off the device. "Thanks, Jayce. We'll find the guy who did this."

"It's the same person who killed Matt Zana." Nick's nostrils flared. "He must think Jayce got a look at him when he stole her truck, that she can identify him."

"If she could identify him," Denton said, "the killer must know she would have by now."

Nick's jaw set. "It's the same person."

"We'll find him," Hernandez said, grim.

The cops departed, their squad car rolling near-silently away from the red painted curb. Nick and I returned inside.

Lenore sat in a large chair, her chin slumped to her chest.

I touched her, and she jerked awake.

"Sorry," she said. "Did I miss something?"

"The doctors are right," Nick said. "At least some of us should get some rest. Are you in any shape to drive?" he asked Lenore.

She smothered a yawn. "I guess not."

"I am," I said. "Lenore, why don't I drive your car? You can stay at my place tonight." I didn't want to be alone tonight, and I knew she didn't either.

She nodded.

I glanced at the clock above the nurses' station. I had to open Ground in three hours.

Yawning, she followed me outside.

"Where's the Volvo?" I asked.

She pointed to a far corner of the lot, and we walked to it. Her car sat beside a stand of redwood trees. Past the macadam, the forest sloped down into still darkness.

I shivered and stepped inside the car, slamming and locking the door.

We drove to my apartment, and I settled Lenore in the "guest alcove," with its wide couch that doubled as a bed. She buried herself beneath the soft throws and fell asleep instantly.

I plodded to my bedroom and its comfortable chaos of throw rugs and wall hangings and colorful pillows. Head aching, I dropped onto the bed. On the nearby table was a basket of river stones. Unable to sleep, I picked one up, feeling the smooth weight of it in my hand. I visualized a glowing light within my heart and expanded it outward, past the room, past the building, in a protective bubble. Then I visualized roots growing down from me into the earth, and branches like a tree's going into the sky.

"Ancient spirit of the Earth, I humbly ask that you share your strength with me now that I am in need. Give me the power to protect the innocent. I ask that you share the power of your mighty spirit."

The rock warmed in my hand, its heat flooding outward, and the blood zinged in my veins.

Something rapped at my window, and I turned, startled.

Early morning darkness filled the window, but dimly I thought I made out a small dark shape. I walked to the window, opened it.

A crow flapped inside and perched on my bed post.

My breath caught, and I edged away.

The bird's head cocked, tracking me with its beady black eyes.

"The last gang of you I ran into attacked me. So if you've been sent by the earth spirit, then I don't get it, because earth and I get along."

It cocked its head, its black eyes impassive.

"Seriously. This is confusing."

It fluttered into the air and soared over my head. The crow rapped me on the skull and soared out the open window.

"Ow!" I rubbed my head. And WTF? If the bird had been a messenger of darkness, my protection spells were working in reverse.

I fingered my bangles, then ripped them off and dropped them onto my dresser. My home should have been locked down, magically speaking. No one had ever gotten inside my upstairs apartment, and I'd never felt any negative presence here.

But there were things bigger and badder than my magic. Someone had gotten inside the café before without me noticing. And the crow... I rubbed my head. The bird had actually attacked me, rapping me on the head with its beak.

I frowned. Or had the knock on the noggin been a wakeup call? The crows in the woods hadn't done me any real harm, though they'd chased me into the labyrinth. I'd taken their inability to penetrate its lavender curves as a sign the crows were evil. Maybe my interpretation was off.

I shook my head, too tired to make sense of anything. Setting my alarm clock, I collapsed, face down, on my bed.

Two hours later, I stumbled down the stairs to my coffee shop. I unlocked the rear door for the staff, the door I'd dragged Karin through. I washed the floor, stained with my sister's blood. My hands trembled.

In the café's tiny kitchen, I combined spring water and vinegar and herbs. I charged the mixture with my magical intent, speaking the words.

"Protect." A tremor of energy flowed from earth and sky into my body and through my hand, into the spray bottle.

I wiped down the tables, spritzed the corners, scrubbed the door and windows, drawing protective pentagrams with the mixture on every door and window.

Striding to the back door, I threw it open, forcing myself to stare out, face whatever was waiting.

On the opposite side of the alley, beside a dumpster, yellow police tape fluttered.

Feet leaden, I walked to the site and gazed at the thin, plastic barricade, the circle chalked on the pavement. Had the shooter fired from that spot? There was a clear line of site from the dumpster to the open, rear door.

If I had Karin's ability to see connections and read auras, I might have detected traces of the person who'd stood here. Auras left all sorts of information. But all I sensed was my own sick fear and guilt.

Defeated, I returned to Ground.

Three of my baristas arrived, and we opened for the morning crowd, business as usual. A hard lump formed in my throat. Karin would recover, and the scent of coffee and the bustle of work should have cheered me. But my smiles and jokes were fake, embittered. Karin had nearly died because of me.

Nick had figured right — I'd been in the Bell and Thistle's parking lot when my pickup was stolen. I'd even shouted at the thief – I see you! He'd probably thought I'd identified him. That's why he'd reversed toward me. He'd only driven away after Brayden had emerged from the pub.

"Chai for Sally?" I called out, sliding the cup over the counter.

But the cops were right too. If I knew who'd taken my truck, the fact that I hadn't told the police who'd dunnit must have tipped off the killer that I didn't know who he was. Did the killer think I was withholding that information from the sheriff for some reason? That I was waiting to blackmail him or her? And it had to be a him. How else would the person have gotten Matt's substantial body into my truck bed?

A barista handed me a tall, paper cup of coffee.

I whirled to deliver it to the customer. The hot liquid splashed my hand, and I bit back a curse of pain and exasperation. Setting down the cup, I wiped my hand roughly on my apron.

On the other side of the counter, the customer tapped his foot, his expression tight with impatience.

I refilled the cup, thankful it was a straight black, nothing fancy, and passed it over the counter.

"Looks like you could use a break," Darla said from behind me.

I turned, my eyes widening with surprise. "Darla? It's not your morning to be here."

Her round face creased. "I heard what happened. How's Karin?" She brushed a loose strand of blond hair behind her ear.

"How did you hear?" The news couldn't have gotten around that fast.

"It's in the morning edition of the paper."

Or maybe it could.

She handed me a rolled up copy, and I crunched the paper in my fingers. "Karin's going to be okay," I said. "She's still at the hospital." Lenore and I planned to drive there together at ten. I glanced at the clock. One hour to go.

"You look exhausted." Darla grabbed an apron from beneath the counter. "And you're spilling coffee. Why don't you take a break? I can manage Ground."

"Thanks. I will." I whipped off my apron and folded it behind the counter. I had an hour before leaving for the hospital. I'd use that hour well.

Hurrying upstairs, I grabbed my green jacket. Lenore, a late riser, was still dead to the world, her chest rising and falling beneath the throw blankets on the couch. One slipped to the floor. I picked it up and laid it atop her. She didn't stir.

I tiptoed from my apartment. As much as I dreaded tackling Melanie Zana again, she'd been the closest to Matt. If anyone knew anything, she would. Melanie had believed her husband was cheating — had accused me of being the other woman. Could she have killed her husband and then come after me, and my sister got in the way? If so, this ended now.

I walked up the hill into Melanie's neighborhood. There was less powder blanketing the gardens and walks today. The snow had melted into patches, wilted stems poking through the earth in gardens and along the cracked sidewalk.

Melanie worked from home as some sort of medical writer, so odds were she'd be there. And I was mad enough not to care about calling ahead.

My footsteps faltered. I don't make smart choices when I'm angry. Was tackling a suspected murderess in her own home the best idea?

Doc Toeller emerged from Melanie's house, and I relaxed. It was a sign from the universe, as green a light as I could hope for.

Head bent, the doctor thumbed through a stack of papers. She pushed open the wooden garden gate with her hip. A robin's egg blue leather briefcase/purse hung over her shoulder.

"Hi, Doctor," I said.

She blinked, the open gate resting against her hip. "Jayce, what are you doing here?"

"I stopped by to see Melanie." And now that the doctor knew that, Melanie couldn't murder me. She was my witness and knew I'd been alive and well before entering the widow's house. I opened the gate wider.

The doctor glanced toward the cottage. "Melanie's pretty busy, but she's home."

"Is she doing some work for you?"

"For the hospital," the doctor said. "She's translating our research into language doctors and the public can understand."

"Interesting," I said, and meant it. Brayden and I both kept up on the local medical journals. You couldn't be an herbalist – or at least not a good one – if you ignored the studies. And though Brayden dealt with emergency medicine, he always liked to go a bit beyond what was required too. "Have you heard anything about Karin?"

"She's going to be fine. I'm surprised you're not at the hospital."

It felt like a reprimand. "Lenore and I are going there in an hour," I said, defensive.

The doctor nodded. "Then I'll see you there." She crossed the street to her red sports car, a Spider, and drove off.

I passed through the wooden gate and up the steps to Melanie's porch, knocked.

The door opened quickly. "Did you forget..." Melanie trailed off. Her red hair was tamed into a bun. She adjusted her purple reading glasses. "Oh," she said in a flat voice. "You."

"I didn't sleep with your husband. I'm sorry for your loss, and I wanted you to know that. I don't know where you heard that, but it isn't true, and the rumor hurts us both. Worse, it may have hurt my sister. Someone shot her last night outside Ground. I think they were aiming at me."

She stared at me for a long moment. "You think someone shot your sister out of revenge on my behalf?" She gave a caustic bark of laughter. "I don't think so." To my amazement, she stepped away from the door and held it wider, in invitation.

I hesitated. "I ran into Doctor Toeller on her way out." So someone knows I'm here, lady.

"The doctor's one of my clients." She nodded. "Come in."

I walked inside. The house was less cluttered today. Boxes were still piled in the green living room, but they'd been shoved into neat stacks in the corners. The hallway was freezing, the living room windows open.

Pulling my jacket closer, I followed her into the kitchen. The tile counter and sink were clean, and the windows were open here too. At least the house had lost that stagnant, unwashed odor. The dishwasher hummed. I stood beside it, enjoying the heat from the steam escaping its door.

"I should apologize," Melanie said. "For earlier. I wasn't myself. And I'm sorry to hear about your sister. Which one was shot?"

"Karin," I said stiffly.

"The lawyer." She nodded. "I didn't shoot her, if that's what you're worried about. I also didn't kill my husband. And I didn't try to kill you."

"Well." I shuffled my feet. "That's good."

"I don't suppose you have any reason to believe me after the way I acted the other day. It was a stupid accusation. I should have known better." She walked to the coffee maker, raised the pot. "Coffee?"

I shook my head, and she poured a mug for herself.

"Why did you think your husband and I were having an affair?" I asked.

"He slept with a lot of women. And then you came here after he died, as if looking for absolution."

"Not absolution, but I was looking for answers."

"I wouldn't mind some of those either."

I gripped the counter behind me. "The boxes in the living room, were those Matt's? I heard he'd filed for divorce."

"How did you—?" A muscle jumped in her jaw. "Yes. It's a matter of public record now."

So it was true. And I could have asked Karin to do a record's search rather than coming here. My heart twisted. Karin would be all right. The doctors had said so. Lenore had said so. It was safe for me to believe. "And is that why you thought he was having an affair?"

"No." Steam rose from the mug in her hands. "There were other reasons."

"Such as?"

"He'd been acting differently lately."

"Differently?"

She looked past me, out the open kitchen window, and I followed her glance. The floral curtains fluttered.

"Who would have wanted to kill him?" I asked.

"Ask Eric," she said, her tone bitter. "He knew more about my husband's life than I did."

Eric? The house flipper? "What do you mean?"

"Those two were up to something. They were always thick as thieves."

"Why do you think they were up to something?" I asked.

"Because when I asked about their latest project, Matt got cagey. I could always tell when he was lying, hiding things. My husband wasn't half as subtle as he thought."

"Did Matt have a lot of secrets?"

She laughed, a harsh caw. "Honey, everybody has secrets."

CHAPTER 15

Karin lay, unnaturally pale, against the white hospital sheets. But she was awake, a faint smile playing across her lips.

Nick sat in the lounge chair beside the bed. He leaned forward, cradling her hand in two of his. Her fiancé wore the same clothing as last night. I wondered if he'd ever left the hospital.

"No organs damaged," she said. "I was charmed."

He frowned. "You were shot. You lost a lot of blood. You could have been killed."

I swallowed, dizzy with relief. She was alive and well and awake. And none of that was any thanks to me.

On the table by her bed, I set a thermos of tea I'd prepared. It contained the usual herbs, plus an infusion of magical, healing energy.

"What's this?" Lenore, beside me, picked up the thermos.

"A healing tea," I said. "And you'd better drink it, or Lenore will have to journey to spirit world and find any lost pieces of your soul."

Karin smiled at her fiancé. "My soul's right where it's supposed to be."

It almost hadn't been. I looked away, tears stinging my eyes.

"This wasn't your fault, Jayce," Karin said, and I jerked, startled. I'd gotten used to Lenore picking up on my stray thoughts, but Karin had never done that before.

She smiled crookedly. "Under the circumstances, it isn't hard to guess what you're thinking."

"I'm so sorry," I said.

"And I told you not to be. You're not responsible for what happened. I'll be okay, and I'll drink that tea."

Someone rapped on the doorframe, and I glanced over my shoulder. Officers Owen and Hernandez stood inside the open door. "Ms. Bonheim," Owen said. "May we speak with you about what happened?"

Karin tried to push herself higher up the mountain of pillows and winced. "I didn't see anything, but sure."

Hernandez caught me with his dark gaze, and I looked away. "Alone," he said, "if you don't mind."

"Of course," Karin said.

It didn't matter if we minded or not. Hernandez was just being polite.

Silently, Lenore and I filed out of the hospital room and into the hallway, painted in soothing sand and wood colors. A minute later, Nick joined us.

"The police aren't going to get much from her," he said. "She really didn't see anything — no one lurking in the alley before the shot, no cars that shouldn't have been there, nothing."

"Neither did I." And I should have seen something. I was a witch, dammit. I was supposed to pay more attention. "I talked to Melanie Zana this morning."

He frowned. "Melanie? Why?"

"She once accused me of sleeping with her husband. I thought maybe she'd been the one to go after me and shot Karin by accident."

"You shouldn't have confronted her." But his heart wasn't in telling me off. He watched the door to Karin's room.

"It wasn't a confrontation. I think she understands now I wasn't involved with her husband. There is one thing though – Matt was divorcing her. Melanie knew it."

"And she told you?" Lenore's brows shot skyward.

"If the papers were filed," Nick said, "it's a matter of public record." He stared at the closed door. Soft murmurs drifted from Karin's hospital room.

"About that," I said, "can anyone see the divorce records?"

"They're on the Internet," he said, "but the online records aren't very detailed."

The deputies left, brushing past us and muttering apologies. The three of us returned to Karin's room.

Karin lowered her chin and gazed at Nick. "You need to go home and get some sleep."

"I'm fine," he said.

"And take Jayce back to Ground. She needs to get to work."

"No," I said, "I don't. I can stay." I fought a smile. Karin was returning to fighting form faster than I'd expected. But not even her bossiness could annoy me now.

Lenore smiled, smug. "I have the day off."

"Good, because you're wearing the same thing you did last night," Karin said. "Go home and change. I'm fine. Oh, and Officer Hernandez said you can collect your truck, Jayce."

I nodded. The sheriff had told me the same thing.

"Nick, will you take her to the police impound lot?"

"For you, anything." He bent and kissed her forehead. "I'll be back this evening."

Her eyes crinkled. "It's a date."

"I'll stay here a little longer, if it's okay," Lenore said. "We can catch up."

Karin looked as if she'd object, but she nodded. "That would be great. I'm already bored with this place."

Nick and I walked to his SUV in the hospital parking lot.

"Ever feel like you're getting the bum rush?" I asked.

He yawned. "I think she wanted to talk something over with Lenore."

A tiny, green-eyed monster coiled in my chest. I told myself I was being stupid. They were probably plotting their next magical foray against the unseelie.

Nick drove me to the impound lot, while I picked his brain on searching Internet records. I collected my truck and parked it in the alley behind Ground.

The lunch rush came and went. I set up my computer tablet behind the register. Between customers, I surfed the county records website.

I typed in Matt's name. My screen filled, a virtual spreadsheet of court filings. I scanned down it, clicking on the links, and whistled. Matt had been suing his wife for palimony. I didn't know how much a medical writer made, but if she really believed he'd been cheating on her, she must have been pissed.

I squinted. Hold the phone. Most of these records weren't about their divorce. Wynter Swanstrom vs. Matt Zana. I clicked on the hyperlink.

"Double mochachino with soy," a customer chirped.

"Right. Sure." I took his money, made change, made the drink, returned to my tablet.

Wynter had been suing Matt. Now that was information worth having, and I kept reading. Correction – the city manager had sued Matt and lost. Unfortunately, Nick had been right about the level of detail available online. I couldn't tell from the scanty records what Wynter's suit had been about. But still, a lawsuit.

How many other suspects were listed in the local court's database?

A plate clattered, and my head jerked up.

Darla grimaced sheepishly. She set a fresh apricot scone on a plate and passed it across the counter to a customer, then picked the fallen scone and plate off the floor.

I sighed. That was one scone wasted, but at least the plate hadn't broken.

I typed in Eric Gertner's name. Hot damn, he was in here too. I whistled. Eric was being sued by the Historical Society and Doctor Toeller. That explained Eric's tension in the yarn shop, even if Toeller had remained unflappable. The dates on those court filings were recent, so it looked like the suit was ongoing. I squinted, frowning at the screen. Again, there was no transcript. As far as I could make out, the Historical Society was suing him over some land development, claiming it was a historic landmark.

Returning to the search page, I scanned down to an article about the death of Eric's first wife. Their car accident had happened fifteen years ago, so I doubted it was relevant. But I was in a new, diligent, no-stone-unturned mode. I clicked the link to a newspaper article about the crash.

WOMAN KILLED, HUSBAND INJURED IN DRUNK DRIVING CRASH

(Angels Camp, CA) Sandra Gertner was killed and her husband Eric injured Friday night after their Porsche struck a tree. Investigators say Sandra was driving drunk when she lost control of the vehicle. Sandra Frances Gertner, 28, of Doyle died when the couple's sports car veered off the highway, the Doyle Sheriff's Department said.

According to investigators, both husband and wife had been drinking at the Bell and Thistle. The car rolled down an embankment, and struck a redwood, killing Mrs. Gertner instantly. Mr. Gertner was able to crawl from the car and signal for help on the road. A passing motorist, Matt Zana, called emergency services.

The metal countertop had grown cold beneath my forearms, and I straightened off it. Strange that Matt had been on the scene of the crash. Had he been drinking with the couple, or was it a weird coincidence? Or maybe it wasn't so weird. This was a small town. We were all in each other's pockets.

I tapped my finger on the counter and thought of my father's accident. Had he been killed by a drunk driver as well? There'd been no evidence of another car — he'd just swerved off the road while racing to the hospital for our births. But there was more to his death than a simple accident – the fairy's curse extended to the Bonheim husbands, but there was always a human element to the deaths.

I called Lenore. It rang twice, and she picked up.

"Are you still with Karin?" For privacy, I walked through the open curtains that formed a barrier between the kitchen and the coffee shop. From here I could still see if anyone approached the counter.

"No, but—"

"Get this! Matt was suing his wife for palimony. She totally had a motive. And Wynter was suing Matt for some reason—"

"Wynter Swanstrom? The city manager?"

"Yeah," I said. "He told me he can't stand Matt. Or he couldn't, but he didn't mention a suit. And did you know the Historical Association and Doc Toeller are suing Eric Gertner?" Our small town was lawsuit happy.

"What does Eric have to do with any of this?" Lenore asked.

"He was best friends with Matt. They flipped houses together. Melanie told me those two were up to something. Everyone's connected."

"This is a small town," Lenore said dryly.

"Yeah, but I saw Doc Toeller coming out of Melanie Zana's house today."

"So?"

"She said Melanie was doing medical writing for the hospital."

"And?" Doubt threaded her voice.

"And isn't it weird?" I asked. "Toeller's suing Matt's best bud and working with Matt's wife?"

"See previous comment regarding small towns."

"No, there's more going on here." And at last I sensed I was closer to the answers.

CHAPTER 16

I locked up Ground and turned off the lights, plunging the coffee shop into darkness. I stilled, listening intently, but all the sounds were routine. The swish of tires on Main Street. The laughter of a couple passing on the sidewalk. The creak of the building, shifting on its foundation.

Though it was only five o'clock, it was dark outside, and I felt my senses withdrawing, wanting to hibernate.

But I had my pickup back, and Karin was no doubt bored out of her mind in the hospital, so duty called. I drove to the grocery store on the main highway and bought some magazines, then continued on to the hospital. With all the suspicions and questions jumping through my mind, I could use a dose of Karin's logic.

I brushed aside the curtains to her room. It was lit only by flameless candles. A white cloth covered her bedside table, and on top of that was a vase of red roses, their scent heady. Nick leaned close to my sister, holding her hand.

They looked up, and I hovered in the doorway. "Bad timing?" I asked, and I swear I could feel the heat from her blush.

Nick turned on a bedside lamp. "Hi, Jayce."

Every spare surface was filled with roses. No wonder their scent was overpowering. I nodded, approving. It was about time the family romance writer found someone who understood romantic gestures. I squashed a pang of envy.

I looked for a place to set the magazines, couldn't find one beneath all the roses, and handed them to Nick. "I won't stay long." I turned to Karin. "How are you feeling? Have the doctors said anything?"

"Everything hurts," she said, "but I'll be fine."

I brushed a kiss across her cheek, smiled at Nick, and left. Three was definitely a crowd.

As I stepped from the elevator downstairs, my cell phone rang in my purse. I dug it out and frowned, not recognizing the number. "Hello?"

"Jayce, this is Phoebe England, the realtor?" Her voice seemed high, strained.

I smothered my irritation. Karin had just been shot, and Phoebe wanted to talk real estate? "We still haven't made a decision on the house." I strode through the hospital's automatic doors and into the frigid darkness. A few pinpricks of stars shone through the cloud cover, and then they vanished, the clouds closing in.

"That's okay. There's something else I want to talk to you about. Are you at Ground? Can you come to my realty?"

"I'm at the hospital, but I'm on my way downtown." Downtown meaning Main Street. "Can we talk over the phone?"

"I'd kind of... It's important. I'm not sure if I'm right or not." Her voice came in a rush. "I found something. It only makes sense if I show it to you."

Excitement sped my pulse. Had she discovered something about Matt's murder? "Found what?"

"The only way it will make sense is if I show it to you."

"If you've learned something about Matt's death, you should call the police. Now."

"But they'll think I killed him!"

"Why would they think that?"

"Because my name is on the deed."

Confused, I fumbled one-handed with my truck keys. "What deed?"

"Matt made things so complicated. I'll explain when you get here." She hung up.

Shoving the phone into my pocket, I unlocked my truck. I wasn't thrilled with Phoebe's cryptic message, and for a moment I toyed with the idea of calling Brayden. But he'd made it clear we shouldn't be seen together until things cooled off. And it was only Phoebe.

I sped along the mountain highway toward Doyle. My headlights flashed across thick tree trunks, monochrome in the night.

An SUV loaded with ski equipment pulled out in front of me, and I slowed. The SUV took its time, probably unfamiliar with the road's curves.

Impatient, I tapped my fingers on the wheel. Now that I'd made the decision to see Phoebe, an urgency sped my pulse. I had a bad feeling. I wasn't worried about meeting Phoebe, but I'd learned to trust my bad feelings.

Finally, the SUV reached the turn-off to Doyle. It continued on, higher into the mountains. I peeled off the highway and sped onward.

The F-150 hit a patch of ice and fishtailed. My breath caught, my hands tightening on the wheel. And then my new tires reclaimed the road. I moved forward smoothly, passing a stone barn that had been converted to a wine tasting room, then veering left onto Main Street. I slowed and pulled over, parking beneath a street lamp across from Phoebe's realty.

Its windows were black.

Uneasy, I bit my bottom lip.

A block away, light and noise and security spilled from a restaurant.

Phoebe had definitely told me to meet her here. There was only one realty in Doyle – I couldn't have confused the address. Had she called me from somewhere else, and now she was late for our appointment? Had she chickened out and ditched me?

Sitting in the truck, I called her on my cell phone. The call went to voice mail.

No, I was absolutely not going to check out the realty. This was getting too much like one of those TV shows, where the heroine rattles the knob and the door is unlocked and a killer is waiting inside. Nope. No way was I playing that game.

The streetlamp beside me flickered and went out, plunging my cab into velvety darkness.

On the other hand, a quick peek couldn't hurt. Could it?

I stepped from my truck and crossed the street. The realty windows were full of flyers for vacation homes for rent. I peered between the flyers, trying to get a look inside. All I could make out were disembodied shadows.

Oh, what the hell? I tried the knob. Locked.

She wasn't there. Phoebe probably had called me from elsewhere and gotten delayed. Maybe she hadn't picked up my call because she didn't like answering her phone while driving. A lot of people didn't. But annoyance sparked inside my chest.

The realty stood at the end of a line of 19th century, clapboard buildings. I walked around the corner to the alley. An exterior light was on above the realty's rear door. I rattled the knob. Also locked.

So that was that.

I turned to leave, but something, an instinct, hooked my gut. Hesitating, I walked to the rear window. I cupped my hand to block the reflection from the overhead lamp and looked inside.

Phoebe England lay on the floor, her blood pooling in the sisal carpet. Her eyes were wide and staring.

CHAPTER 17

I gaped at Phoebe, prone on her office floor. A near-black stain spread from her chest. Her wide eyes, so lovely in life, were lifeless.

I fumbled in my purse for my phone. Hands shaking, I dialed nine-one-one. The conversation went much as it had the last time I'd phoned. The shock of finding Phoebe's body, the thought the killer might still be nearby, strained my voice, and my breath came in hard, painful gulps.

Minutes later, the first officers arrived. The lights from their black-and-white bathed the darkened alley in shifting blue and red light. Tall, dark and grim Hernandez and his baby-faced partner, Owen, stepped from the car and strode toward where I huddled beneath the exterior light.

"She's inside, on the floor." My voice cracked.

The two men rattled the knob.

"She called me thirty minutes ago," I said, "maybe a bit more, asked me to come over. She was alive then."

"Stand back." Hernandez kicked the door, and it splintered inward. Something metal clanged to the floor.

I moved forward, but Owen laid a gentle hand on my arm. "Wait here."

The two officers rushed inside. A few minutes later, Hernandez emerged. He clicked a button on the plastic recording device attached to the collar of his parka. "I'll be recording us again, okay, Ms. Bonheim?"

"Okay. Is she...?"

He shook his head, and I took an involuntary step backward. My neck muscles corded. She was dead. I'd known it, but had hoped by some miracle I was wrong.

"I'm interviewing Ms. Jayce Bonheim," he said into the recorder. "Did Ms. England call you on your cell?" he asked me.

"Yes."

"May I see your phone?"

"Sure." I handed him my cell phone.

He checked the call history. "I see you received a call from Ms. England at six-sixteen. It lasted approximately two minutes. And it looks like you called her back at six thirty-two."

"My call went to voice mail," I said.

He nodded. "We'll be able to confirm that when we find her phone. Why did she ask you to meet her here?"

"I'm not sure," I said. "She told me she'd found something and needed to talk to me about it. She was worried that the police would blame her for Matt's murder."

"She said that to you?" he asked sharply.

Red lights flashing, an ambulance pulled into the alley.

Hernandez pointed the EMTs to the door. Brayden was one of the paramedics, and I straightened, my heart beating more rapidly. His movements were sure, his muscles straining against his black uniform jacket.

His gaze drilled into mine, then his mouth compressed, and he hurried inside the realty office.

My heart dropped into a briar patch of emotions. What had I expected? For Brayden to sweep me into his arms and tell me everything would be okay? Brayden was on duty, his first duty was to the victim, and he'd told me we shouldn't speak.

"You were saying?" Hernandez asked me.

"What?"

"Ms. England thought she was a suspect in Matt Zana's death?"

I swallowed. "Not in those words exactly, but yes. She said something about her name being on a deed."

"What else did Ms. England tell you?"

"Only that I should meet her here. I told her if she knew something about Matt's death, she should tell the police, but..." I shrugged helplessly.

"What time did you arrive?"

"I parked across Main Street and saw the lights in the realty were off. That's when I called her back. Like I said, Phoebe didn't answer. I thought maybe she'd called me from somewhere else and was on her way here."

"So why did you check the alley door?" he asked.

"I guess I got impatient," I said, my voice stilted.

The sheriff's SUV pulled into the alley, and Sheriff McCourt stepped out. She was in uniform, and she didn't look happy. "Jayce Bonheim. Again. I think we'll complete this interview at the station."

"How long did the police hold you last night?" Lenore asked.

"Three hours." I groaned and set another container of my "special" tea on the end table by Karin's hospital bed. "Poor Nick. With all the business I've been giving him, he's going to regret that friends and family discount he promised." And he hadn't blamed me for Karin's shooting either. He didn't have to – I still blamed myself.

"Or he'll be a part owner in Ground." Karin smiled. Her hospital bed was angled so she could sit up, a step forward in her recovery.

The scent of roses hung heavy in the air. Nick probably didn't know that roses were associated with healing and protection as well as love. Karin could use all the help she could get – magical and medical.

Lenore, her white turtleneck rumpled, sat cross-legged in the window seat. Gray morning light, filtered through clouds of iron, lit her golden hair. I should be at Ground now. But I'd taken the day off, thanks to Darla. At this point, I didn't care how many coffee mugs she broke. My luckless assistant manager was a champion, and I was grateful she was on Team Jayce.

Anxious, I studied Karin. The doctors had marveled at her recovery, but her face was an unhealthy shade of bone. "Never," I said. "I'll pay Nick. Don't you worry." I stood and grabbed a vase of roses, refreshing its water from the nearby sink.

"I'm not worried about the money," she said.

"No," I said. "We've got bigger problems."

"Why would someone kill Phoebe?" Lenore's eyes, more gray than blue in the room's unnatural fluorescent light, widened. "Because she was having an affair with Matt?"

"If that rumor was true," Karin said.

"It was," I said. "She basically admitted it to me."

"We know Phoebe wasn't the killer," Karin said. "But Matt's wife had good reason to kill them both."

"When Phoebe called me," I said, freshening another vase, "she told me her name was on a deed. But what deed?"

One corner of Karin's mouth angled upward. "Just go to the county clerk's office online. You can search property records by name."

"Where's your laptop?" I dumped water from a third vase and refilled it.

Karin gave me a look.

"I know you haven't been in the hospital all this time without working on your laptop." I returned the vase to its place atop a dresser. She was a writer first. Karin without a laptop was like me without a glamour spell. I never left home without one.

She dug beneath her covers and pulled out a slim tablet. "Nick brought it to me. Take it."

"Fantastic." I flipped it open — the computer was already booted up and in sleep mode. Quickly, I navigated to the website for the county records and typed in Phoebe England's name. A list of records popped onto the screen. "There's gotta be twenty here," I said, dismayed.

"Let me see." Karin held out her hand.

I handed her the computer, and her fingers skimmed across the screen. "Okay. The good news is all these records seem to be for a single piece of property at 329 Freeman Street." She frowned. "I wonder what's there?"

"Map it online," I said.

"I will, but... Here." She returned the computer to me. "Phoebe's not the sole owner, not on the deed at least. Eric Gertner's name is on it too."

"Eric Gertner?" I asked. "But he's... He was best friends with Matt. Matt's wife said the two were up to something," I muttered. But this couldn't have been it – Phoebe was on the deed, not Matt.

"It looks more like Eric was up to something with Matt's girlfriend," Karin said dryly.

"A possible motive for Matt to kill Eric and Phoebe," Lenore said, "not the other way around."

"Or for Rasha, Eric's wife, to murder Phoebe?" Karin said. "How was she killed?"

"Shot," I said. "But even if she wanted Phoebe dead, she had no reason to kill Matt."

Karin rubbed her temple. "Sorry. I was getting lost in what-if land."

Lenore shot me a worried glance, then said to Karin, "A normal place for a writer to spend time in. How do you feel?"

"Fine," Karin said. "I can't wait to get out of this mausoleum."

But our sister looked tired, something I should have noticed sooner. I cleared my throat. "It's not that bad. Has the doctor said when you'll be released?"

"No." Karin shook her head against the pillow. "They're hopeful I'll be out in a few days, but they said they have to assess my condition." She rolled her eyes. "I hear that a lot."

"I'm so sorry," I said. "If I hadn't—"

"Oh, shut up," she said. "Stop thinking this was your fault. It wasn't. So what's at 329 Freeman Street?"

I hesitated. Karin needed to sleep, but she'd kill me if I used that as an excuse to keep her out of the investigation. But she wasn't going to be doing any investigating from the hospital. It didn't matter what I told her.

I entered the address into the mapping website and clicked for a street view. An image of an empty lot and a tangle of manzanita flickered onto the screen.

Frowning, I clicked back to the map. It looked like the site of the old wellhouse, but I couldn't be sure. Why would Eric and Phoebe want this ruin?

"Well?" Karin asked.

"It looks like an empty lot," I said.

"Maybe they planned to build something on it?" Lenore asked.

"Maybe," I said. "I'll go check it out."

Lenore glanced at her watch. "I've got to get to the bookstore, but I'll return to the hospital this evening. Do you want anything, Karin?"

"Could you plug in my computer before you leave? It's running out of juice."

"Sure." I plugged it in and set it on the adjustable table near her bed, within easy reach.

We said our goodbyes, and Lenore and I left.

"What do you think?" I asked in the elevator.

"She's going to be fine, and you need to stop blaming yourself." Lenore smiled.

"That bullet was meant for me," I said grimly. But I didn't feel grim. I felt scared and guilty.

"You couldn't have known what would happen."

No, my magic didn't work that way. Maybe if I'd more common sense, been more like Karin—

She grasped my shoulders and shook me. "Stop it. By the way, Karin told me about the engagement, so you don't have to keep it a secret anymore."

The elevator doors slid open, and we stepped into the modern tile hallway. Through glass walls, an atrium filled with ferns and a stand of three pine trees glistened, damp from last night's rain.

I forced a smile. "That's a relief. She was going to tell you sooner, but..." Someone had shot her before she'd had the chance.

"Right." Lenore's lips flattened.

We went to our separate cars, and I followed Lenore up the winding highway into Doyle. I peeled off and onto Main Street and wound my way to Freeman, a residential road lined with grand homes set back from the road and hidden amidst the pines. In Doyle, this was the good side of the tracks, though we didn't have any actual tracks. The doctor lived in this neighborhood — we'd all gone to a holiday party at her house when we were kids.

I slowed at 327 Freeman, a house straight out of Gone with the Wind. The lot beside it was a tangle of brush and pine. I stopped on the side of the road.

Stepping from my car, I pulled my long, fringed green cardigan tighter. It was cold enough this morning that I could almost believe it would snow here today, even though this was the lower elevation. Snow in west Doyle was rare.

There were no sidewalks here, a trick to discourage the proletariat from strolling and staring at the mansions. I couldn't entirely blame the homeowners. The massive houses were gawk-worthy.

I walked down the damp road. Brown pine needles lined the shoulder. I paused, scanning the lot. It looked like the scene from the picture. The manzanita leaves had dropped, and its smooth branches were the color of dried blood. They made a seemingly impenetrable barrier.

But I knew better. As a child, I'd played here and found the mazelike deer paths through the manzanita.

Behind the brush and to the right rose an octagonal stone structure with a red-tile roof — the old wellhouse. A shimmer of gold glinted through one of the arched openings.

I wound through the manzanita, following the trail I knew would be there. The wellhouse had been an irresistible draw when we were kids. Our aunt had warned us away from it with stories of children who'd fallen through the wood floor, never to be seen again.

I pressed my hands to both sides of a cold, stone arch for a window and leaned through. The wooden floor was cracked and gray with rot. Someday, my aunt's horror story would come true. A child would fall through and never be seen again.

Green and gold mosaic tiles surrounded a tap in the wall. No well water trickled from its rusted pipe now.

What had Phoebe and Eric planned to do with this property? There was one way to find out — ask Eric. But instead of turning and leaving, I walked around the small, eight-sided building to the entryway.

Memories of my childhood flooded me. Playing here with my sisters. Conjuring stories of lost princes and evil witches, ignorant that we were witches. I'd believed this place had been magic then, even before we'd learned of our heritage. Maybe a part of me had always known.

No. I swayed, shocked. I'd done magic here.

We'd made this our fort, decorating it with pine cones and other forest treasures. And then the property had changed hands one hot summer. No Trespassing signs had gone up, and we'd been warned away, our prizes scattered. The three of us had snuck back at twilight one evening and loosed our rage in a childish rain dance. To our delight, the rain had come, a storm that shook the mountains and widened the streams.

Soaked to the bone, we'd fled to our aunt's home. She'd said nothing to us, but my sisters and I never again spoke of that day. In fact, I'd never remembered that day until now. Had our aunt put a spell on us to forget?

I knit my bottom lip. It was possible. She'd done that sort of thing before. But we had called the storm. I'd felt the power flowing through us, energy sparking through my veins.

My gaze clouded. How could I have forgotten?

Something creaked beneath me, and I looked down.

My breath seized. I stood in the center of the wellhouse floor. Its wooden boards sagged beneath me.

"Crap!" I leapt backward.

There was a creaking, splintering sound. The board gave way beneath me.

I stumbled and fell sideways, tumbling to the cold earth.

A clunk. A hollow, echoing thunk.

Hairs lifted on the nape of my neck. I'd walked inside the wellhouse and not noticed. How had that happened?

Heart pounding erratically, I clambered to my feet and tried to brush the pine needles from my sweater. They clung to every knitted loop.

I walked to the stone entrance and peered inside. One of the floorboards was missing, leaving a dark gap.

Now, this place really was a hazard. And I was pretty sure I wasn't the only kid whose imagination had been captured by the Moorish building. There would be others.

I could call the police, but who knew how long it would take for them to fix the problem?

I called Brayden.

"Jayce," he said, his voice cautious.

"I'm at the old wellhouse on Freeman Street," I said, businesslike as Karin, but my pulse thumped. "One of the boards has fallen through. I'd like to fix this before anyone gets hurt. Do you have any scrap lumber we could use to cover the hole?"

"I'm off duty. I'll be right there." He hung up.

I got on my knees in the stone entrance. Cautious, I crawled onto the floorboards, testing the weight. Most of the boards seemed steady, but I could see the rot. They'd all need to be replaced — a job too big for Brayden and I today. If we could do a quick repair on the worst of it, maybe put a warning sign near the entrance...

I hadn't thought to ask him to stop by the hardware store and get one. Well, I could return later and erect a sign. But I'd let the police know, and... And that would make a good excuse to call on the city manager, Wynter Swanstrom, and learn more about the lawsuit.

I peered through the rectangular gap in the floor. A musty, earthy smell rose from it, enveloping me. I sniffed. The odor wasn't bad exactly, just different. And there was something else. A current of air from below stirred my hair, and my skin tingled.

Magic.

Curious, I extended my senses, closed my eyes. A twisted, black and white landscape. Dead oaks and lightning flashes and dark, dark, dark. A broken castle and water streaming, ripping the earth, tearing at roots. Groaning trees, tilting, falling.

And someone. Something. A feral power, wild beyond my understanding. A gold light tinged rose expanded before my gaze. The magic overwhelmed me, racing like a wildfire across my skin. The light swelled, hot, beyond my control, and—

"Jayce!" Firm hands grasped me, and I was sitting up.

I gasped.

"Jayce, what happened? Did someone hurt you?" Brayden's voice rumbled through me. My side pressed to his chest, and his muscular arms encircled me. If I tilted my head, I could lay my ear against him, hear his heartbeat. Above us, pine branches swayed in a cold breeze.

"I'm okay," I choked out and tried to pull away, but he didn't let go.

"You're not okay. You were unconscious a minute ago." He flicked a pocket flashlight into my eyes. "I'm taking you to the hospital to get checked out."

"I'm fine."

"Passing out is not fine."

"It was magic," I blurted, exasperated. "The doctors won't find anything.

They'll tell me to get something to eat and rest."

He released me, and I wobbled, losing balance at the sudden absence of his touch. "Has this happened before?" he asked.

Had I ever gone back for a second helping of trouble before? Oh, yeah. "I was in a trance state, not unconscious." That, I think, was true. I'd opened myself to a light trance, but it had taken me somewhere deeper and terrifying.

"Like Lenore's shamanism." He got to his feet.

Mouth open, I stared up at him.

One corner of his mouth twisted upward. "Can you blame me for being curious about you three?" He extended a hand and helped me rise, yanking hard enough that he almost lifted me off my feet.

I lurched toward him and braced one hand on his chest.

We stood frozen, desire flowing between us. His chest rose and fell. I stepped away, his touch suddenly unbearable.

"I guess I can't blame you," I said. "Thanks for coming. I wasn't sure you would."

He nodded to a tumble of rough lumber and a tool box lying near the stone wall. "I don't want a kid to fall in either."

"And that's the only reason?" I asked and heard bitterness in my tone.

"No." He reached for me. At the last moment, he dropped his hand. "You found Phoebe."

"Too late," I said. "She'd called me, wanted to talk."

"And you went." Emotion filled his voice. Anger. Frustration. Fear.

"Something bad is happening in Doyle," I said. "Not just the murders. I can't—"

"He was blackmailing me."

I stared.

"Matt Zana," he said.

Confused, I looked from the swaying pines to him. A wounded bird fluttered beneath my ribs. "Blackmail? But what—?"

"I didn't want to tell you. I told myself it didn't matter. I wasn't responsible, and I was only a kid when it happened. But somehow he found out. And then he began twisting the knife. He knew how I felt about you, what it would do to us."

I grasped his wrist, my movements herky-jerky. There was nothing he could say that would change how I felt about him, because I knew Brayden. He was a good man. "What are you talking about?"

"My father was a drunk, and when he drank, he got angry."

I already knew this. Or bits of it. Brayden didn't like to talk about his father. His parents had separated when he was young, and he'd told me he had few memories of the man.

"One night my mother had had enough." He stared past me, through the open arch of the wellhouse. "She packed me into the car and ran. She was frightened, not really thinking. He chased us in his truck. I was nine." And then he looked at me, as if this last bit of information was somehow significant.

I shook my head. "I had no idea things had been so violent. I'm sorry."

"Don't say that," he said roughly.

"Brayden—"

"She was driving badly. They both were. My father tried to pass, and she swerved to block him. There was another car coming in the opposite direction. It veered off the road, hit a tree. My mom kept driving. She was afraid if she stopped, my father would kill us both."

"Given what you've told me about your father," I said, "that wasn't exactly a crazy idea."

"She finally did stop, here in Doyle. My father kept driving, and I never saw him again. The police station was smaller then. But they already knew about the accident. So my mother said nothing."

"The accident..." I shook my head. "You mean the other car?"

"My mother didn't report it."

"And the police never found out," I said.

"No. She took the secret to her grave, and I kept it for her."

What must it have been like to keep that secret? To have held onto that awful knowledge as a child? "And Matt found out about the hit and run? How?"

"That's not the important part of the story." His rugged face creased, anguished. "The other driver was killed. He was on his way to the hospital, where his wife was giving birth."

I felt the blood drain from my face.

"To triplets," he said.

CHAPTER 18

"Your parents killed my father?" I stared, stunned. "That's what you're telling me?"

The woods had fallen silent. A pine cone struck the wellhouse's red-tile roof and tumbled to the earth.

"I didn't know how to tell you." Brayden looked at his booted feet. "I can't tell you how sorry I am."

"And you paid Matt to keep silent," I choked out.

He looked up, his green eyes intent. "No, I didn't pay him. I threw him work. I think for Matt, blackmail was about enjoying his power over people, not getting actual money."

Tucking my hands around my elbows, I turned from him. He'd known all this time the truth behind my father's death, and my sisters and I had blamed it on an unseelie curse. I laughed. All this time.

A distant part of my brain reminded myself this wasn't his fault. He'd only been a kid at the time of the accident and carrying a terrible, adult secret. But hurt and anger coiled inside me, and I squeezed my mouth shut, terrible words rising in my throat.

"Jayce—"

"I can't talk about this now. I have to go." I walked to my truck and didn't look back. But his pained gaze scorched the flesh between my shoulder blades.

Leaving was the best I could do. I couldn't think about this now.

Starting the F-150, I drove toward downtown. I couldn't return to Ground. It would be too easy to fall into a work pattern and start thinking about Brayden and my father's death. Talk it over with Lenore? No, I had to get this straight with Brayden before I told my sisters. Between Brayden's bombshell and whatever magic had happened at the wellhouse, I was too rattled to figure out anything that mattered.

I drove past the park and its gazebo, abandoned in the winter, and rubbed a curled knuckle against my bottom lip.

I couldn't think about Brayce now, but what had happened at the wellhouse? I'd been drawn inside in a trance state and nearly fallen through its plank floor. Had that vision been part of the unseelie's magic?

My leg muscles twitched, restless. Unlike a dream, the vision hadn't faded. I could still see that twisted landscape, the ruined castle, the unnatural light.

The place I'd glimpsed hadn't been of this world. Was this one of the other worlds Lenore journeyed to in her shamanic trances? My hands tightened on the wheel. That answer didn't feel quite right to me.

And the power I'd felt there — what the hell had that been? It hadn't felt heavy or bad. It had felt beyond good and evil — wild, primal.

I turned left on Main and drove to the two-story city hall. Like everything else in Doyle, it was old. Built in the 1890s, its bricks had faded to a golden brown. Thick swags of holly garlanded the building, giving it a festive feel. A twenty-foot tall Christmas tree stood on the small patch of grass in front of the town hall, its red and green lights dim.

I walked up the brick steps and pushed through the wooden, double doors into a high-ceilinged hall. Doors lined the paneled walls. A polished, oak help desk stood in the center of the room. Two poinsettias bracketed each end of the desk.

Behind it, Mrs. Steinberg touched her silvery hair, and smiled. A pair of reading glasses hung from a chain around her neck. Like everyone else in Doyle, she was well-preserved, her age showing mainly in the depths of her brown eyes. I couldn't say how old she was, but she'd seemed to have been around forever.

"Good morning, Miss Bonheim. What brings you to town hall today?"

"I'm here to see Wynter, the City Manager."

"Second floor. Room two-three-two."

"Thanks," I said, glad she hadn't asked if I had an appointment.

I climbed the marble steps to the second floor gallery. It smelled of lemon furniture polish and thwarted power. Running my hand along the gleaming wooden balustrade, I made my way to room 232. The door stood ajar, so I walked into the receptionist's room with its green carpet and sleek, modern furniture.

"May I help you?" the young man behind the desk asked. I recognized him from Ground. He always ordered a flat white – name on the cup: Mark.

"Hi, Mark. I'm here to see Wynter."

"Do you have an appointment?"

"It's about the wellhouse."

He frowned at his computer. "But do you have an appointment?"

"It won't take long."

"You need to make an appointment."

"But—"

An interior door opened. Wynter, his blue eyes cheerful against his near-albino skin and hair, strode into the room. "Mark, can you fix this presentation for me? Maybe come up with an infographic too?" He handed the receptionist a thumb drive and smiled at me. "What are you doing here?"

"There's a problem with the old wellhouse," I said.

Wynter groaned. "Not again."

"Other people have complained about the hole in the floor?"

His pale brow furrowed. "The floor?" He jerked his chin toward the open office door. "Come inside and tell me about it. I've got a few minutes before my next meeting."

"Thanks."

The receptionist scowled at me.

I smiled back and followed the city manager into his office. He'd retained its 19th century vibe. The molding on the ornate wooden desk matched the curlicues on the wood-paneled walls. Sturdy, antique chairs with crimson and gold-check cushions mirrored the striped, burgundy and gold curtains.

"Wow," I said.

He grinned. "You can't work in a historic landmark and just chuck the history away."

"The town did in your reception area."

He shrugged. "Water damage. We had to re-do everything, and Mrs. Steinberg wanted ergonomic furniture. I can't say as I blame her, and no one crosses that woman. So what's this about the old wellhouse floor?"

"I was there earlier today and nearly fell through it. A friend of mine is there now doing a patch job but there are no warning signs—"

His forehead creased. "Unless he works for the owner, fixing the floor isn't his job."

"Which is why I'm here."

He sat in the massive leather chair behind his desk. "I guess I can't complain too much about your friend's initiative. The land the wellhouse is on is privately owned. I'll send a warning notice to the owner."

I plopped into a chair opposite. "You said other people have complained about the wellhouse?"

Wynter ran his hand along the brass thumbtack studs on the chair's arm. "I take it you're not a member of the Historical Association."

"No."

"They're spearheading a drive to declare the wellhouse a historic landmark."

Ah ha. So that's why they were suing Eric. "What's wrong with that?" I asked, feigning innocence.

"It puts them at loggerheads with the new owners, who plan to tear down the wellhouse and develop the land."

"Where does the town council stand on this?" I crossed my legs. The antique chair wasn't built for comfort. Maybe it was Wynter's trick to keeping his meetings short.

"The town council is divided. Some, like the mayor, value preservation. But housing is tight in Doyle due to various environmental restrictions. The new development would bring more badly needed middle-income housing to the town."

"Middle income?" The wellhouse was in a fancy neighborhood, too high class for anything less than upper-income homes. "How do the wellhouse neighbors feel about that?"

"NIMBY."

"Pardon?"

"It stands for, 'not in my backyard.'"

"One of the owners of that property — Phoebe England — was murdered last night," I said. "I wonder if that will change things?"

His expression flickered. "Death always changes things."

"Have you spoken with the other owner, Eric, about this?"

"I really can't say." He rose, but I stayed seated.

"I've heard Phoebe and Matt were close," I said, "and now they're both dead."

"It is strange."

"You sued Matt once, didn't you?"

A door clanged shut behind his arctic gaze. "Ancient history."

"What was it about?"

"I'd rather not say."

And I had no way to force him to tell. "But you hinted to me that he was a snoop. I've heard from other people that he might have been a blackmailer."

"You don't sue people who are blackmailing you, Jayce."

"No," I said. "I guess you don't." But the lawsuit had been years ago. Had Matt held something else over Wynter? Something worth killing over?

Outside the town hall, I sat in my truck and thought. Brayden's parents and mine. Brayden's secret. Brayden lying to me... I shook my head. Enough. The past was done with. The present had nearly gotten Karin killed.

The truck's cab was a refrigerator, and I blew into my fisted hands.

The motives for the murders were piling up. The Historical Association, led by Doc Toeller, were suing Eric and Phoebe over the wellhouse. Matt had been having an affair with Phoebe. So far, Matt's wife was the only one I could see who had a motive to kill them both. But a piece felt missing. Had Matt been blackmailing Wynter?

I turned the ignition and pulled from the curb. Eric was flipping a home on Bean Blossom Road. There'd be workers about, and that made the house a perfect place to ask Eric what he knew.

On Main Street, a handful of tourists getting a jump on the weekend wandered the raised sidewalks. The windows glittered with Christmas displays. Sandra, who ran one of the wine tasting rooms, turned the sign in the window to OPEN, and paused to pick a dead leaf from the mountain of poinsettia plants on the porch. She went inside and adjusted a Santa Claus wine cozy in the window.

My stomach growled. If she was opening the tasting room, it was eleven o'clock, too early for lunch. But the vision I'd had at the wellhouse had worked up an appetite.

Ignoring my hunger, I drove to Bean Blossom Road. It wound above the snowline, and thin powder covered the gardens. Small Victorians — no more than ornate shacks — lined the narrow street. A work truck, its bed filled with equipment, squatted in the narrow driveway of a ramshackle cottage with a steep roof. Eric's red sports car sat parked on the street.

I pulled up behind the car, parked, and stepped from my truck.

Opening the picket gate, I walked up the brick path and the three low steps to the porch. An antique rocking horse, its paint flecked, its eyes sad, braced open the front door.

I patted the horse's wooden head. The toy swayed eerily, scraping against the door.

Hammers and saws banged and scraped from within. I grit my teeth against the aural assault. "Hello?" I called and stepped inside.

The walls and floors were bare, and new drywall had been nailed into place. Strips of the original crown molding lay on the floor near a fireplace and I wondered what they were going to do with it. "Hello?"

Eric ducked his head and passed through an open doorway. He wiped his hands on a damp rag. Our gazes met, and he stopped short beside a sawhorse. "Jayce? What are you doing here?"

"I hope it's okay. I was driving by and saw you were here. My sister, Lenore, is looking to downsize." I sent her a silent apology. "I thought this cottage might be just right for her. When do you think you'll be putting it on the market?"

"Downsize?" he blinked and turned toward the door he'd come through, turned back to me.

"Our aunt's house is so big," I said. "It was great when we were all living there, and of course my aunt would never sell, but now that she's gone..." I trailed off, a sudden rush of anguish threatening to engulf me. The loss of our aunt, our only real mother figure, still hit me at random moments. My lips compressed.

"Right." He nodded. "Sorry. I heard about the attack on your sister, Karin. When you started talking about Lenore, it threw me. How is Karin?"

"She'll recover. She was lucky."

His head fell back, and he stared for a moment at the ceiling. "I'm glad to hear it. Matt's death seems to have had a ripple effect. I hope whatever's happening ends soon."

"You think her attack is connected to the murders?"

He dropped the rag on the paint-flecked sawhorse. "The police do. They asked me where I was at the time of the shooting. Is that why you're really here?" he asked dryly.

I grimaced. "I'm that obvious?"

"I can't blame you. You're worried about someone you love. But I wasn't anywhere near Ground that night. I was meeting with one of my business partners in Angels Camp."

Something in the way he'd said "that night" made me study him more closely. "But on the night Matt was killed?"

He rubbed his scar. "I wasn't anywhere near him either."

"Do you mind if I ask where you were?"

He shrugged. "I came clean with the police. I may as well tell you too."

"Came clean?" What had Eric been up to?

"Matt had called me to meet him at the Bell and Thistle. I didn't go. I had some things on my mind, so I drove around to clear my head."

He'd lied about his alibi. Why? Did he worry he'd be a suspect? If so, he had to have a motive. "The police couldn't have been happy about that alibi."

"They weren't, but it's the truth. And now that another one of my business partners is dead..." He shook his head. "I'd like to know what's going on too."

"I'm sorry about Phoebe. I know she was a partner in the wellhouse property. Was she involved in any others?"

"No. Only the wellhouse. She told you we were partners?"

"Phoebe mentioned she was on the deed," I said, probing. She'd said she was on a deed, and Eric's was the only one I'd found online. How was the wellhouse property connected to the murders, if at all? "You must have known her well."

"No. We were business partners. But you never imagine someone you know dying like that, murdered."

"How did Phoebe come to partner with you on the wellhouse property?"

He crossed his arms over his muscular chest. "What did she tell you?"

"She was a little nebulous," I said.

The rag slipped from the sawhorse to the rough floor. He stooped and replaced it. "She was a realtor, and she had connections. She also had a little money saved and wanted to invest it somewhere."

"It's too bad about the lawsuit. Does the Historical Association have a case to block the wellhouse development?"

"I don't think so. I hope not." He angled his body away from me and looked out a window. "Tell me the truth. Is Lenore interested in this house?"

I shoved my hands in my pockets. "Um, no. Sorry."

He shook his head, his mouth twisting.

"But I'd love to look around," I said quickly, "if that's okay."

The saw was still whining in another room, so I wasn't worried about him hitting me over the head and burying me in the backyard. Someone else was working here, so I had at least one witness.

He sighed. "Come on then."

Eric gave me a tour, explaining the modifications and improvements. "We're keeping the Victorian feel," he said. "But we're enlarging the rooms to modern standards and upgrading the bathrooms and kitchen."

I made appreciative noises. And I did appreciate the cottage. It would be a jewel when finished, but I couldn't imagine living anywhere other than above Ground.

"I suppose Phoebe would have helped you sell it," I said.

He sat against a windowsill, his posture loose, his shoulders slumped. "Yeah. Now it will be for sale by owner, but I'm not expecting selling it will be difficult. There's no new housing in Doyle, and demand is high. People – especially retirees – are looking to get out of the cities. We're getting our share of tech workers too, folks who can work from home and earn a living."

It sounded like a speech he gave often. "Hence the wellhouse development," I said.

"Which isn't going anywhere until that damned lawsuit is over. People need places to live. That old wellhouse is a hazard. If the city won't take care of it, then it isn't fair to make me do it."

"Now that Phoebe's dead, what happens to the property?"

"I don't know," he said, his words clipped. "It's too soon. I can't think about it now."

"I guess it is." I hesitated. "You knew them both, who would have wanted to kill Matt and Phoebe?"

He looked as if he would say something, then shook his head. "I can't say."

I left, dissatisfied. Eric had pretty much confirmed what I'd guessed about her connection to the wellhouse. But I felt no closer to the truth.

CHAPTER 19

I closed Ground for the evening and drove to the hospital.

Karin was alone and sleeping. The scent of Nick's roses hung faint in the air. Machines bleeped. Two nurses murmured in the hallway outside, their voices and footsteps growing fainter.

I picked up one of the knitting magazines I'd brought her and dropped into the armchair by the bed. I preferred fashion magazines, but the knitting mags had some cute designs. I skimmed an article on a woman who designed fairy-inspired patterns. None appealed. My view of fairies had taken a turn for the dark and dangerous.

Karin sighed. "Ask the rose rabbit."

I looked up.

She was still sleeping.

My scalp prickled. The "rose rabbit" probably meant nothing. Karin had gotten this business about a rose rabbit into her head and was dreaming about it now.

But… That didn't explain how I'd heard those words in the beating of the crows' wings.

There was a soft sound near the door. I gave a start and glanced toward the parted curtains.

Brayden stood inside the doorway, his broad shoulders hunched beneath his green flannel shirt. He held a potted poinsettia in one hand and glanced down at it. "There aren't many options this time of year. Roses didn't seem right."

My heart thudded three times, then settled into its natural rhythm. "Hi," I said in a low voice.

"This looks like a bad time," he said.

"No." I stood.

We watched each other for a long moment. He smelled of cedar and sawdust and sweat. Everything I wanted to say – to shout – at him and wouldn't roiled inside me. And none of it mattered.

I moved to him.

He set the flowers on the counter by the sink, and we stepped into the hallway.

I reached to touch his hand but stopped myself, dropping my own to my side. He'd kept so much from me. It was only because of murder and blackmail that he'd finally told the truth. I stared at the carpet. Had he really thought I was the kind of person to blame him for something he hadn't done? But here I was, looking for reasons to do just that. "I didn't expect to see you here."

"Karin's a good person," he said, gruff.

"She is." So was he. "Thanks for taking care of the wellhouse."

His shoulders loosened. "Not a problem, but it's only a temporary fix."

"I stopped by city hall," I said casually. I didn't know what to say about anything that mattered, but I kept talking, unable to stand the thought of him going away. "Wynter said he'd send a notice to the owners."

Brayden snorted. "Who knows how long that will take? Better we deal with it ourselves."

And just like that, we were a team again. I warmed, swaying toward him like a sunflower. "Brayden—"

"Will you tell her? About the car accident?" His gaze was probing, worried.

Angry heat flushed through my veins. So that was why he'd come. "Karin deserves to know. Both my sisters do."

His broad fingers twitched. "You're right, but I'd like them to hear it from me."

My arms tightened against my body. "That's fair." It would also allow him to control the message. Much easier to garner sympathy when— No, that wasn't Brayden. He was better than that, and I wasn't being fair.

A nurse rolled a food cart down the hallway. She paused in front of an open door, consulted her chart.

I couldn't blame Brayden for any of this, but a part of me couldn't let this alone.

"I'll come back tomorrow." Lightly, he touched my arm.

I shivered but said nothing.

Miserable, I watched him disappear around a corner. I returned to Karin, still sleeping. My blood hummed, agitated, and she didn't need to be around that kind of energy when she was recovering. I grabbed my blue, wool shawl from the back of a chair and strode into the hallway. I needed air, somewhere to pace, to get my head clear.

On impulse, instead of taking the elevator to the lobby, I turned right and walked through the glass doors onto the patio. The night was cloudless, the sky filled with stars. I lifted my hand, sketching the Milky Way's wavering trail.

Alone, I paced past concrete planters filled with ivy and rosemary. I brushed my hand across the top of a rosemary bush and rubbed my fingers together. Its tangy scent rose around me, and I smoothed the oils over my hair.

I replayed the conversation with Brayden in my head. True, I hadn't said anything awful to him, but things between us had been stilted.

He was trying. I was trying. We'd get through this. He had to understand I needed time to process his confession.

Dammit, I hadn't exactly told him that.

I shook my head. I needed to stop dwelling and start doing. Since I wasn't going to get any detecting done on the third-floor hospital patio, my only alternative left was magic.

I sat on a concrete bench. Trying to ignore the chill seeping through my jeans, I folded myself into a cross-legged position. One of the crows that had attacked me had escaped with a lock of my hair in its talons. If the unseelie/fairy/whatever had sent those birds, then it had made a mistake.

Scrabbling in my purse, I dug out a crumpled envelope and pen. I peeled the return address sticker from the envelope, so my spell wouldn't attach to the sender (my car insurance broker). Rosemary and ivy were both for protection and healing – suspiciously ideal for a hospital, and not bad for my plans either. I broke off short stems of both from the planter behind me and twined them together.

"Now, I invoke the law of three, that what was taken is shown to me."

I drew the symbol for the planet Mercury and the Moon on the back of the envelope. Wincing, I plucked a long hair from my scalp and put it inside.

The herb's scent coiled around me. I visualized it lifting me into the sky.

Where is it?

And then I was flying, soaring away from the hospital, over the tops of redwoods. Lights faded behind me, and I was above the Sierras, the air cold enough to blister my skin. I descended, and the trees changed to oak. And then I hovered above one oak, a murder of crows roosting in its branches.

The ebony birds shifted, cawing, as if they'd sensed my presence. But they couldn't hurt me in my astral form, and I floated closer.

A nest wedged in the tree. The twigs were lined with pine needles, dead weeds, and strands of long, brown hair.

"Jayce?"

I jerked from the vision and was back on the hospital patio, my butt numb from the cold concrete bench.

Lenore sat beside me, her white jacket zipped to her chin. "Karin's still sleeping."

"How...?" My muzzy brain fumbled, struggling to understand the change in realities.

"I figured you came out here when you found her asleep. What were you doing? Meditating?"

My chest tightened with an entire swamp forest of guilt. "Spell casting." I folded the envelope and stuck it in the rear pocket of my jeans.

Her blue eyes narrowed. "For what?"

"For my hair. The crows that attacked me stole a few strands. I thought the unseelie was behind it, but..."

"But what?"

"But I saw it in a nest."

She stuffed her hands in her jacket pockets. "That's weird."

"It's a relief. It means the unseelie can't use my hair to curse me." Fingernail clippings or hair from an intended victim were classic ingredients in curses. I didn't know why the fairy would need mine. She'd already zinged us good with her birth-death curse.

"No, it's weird," Lenore said. "This isn't the season for nest building."

I bit my lip, chagrined. I knew that, but I'd wanted to believe all was well. "It was a trick." I drew a deep breath, sucking in my annoyance. "She showed me what I wanted to see."

"You think the unseelie figured out what you were doing and sent a vision to throw you off track?"

"Something sent those crows after me. There was magic in their attack."

She canted her head. "But they didn't hurt you."

"They got my hair. God knows what the unseelie will do with it." I'd made such a mess of things. And now I knew the truth about our father's death, a truth that Lenore deserved to know sooner rather than later. A truth I couldn't tell. I changed the subject. "What do you think of Karin's rose rabbit?"

Her pale brows rose. "Is it Karin's now? I thought you said you'd heard it too."

"I thought I'd heard the words in the crow attack. If I did, then the rabbit must be connected to the fairy. Or maybe rose rabbit is another name for the unseelie." I straightened. Or maybe it was something else entirely.

"What are you thinking?" she asked.

"What if the crows were sent by the rose rabbit and not the unseelie?" I asked, feeling my way. "Because you're right, they didn't hurt me. What if the birds were a warning?"

"Then why take your hair?" she asked. "That's just creepy. Karin's looked everywhere online for references to a rose rabbit. I've looked too. There's nothing."

"But Belle's a lot older than the Internet. What if there isn't anything online because the rose rabbit predates digital records?"

She ran her hand along the tops of the rosemary bush. Its scent lifted into the air, twining around us. "Tons of people are doing supernatural research and posting their findings," she said. "And there's lots of stuff online that was written before the Internet existed. You'd think we'd find something."

"Not if this is a local legend," I said. "But with Aunt Ellen gone, there's no one else to ask about local folklore."

"You could try the library."

I blinked. "Library?"

"You know, that big building with all the books?"

My cheeks warmed. "I didn't even think to look. It's been so long since I've been inside one."

"Not since you were a kid, I'll bet."

"I did hit the books a few times in college."

She snorted. "Very few."

"So you think it's possible? That the rose rabbit isn't only in our imagination?"

"There's something to it. Both you and Karin have encountered this thing."

"But you haven't?"

My sister bent to sniff the rosemary. "Mm."

It wasn't an answer, and my eyes narrowed. "Have you been experiencing anything, well, weird?"

She blinked rapidly, then turned, wide-eyed, to me. "I've been dreaming poetry, does that count?"

"You're dreaming poems?" I laughed. Only Lenore. "No. It doesn't count." But I wondered about Lenore's dreams, and about what she wasn't telling me.

CHAPTER 20

Karin finally woke up. Settling around her hospital bed, we talked about the murder and the unseelie and the rose rabbit.

And we got nowhere.

Then Nick arrived, roses in hand. Lenore and I left the lovebirds alone.

Lenore followed me to my truck in the hospital parking lot. A waning crescent moon curved like a scimitar over the sawtooth mountains. The night was still and brittle with cold.

"What's going on, Lenore?" I asked.

"Regarding magic or murder?"

"Regarding you."

A lamp in the parking lot flickered amber, making her face look jaundiced.

Lenore bit her bottom lip. "I didn't want to say anything until I was sure. I wasn't sure if it meant anything or was just my subconscious in overdrive. But I've been dreaming strange things."

Dread rooted in my stomach, and I slumped against the F-150. "What sorts of things?"

Her hands fluttered, mothlike. "Real things, but not real."

"What does that mean?"

"I've been going to the same place, over and over. And each time I go, the place changes, as if it's decaying."

"Where do you go?" I asked.

"I'm not sure. It's not this world, or Upper or Lower World. And it's sure not Middle World."

A bat fluttered above us.

"How do you know what Middle World looks like?" I asked. "I thought Middle World was too dangerous for journeying."

Her fair skin darkened. "I'm not a beginner anymore. It was time. And it's not dangerous, not really. It's just difficult."

I raised my hands in a warding gesture. "Hey, I was just asking."

We didn't say anything for a long minute.

"There was a man there," she said.

"A man?"

"I think…" She took a deep breath. "I think it's the Rose Rabbit."

"He's been contacting you?"

"I don't know."

"Why didn't you say something sooner?"

"I don't know," she repeated miserably. "It's strange, but I just didn't want to say anything to either of you. I wanted to keep it private. And I know that doesn't make any sense."

"It does if whoever he is, he's been influencing you."

"I know. If Karin hadn't been shot… I still might not have said anything."

That's us Bonheim sisters. It takes only a complete disaster to get us to budge. "I saw something too," I admitted and shifted against the pickup. My jeans made a squeaking sound. "At the wellhouse. A vision of a place that was… strange. Decaying was a good word for it."

"You don't have visions," she said.

"No." But I'd had two today. Something was changing. Was it me?

Again, we fell silent.

"I've tried to ask my spirit guides," she said, "but they haven't been around. There's been a new spirit hanging around, a white wolf, but he's not talking."

"That's not right. White wolves are supposed to be messengers. So what's the message?"

"I'm thinking the messenger is the message."

"That makes zero sense."

A second bat joined the first. They wheeled in a palsied dance.

"If I help you find the rose rabbit," she said, "will you do something for me?"

"We're trading favors now?" This wasn't like Lenore. We were sisters. We always helped each other, no questions asked.

"Will you?" she insisted.

"Why try to find this rose rabbit? Why not go after Belle?"

"Because the unseelie's too strong to tackle, even for the two of us," she said. "But I think if we chase this rabbit together, we might have a chance to figure out what it means."

"And what if the rose rabbit is the unseelie?"

"Then we'll find out now."

"Okay then." Uneasy, I crossed my arms.

"I think, together, we can journey and find the rabbit."

Now I knew something was wrong. Lenore was the journeyer, not me. "Together? You mean, you would guide me?"

She nodded. "I'd have to, since you aren't familiar with this on your own, but we'd be together the entire time."

I didn't like it. But she was right – we were magically stronger when we worked together. "You'd see what I saw?"

"I should. So? What do you think?"

It was high time I made headway, somewhere, somehow. I nodded. "Let's do it. I'll follow you home."

I trailed her Volvo's taillights to our aunt's shingled house. Blowing into my hands, I waited on the front porch while Lenore unlocked the door.

Stepping inside, I wiped my feet on the blue rag rug. The smell of home — indefinable, protected — hadn't changed, even though Ellen was months gone. My muscles unknotted.

Lenore shut the front door.

"So where do we do this?" I asked. "The attic?" That was where Ellen had practiced her magic, and her power and protection still lingered.

"The attic's freezing. It's not comfortable enough to relax for a journey. Why don't we use your room?"

"Why not?" I climbed the stairs to my old bedroom. Even though the room had been redecorated, its shape, its feel, was still mine.

I sat, rumpling the bamboo-colored spread on the twin bed. On a high shelf, antique hats perched on their forms. The hats had been fashionable in their day, and belonged to our ancestresses. None of them had lived long enough to settle into an unfashionable old age.

But I will.

Unease whispered against my skin, revealing the lie.

"Lie down and get comfortable," Lenore said. She left the room and returned with a gourd rattle. My sister pulled a wicker chair to the side of the bed. "You know the drill."

I knew it, but it had been a long time since she'd practiced her shamanism on me. My earth witchery had its own shamanic bent, working with the spirits of the plants and earth. But I didn't like visions. I never felt in control with them, so I wasn't a fan of shamanic journeying. There was something floaty, disconnected about it that didn't sit well with me, and I wondered if this was a good idea. I straightened my shoulders. Wondering had never stopped me before.

I toed off my shoes and lay on the bed, closed my eyes.

My sister rested her arm on the bed so it lightly pressed against mine. With her other hand, she rattled the gourd in a rhythmic beat. "Go to your starting place, to the beginning of your journey."

The rattle faded into the background, becoming white noise.

I visualized myself standing in my aunt's front yard, beside three aspen trees. As a child, I'd loved playing there, loved the feel of their papery bark, the way their leaves turned to gold in the autumn. The few times Lenore had talked me into journeying, this was where it had begun. Sinking through the earth, I'd followed the tree roots to Lower World.

Now I imagined myself stepping into the center of the three trees, pressing through a shiver of magic as I crossed their invisible boundary. The ground was damp and soft beneath my feet. Night had become day, and puffy clouds floated in the sky.

I didn't sink into the earth, and I turned, puzzled, toward the house. A sparkling gold line of energy, as wide as a road, flowed straight from the house and towards Doyle.

I'd never noticed that before, and I rolled my shoulders. This was my vision. I was in control. Through the roots. Down through the roots.

A crow flapped above me and settled at the top of one of the trees. It clicked its beak at me.

My vision. I swallowed. Down through the roots.

The crow cawed, a grating sound. So maybe the bird was here to take me to Upper World. Or maybe—

With a sickening lurch, I shifted sideways. The trees and houses blurred, and I was on my knees on a cracked sidewalk.

I'm safe. I'm safe here. This is only a vision. But it didn't feel like one. Cautious, I rose to my feet.

Lenore's rattle continued, a steady drone at the edges of my consciousness. My sister knew these things, I didn't, and I had to trust her. She was with me on this journey, even if I couldn't see her. I really wanted to see her.

Across the street, the grass grew thick in the park. It was a green that glittered like a dragonfly. The sky was electric blue-white, bright enough to make me wince. Inside the gazebo, a band in tattered uniforms played an eerie tune. The town pharmacist knelt on all fours and grazed on that strange, glimmering grass, her head bobbing in time to the music.

I'd never been on a drug trip, but it sure felt like I was on one now. The colors were too intense, and everything was… strange.

I turned around. At my back the golden line extended toward my aunt's house. The shimmering path ended at the road. Had that strange, gold path brought me to this place?

I twisted the bangles on my wrist. This was Doyle, but it wasn't, and it sure wasn't Lower World. I didn't believe it was Upper World either. And that only left… Middle World. My breathing accelerated.

I could be injured in Middle World. There was a reason only shamans with years under their animal-hide belts traveled here.

"Lenore?" I shouted.

The band gave a blast of their wind instruments, mocking. Mrs. Fitzpatrick hee-hawed.

I didn't understand any of it, but I'd been brought here for a reason. Unclenching my fists, I walked slowly up the hill toward Main Street, the road cold and sharp beneath my bare feet.

On the sidewalk, the town mayor, his bald head slick with moisture, popped a paperclip into his mouth. He chewed, swallowed. "Where are your shoes?"

"I left them…" What was this place? Fear pounded in my head, and I could no longer distinguish my pulse from the rattle. "Lenore?" I shouted, brushing past him.

A buggy sped down Main Street, the miner whipping his horses furiously.

Where the hell was Lenore? I continued down the sidewalk on autopilot – toward Ground.

Another shimmering cable of light, wide as the road, cut across the town and passed through my café. Bizarre. I walked on, drawn to the light and home.

Customers formed a zigzag line in front of my coffee shop. The house flipper Eric Gertner and his wife, Rasha. The city manager, Wynter Swanstrom. Melanie, Matt's widow.

Melanie turned her sad gaze toward me. "He knew too much, pushed too hard."

Unthinking, I stepped into the gold path of light and swiftly shifted sideways again.

I was inside my café.

Heart pounding, I stood frozen, too shaken to move.

Ground's red brickwork was covered in orange lichen. My tapestries and carpets hung in rotting tatters.

A log stood at the counter and ordered a double espresso.

My assistant manager Darla took his (its?) order. A butcher knife, sharp and gleaming, floated above her head.

"Darla?" I asked, my voice faint.

She looked up. "Oh, hey, Jayce. What are you doing here?"

"I'm not… sure."

The only thing "normal" in this Ground was the scent of coffee. I inhaled deeply, grateful for this bit of sanity.

Lenore's rattle submerged into the clatter of plates and mugs.

At the table where Karin usually sat, a knight in dented armor drank a mochachino. I frowned. How could he drink anything with his visor down?

The knight set down the mug, his armor groaning. "I wondered when one of you would arrive. However, I did not expect it to be you."

I walked to him, the wood floor a caress after the cold sidewalk. "Are you my spirit guide in this place?" I asked.

He laughed, a rusted sound. "I thought you were here to guide me." He leaned forward. "Where is she? Have you seen the queen?"

"I'm not... I'm looking for the rose rabbit."

He leaned back in the wooden chair, and his armor squealed. "The rose rabbit. I haven't heard that name in ages. Where did you learn it?"

"Do you know where it is?"

"Do you know what it is?"

"I'm asking the questions," I snapped. "This is my vision, buddy."

"Are you certain?"

I wasn't, and I didn't reply.

"Lenore brought me here," I finally said.

"Did she? Clever girl."

My voice trembled, an awful idea growing in my mind. "The rose rabbit, what is it?"

"A faithful vassal, betrayed. A doomed soul. Lost hope."

"I don't have time for riddles. Lenore's arm is going to get tired shaking that rattle, and—"

He sighed. "Why do you want to find the rabbit?"

"We've been receiving signs, omens, word of a rose rabbit. And we thought the rabbit might be connected to the strange things happening in Doyle."

"Doyle?"

"This town."

"Town." He rolled the word in his mouth, savoring the round tones. "But the blight is in the woods, at the spring, sacred no longer."

"What do you know about the blight? I saw it too. It's infected the redwoods."

The noise in the café rose to a roar, but I could hear the knight's words as if we were alone in the woods.

"The curse spreads," he said. "It will destroy your world as it has ruined mine."

"Curse? It's a curse?"

"Metaphorically."

Metaphors, I thought, disgusted. This entire vision was a metaphor and I understood none of it. "And realistically? What did you mean by destroy?"

"You needn't worry. You burn too hot. Soon, you will be ash."

My palms grew damp, and I rubbed them on my jeans. "What the hell does that mean?"

"We are not in our proper places. The world is wrong. I must find the queen. And you are not the one."

Enough with the mystery! "Are you the rose rabbit? Do you know who the unseelie is?"

"She is my queen."

Horror swelled my throat.

Black wings fluttered at the edge of my gaze and thudded into the window. I gave a little jump and whirled toward the movement. A smear darkened Ground's front window. I leaned toward it, pressing my hands to the glass, and peered down.

A dead crow lay on the sidewalk, its neck broken. I sucked in my breath and stepped away, the room growing shadowy and silent.

The knight and customers and Darla had vanished. I stood alone in Ground – the real café, not the imaginary one – and my feet burned. The lights were off, the chairs upside down on their tables. A police car cruised down Main Street, its headlights illuminating empty sidewalks.

In my fist were clenched three, long dark hairs. My own.

CHAPTER 21

"About time!" I locked the alley door behind me and hobbled across the pavement to Lenore's waiting Volvo, pebbles pressing into the soles of my feet. "Ouch, ouch, ouch!" I half-fell through the open door into the passenger seat and brushed the dirt from my feet.

"What happened?" Lenore asked, pale and anxious.

"You tell me! How the hell did I leave the house? This was supposed to be a vision, not a barefoot walk across town. And look." I unclenched my fist revealing the three, long, brown hairs. My pulse beat in my skull, throbbing, painful. This hadn't been a regular shamanic journey. I'd gone somewhere in the real world – to Ground. Had I been stumbling around in a trance?

"Let's talk inside," she said.

"Did you bring my purse?" The keys to my apartment were inside it. I don't know how I'd gotten into Ground, but I was locked out of my own apartment.

"Your purse?" she asked blankly.

"With my keys." Irritated, I plucked at my knit top.

"Uh, no. You didn't tell me on the phone you wanted them. I should have thought—"

"No, we were both freaked out." I was still freaked out. This shouldn't have happened. It was impossible. How had I walked to Ground, gotten inside…? I shut the door and buckled up.

"So what happened?" I asked more calmly.

She drove down the alley and turned at its end. "I was in trance, in a deep fog, searching for you, calling. And then when I finally snapped out of it, you were gone."

"No kidding. But how? How did I just… leave?" Though I hadn't just left. The dirt and cuts on my feet were proof some walking had been involved.

A vein throbbed in her jaw. "I wish I could answer that. I can only assume you walked out of the house while in a trance. But I checked the clock. Only ten minutes passed while we were both in trance. And it takes longer than that for you to walk to Ground."

"Well, I walked somewhere outside." But I'd also shifted, traveling swiftly along that energetic highway.

"What exactly did you see?" she asked.

Soon, you will be ash. My heart raced and tumbled like a mountain stream.

Ash. It didn't mean anything. You couldn't always trust the spirits, and I'd never gotten the hang of metaphors. "I was in Doyle, but it wasn't Doyle. It was like a filter was laid over the town, and everyone was acting or looking weird. There was a ghost band at the park, and Mrs. Fitzpatrick eating grass. The mayor, Steve Woodley, was eating paperclips."

"Woodley?" she asked sharply, turning the Volvo into her neighborhood of oaks and gentle hills.

"Yes, why?"

"Karin told us she once saw him eat a piece of plastic. She thought he had that disease that makes you eat weird things — pica."

"So you think I saw real things, the truth behind the town?"

"I think you were in Middle World, but not the way you should have been."

"Should have been?"

"I told you Middle World was dangerous. You can't just wander around in a daze."

"I wasn't wandering."

She pushed out her jaw. "I'm sorry. This is my fault. It never should have happened."

"I didn't have much choice. Was it normal? What I saw? What do you see when you travel to Middle World?"

"Doyle." The word came slowly, reluctant. "This is Middle World. Shamanic journeying through it is just a different way of seeing our world."

"Oh." I thought about that. Was seeing the world differently that hard? What I'd seen was certainly different.

"What else did you see?"

"I went to Ground. It was packed. There was a knight sitting at Karin's table, and he knew about the blight. He said the curse was spreading." A chill rippled my skin, and I pressed my toes into the Volvo's thin carpet. "He was looking for his queen."

She darted a look at me. "She's his queen?" She swore softly. "Then he works for her. No wonder he wanted me to keep our visits quiet."

"Did he say anything to you in your dreams?"

"No. He just made me feel sorry for him," she said. "He looked so… pathetic. What about you?"

"The knight seemed lost. He thought I might be his guide, then said I wasn't. And he said…" I swallowed.

"What?"

"He said I'd soon be ash."

"You can't interpret that literally." She pulled into her driveway, the gravel crunching beneath her tires. "The journey speaks in symbols and metaphors. The knight was probably speaking of some sort of internal transformation, a loss of self."

"But we both know this was no ordinary journey." My voice rose, shrill. "I was in Middle World. I left the house without you seeing, and I got here way too fast. I saw these thick lines of energy, like roads, flowing from Ellen's house. And when I stepped into one, suddenly I was in Doyle."

"You mean like ley lines? The energetic lines of the earth?"

"I don't know. I don't see lines and connections. I'm not Karin." And yet, I'd seen something. "And the knight said said – well, implied – the crows were working on his behalf."

The Volvo drifted to a halt. Light streamed from the windows of the gabled house.

She sat, her hands on the keys in the ignition, unmoving. "He said he was looking for his queen? If he was one of the fairy queen's servants, and the crows work for him, that might explain the crows attacking you."

"But the hair!" I waved my fist in the air. "He returned it to me. Why would he do that if he was working for Belle? Having a little piece of me would give her tremendous power."

"We don't know how unseelie magic works," Lenore said. "Maybe she doesn't need your hair. She's already damned us. Okay, so you were in Middle World. Did you see anything that referred to Matt and Phoebe's murder?"

I stepped out of the car and winced. Gravel. Did it have to be gravel? "I told you everything. They were there — all the suspects — but they looked normal. Only Melanie spoke to me and said that he knew too much. But that just confirms what I suspected, that Matt was a blackmailer. Both Wynter and Brayden caught him snooping."

Lenore walked up the porch steps and unlocked the door. "How does that make Matt a blackmailer and not simply nosy?"

Sighing with relief, I stepped onto the blue rag rug and brushed off the accumulated pebbles. "It's just a feeling I have." I couldn't tell her the truth about Brayden's parents. He had to be the one to tell that story. But if Matt had blackmailed both Wynter and Brayden, had he tried the same trick with others? I needed to learn more about the suspects, and I needed a drink. On a mission, I strode to the kitchen.

"So the knight said he was looking for his queen." She shut the front door and followed me. "But he didn't specifically say he was her servant. What about the rose rabbit?"

I found a dusty bottle of Rioja in the cupboard over the fridge and tore off the metal wrapping around the cork. "The knight said he'd heard the name. I got the feeling he was the rabbit — or he knew more about the rabbit than he was telling."

Lenore frowned, and I knew what she was thinking — that my feelings weren't enough.

But they should have been.

I cocked my head, studying her. Something had come between Lenore and I. Maybe it was my fault, because I hadn't told her the truth about Brayden. But there was something she wasn't telling me. I scrabbled in the kitchen drawer. Where was the damn church key? "Is something bothering you?" I asked.

"We're neck deep in another murder, and I sent you on a journey to Middle World. It's only dumb luck that nothing bad happened to you there." She laughed, a flat sound, and rested both hands on the butcher block work island. Dried herbs lay in bundled rows atop it. "My sight's gotten so fogged lately, I thought if the two of us went together, it would clear things up. But I ended up stuck in a real fog, and you were put in danger. I'm sorry. I don't know what I was thinking. What I did was wrong and reckless."

I uncorked the bottle and grabbed two wine goblets from the cupboard. "Hey, reckless is my line." I poured two glasses and drank half of mine in three gulps.

"Feel better?" she asked.

"No, but I might be able to sleep now." I sipped more slowly this time. "Maybe the journey will make more sense in the morning."

"Maybe."

I finished my wine, then jogged upstairs and retrieved my shoes and purse. Suddenly, I wanted to go home, be alone. I slipped into my shoes and walked downstairs.

Lenore still stood in the kitchen. She stared at nothing in the corner, the wine goblet clutched to her chest.

"Are you really okay?" I asked.

She shook herself, as if waking up. "Yeah. Only. I'm sorry."

"Stop saying that. It will be better in the morning." I walked down the hall. Lenore trailed behind me.

I grasped the front door's knob. A cold shock ran through me, then, hot, twisting, coppery rage. I gasped.

"What's wrong?" she asked.

I shot her a quick smile, but my stomach quivered. "Nothing. Just a shock from the metal."

"Wait." She placed her hand on my arm and closed her eyes, extending her aura, probing for danger.

Shutting my eyes, I did the same and visualized a hawk, soaring high above, hunting. From a spot over its head, I saw what it saw, sensed what it sensed. Light from the homes below flared, disturbing, in the night. A mouse rustled in manzanita. A murder of crows roosted in a high redwood. But I sensed no magic aside from our own and no humans lurking. On the other hand, I hadn't sensed anyone in my café either.

I opened my eyes.

"It's safe," she said. "There's no one there."

I hoped Lenore's magical senses were sharper than mine. "Like I said, static." Shocks were easy to come by at this altitude. But I kept my keys clenched like spikes between my fingers as I walked to my truck. I got in quickly, locking the doors, and drove off, watchful.

No one passed me. No headlights gleamed behind me. No animals darted in front of my truck. I was alone, and for the first time in a long time, I felt lonely.

The dash clock read midnight — too late to stop at one of the bars, not when I had to open Ground tomorrow morning.

I turned down the alley to Ground and parked, flipping off my headlights. The light by the exterior stairs was out, bathing the alley in blackness. I sat for a long moment, my disquiet growing.

Gathering my macramé purse, I stepped from my truck and let my eyes adjust to the dim light. I didn't see anyone. Paranoid, my gaze darted around the gloom as I walked to the base of the stairs. My foot crunched on something.

I edged sideways. At my feet, moonlight silvered triangles of broken glass.

The wooden stairs creaked above me, and I drew in my breath.

Someone was on my stairs.

Someone was breaking in — had broken in.

Blood pounded in my ears. My hands clenched, my keys pinching my fingers. Enough! I raced up the stairs. My skin burned with energy. I was going to rip this guy's face off. The taps inside me opened, magic spilling through me from the earth and sky.

A dark shape rushed down the steps.

I gathered my will and shrieked words I didn't know. Hot wind tossed my hair. The dark shape stumbled, plowed into me.

I flew backwards. At the last moment, I remembered to tuck and roll.

We bounced together down the stairs.

An elbow in my gut. A boot striking my shoulder. My head struck something hard, and the world dimmed.

I blinked.

I lay on cold pavement. Sharp, uncomfortable things dug into my flesh. Stars spun above me. The earth was moving.

A shuffling sound.

Not me.

Him. Her. It.

I smelled the sharp tang of my own fear. Whoever had been on the steps was still out there. I groaned and tried to sit up. But I couldn't gain purchase in this new, tilting world.

The sound came closer. Footsteps.

Something stirred inside me. The spell. I had never released my spell, and it coiled, a burning spring.

I sucked in painful gulps of frigid air. The spell was a hot iron, stabbing my core, agonizing. I had to do something with it. Get rid of it. Stop the pain.

A dark figure loomed over me, something long and narrow in its hand.

I tried to escape, but my legs skidded, helpless, on the pavement. Move,

move, move.

The shape knelt beside me, raised a hammer.

I flung out my hand and released the spell. Electric fire flowed through me. I shrieked, pain jumbling the words.

CHAPTER 22

I woke up with Picatrix on my chest.

She sneered at me in that regal way cats do. Then she yawned and arched her back, digging her claws into my skin.

"Ow!"

She sprang from my chest and trotted beneath the stairs.

The sky had lightened, the stars fading. Abruptly, I sat up, remembering. I looked around wildly.

Aside from Picatrix nosing about the garbage bins, I was alone in the alley.

Holding tight to the railing, I climbed the wooden stairs to my apartment. Bits of glass lay scattered across the landing, but most of it had rained straight down onto the pavement. I hoped Picatrix was careful where she set her paws.

I studied my broken window, to the left of the staircase. The burglar had been nuts to think he could get through it. It was a good three feet from the stairs – close enough to reach with his hammer, but a stretch to climb through. If he'd successfully made the leap, or if I'd been home…

I looked away, nauseated. The shamanic journey had brought me here. If I'd had my keys on me, I'd have gone straight upstairs and to bed. If Lenore hadn't forgotten my purse…

Jamming my key into the lock, I thought back to the struggle on the stairs. He'd knocked me flat before I could use that spell — the spell with words I didn't know and outcomes I didn't understand. Had there even been a spell? My memories were fuzzy, gray. I remembered the feelings — the pain and the power — but that was all.

I didn't know what scared me more – my attacker or that weighted spell.

I'd think about it later. Scarlett O'Hara had nothing on me. Whatever had happened, my attacker was gone. I hadn't disabled him or her. No fallen bodies lay beneath me.

Dammit.

I stumbled inside and hit the light. Thanks to the broken window, the living room was the same temperature as outside. Shards of glass glittered on the distressed wood floor. But the room itself appeared undisturbed.

I extended my senses. The atmosphere felt undisturbed too. No intruder had gotten past the wards I kept on the upstairs apartment. But I'd been wrong before.

Outside, a garbage can lid clattered, and I jumped.

Swearing, I got a broom, dustpan, and old newspaper and walked downstairs. Picatrix had made her way inside one of the garbage bins, her tail a question mark.

I left her to it and swept up the glass. Wrapping it in the newspaper, I deposited it in a cat-free garbage can.

Weariness hit me, and I grasped the stairway banister, closed my eyes, drained.

I trudged upstairs and swept up the glass inside my apartment.

Abandoning my broom, I stumbled to the kitchen. I poured a dram of our aunt's Four Thieves potion, and shot it back, grimacing at the vinegar-garlic mixture. My magical malaise lifted, energy flooding my veins.

I showered, ignoring my bumps and bruises from the tumble down the stairs. I should call the police, but I'd already cleaned up most of the mess and had probably ruined the crime scene. Besides, I was sick of deputies. Sick of being stared at like a criminal. Sick of being dragged to the sheriff's station for "a few more questions."

Either Matt's wife had killed him, or Matt had been killed because he was a snoop who got a kick out of blackmailing his clients. Even if it was only a gentle blackmail — like he'd pulled with Brayden — one of his victims might have snapped. I needed to find out what was blackmail-worthy in my suspects' pasts.

Unfortunately, I had no idea how.

Friday rush. I poured an espresso and eyed Darla, working the cash register. No matter how I squinted, I couldn't see the knife hanging over her head from my journey in Middle World. If Darla's bad luck was part of the unseelie's curse, was the knife a metaphor for her misfortune?

And what about the knight? I glanced to Karin's window table and away. The table had remained strangely unoccupied all day. All the other tables were taken, the coffee shop packed, yet people avoided a primo window seat.

"Joy?" I called out, clapping a plastic lid on a double espresso.

A young tourist in a blue parka and scarf stepped to the counter. "That's me."

I handed her the drink. She moved away, looking around for a spot to sit. Her gaze passed over the empty window table and moved on. She shrugged. Sipping her espresso, she walked out the red-paned front door.

I shifted my weight. Weird.

The lunch rush ended, leaving us with the work-from-home crowd — men and women typing on laptop computers.

I wondered what Karin would have made of the table. Would she have avoided it as well?

I wandered to the empty table. Casually, I wiped it down, reaching out with my senses and feeling for magic.

I felt nothing.

That scared me even more, and I scuttled to the safety of the counter. Customers moved down the line, and I tried not to look at the empty table.

My stomach growled, and I glanced at the clock on the distressed brick wall. Two o'clock.

Darla smiled and took a cup from my hands, passed it to a waiting customer. "You haven't taken your lunch break yet."

I wiped down the espresso machine and tossed the washcloth in the sink. "No, and I've got errands to run. Do you mind?"

"You're the boss."

I grimaced. "I've been taking off a lot lately, haven't I?"

"Your sister was shot. Someone stole your truck and used it in a murder. I get it. Go and do what you need to do. You know the afternoons are light. I'll be able to manage on my own." She grinned. "Besides, I need the hours."

"As long as you're happy." I whisked off my apron. Hurrying upstairs, I grabbed a black wool coat, gloves, and purse.

The Historical Association was only a few blocks away. So I walked, enjoying the cold air on my cheeks, the bustle of tourists in winter ski wear, their noses red from wine tasting.

I strolled past a brick, two-story hotel. A vacancy sign sat in the window. Most of the tourists would head higher into the mountains, spending the night at a higher elevation and ready to ski in the morning.

The Historical Association was in a two-story Victorian a block off Main Street. Behind the picket fence, dormant rose bushes awaited winter's end.

I walked up the brick path to the porch and stepped inside.

An elderly lady, Mrs. Parks, looked up from behind the desk and smiled. Her skin seemed to glow from within, and her eyes were a startlingly clear blue. She adjusted her red cardigan.

"Hello, Jayce. What can I do for you today?"

I sat in one of the green chairs in front of her. "I'm doing some research on the old wellhouse."

She opened a drawer. "A lovely bit of local architecture. I have just what you're looking for." She slid a sheet of paper across the desk to me. "I assume you're here about the petition?"

"Petition?" I scanned the paper, a one-sheet on the wellhouse history.

"The wellhouse was built in the mid-nineteenth century. It's an extraordinary example of Victorian Moorish architecture and highly unusual in this location. And Mr. Gertner wants to tear it down for a housing development!" Her mouth twisted.

"He said no one was taking care of it," I said.

Her eyes flashed. "Well, we'd like to!"

"Of course," I murmured.

She toyed with the reading glasses dangling around her neck. "Unfortunately, the Historical Association has had its hands full with other projects. We'd like the city to buy the property and put it into a public trust. Our organization of volunteers is quite willing to manage the wellhouse's upkeep. We simply can't lose such a lovely piece of history."

"Who built the wellhouse?"

"A miner named Alpheous Wright." She arched a white eyebrow. "He must have been quite a fanciful man. Sadly, he died of consumption not long after he built the structure. He never enjoyed the fruits of his labors."

"What happened to the wellhouse?"

"The property passed to his heirs, who eventually moved away."

"And now Eric Gertner owns the property."

She sniffed. "Mr. Gertner doesn't appreciate what he owns. It would be simple to turn that property into a park and tourist attraction. People are looking for things to do in Doyle, places to snap photos of themselves. The wellhouse is ideal."

If someone didn't fall through the floor first. Still, losing the wellhouse did seem a shame. Old Doyle was a sturdy gold rush town. The Moorish wellhouse was a whimsical dash of fantasy. "I'll sign," I said.

"Excellent!" She shoved a clipboard at me, and I signed beneath the row of names.

She glanced at my signature and smiled. "The fairies will be grateful."

My mouth went dry. "Fairies?"

"Oh, another funny old legend attached to the wellhouse. The story goes, that the fairies weren't happy when the well was built. They cursed Mr. Wright with consumption."

Fairies.

"Are you all right?" She leaned across the broad, polished desk, her face creasing with concern. "You look most peculiar."

I cleared my throat. "Is that the only legend attached to it?"

"There are happy stories as well. The women of Doyle used to go to the wellhouse to take away their love sickness."

"Love sickness?" I asked.

She laughed. "An old-fashioned way of describing pining after someone you can't have. They believed the wellhouse would cure them of that terrible feeling. Of course, now we know something about psychology. The well water worked to cure love sickness because women believed it would."

"That makes sense," I said slowly. Why hadn't I heard this story before? "Aside from the fairy spring in the woods, are there any other local sites connected to the fairies?"

"No. Well, that's not entirely true. There's the Bell and Thistle. But I'm not sure why that has a fairy connection."

"The Bell and Thistle? The pub?"

"They have such a lovely happy hour. Perhaps it was the Bell and Thistle's connection to the green fairy, absinthe, that led to the legend. They used to brew the stuff, you know. I believe the new owner is talking of opening a new absinthe distillery. Wouldn't that bring tourists to Doyle!"

"Yes," I said, disconcerted. My problems had started at a local fairy site. It wasn't a coincidence.

CHAPTER 23

Bing Crosby warbled from the jukebox about White Christmases. Twinkle lights reflected in the mirrored shelf behind the bar. They glinted on the rows of bottles and made a halo around my reflected, acorn-colored hair.

I braced my elbows on the ornate, wooden bar and made small talk, my flirting automatic. The door opened, and I turned, my thirsty hope surging.

Brayden didn't walk inside.

Stupid. My hands tightened on my cocktail glass. Why would he show up? I hadn't invited him to join me at the Bell and Thistle, or even let him know I'd come. If I had invited him, he'd probably have declined.

I speared an olive from my drink and hooked my stiletto heels on the rung of the barstool. I wasn't here for romance. The Bell and Thistle had a fairy connection, and that made this martini a work expense.

A bead of sweat trickled down my back, and I adjusted the collar of my emerald v-neck sweater. The crush of tourists and locals had raised the temperature in the noisy pub, the fire in the corner unnecessary.

Knit cap pulled low, Rasha Gertner, pushed past me to the bar. A red scarf wound around her throat, and she was bundled in gloves and a bulky sweater. How did she stand them in this heat?

She motioned to the bartender, Rafe. "Another Irish coffee." Her words slurred.

Rafe, a sunburnt ski bum, nodded and ambled to the other end of the bar.

"Hi, Rasha," I said. "How have you been?"

She swiveled toward me, her gaze an uncertain trail. "How have I been? I'm alone, just like you. Men are completely unreliable. You think you can trust them, but no, you can't."

Taking advantage of a drunk was wrong, but these were desperate times. "What happened?" I asked, squeezing sympathy into my voice.

"Matt happened," she said darkly.

The door opened, and my heart leapt again. I glanced toward the door, and my hopes crashed and burned.

Lenore, wrapped in a white parka, walked inside. She paused in the entry way and squinted at something on the wall.

"You mean Matt's murder?" I asked, tearing my gaze from my sister.

"I mean his life," she slurred. "Did you know he and Phoebe were having an affair?"

"Well—"

"And he put her… put her up to being his front on a real estate deal with my husband. Phoebe's name was on the deed, but the property belonged to Matt. And do you know why he did that?"

No, but I was dying to find out. "N—"

"To keep the property out of his divorce pro… pro… proceedings against Melanie." She hiccupped. "Matt was suing Mel for half her income and assets. She would have had to pay him a monthly stipend, pay his rent, treat him like a kept man. And all the time, he had a share in the wellhouse property, and he was hiding it. And my husband knew." She poked my shoulder for emphasis. "He knew about everything."

"Oh." Absently, I rubbed my shoulder. Rasha had put some muscle behind that finger.

She rubbed her parka sleeve across her reddened nose and sniffed. "Can you believe Eric told the police before he told me? How am I going to look Melanie in the eye? How could Eric have looked at her with a straight face and acted like everything was all right?"

Lenore drifted to the bar. "Hi, Jayce, Rasha. It's good to see you."

"Is it?" Rasha snapped.

The bartender slid her Irish coffee across the bar.

Rasha snatched it up, slopping liquid across the counter, and lurched to her corner.

"Bad timing?" Lenore asked, peeling off her parka to reveal a gray sweater so pale it was nearly white.

"One of us is going to have to make sure she gets a ride home," I said.

"Don't sweat it," the bartender said, his reddened face crinkling. "I'll take care of her. What can I get for you, Lenore?"

I raised a brow. Lenore wasn't a bar person, and Rafe was only here for the winter season. How did the sexy bartender know my sister's name?

"I'll have a cider," she said, barely audible over the music and the roar of the crowd. Dean Martin had replaced Bing.

Rafe walked to the low refrigerator on the other side of the bar.

"Come here often?" I asked her and arched a brow.

"No." She shrugged beneath her pale, turtleneck sweater and smiled. "You know how I feel about crowds."

Yeah, she hated them. I'd had to use a promise of a free dinner to lure Lenore from the house. So how did the bartender know her? He didn't strike me as a big reader.

She looked around the crowded pub. "How are we going to get a table?"

"Don't worry. I always find one." Confident (because you can't do magic otherwise), I sent my will into the pub — a free table for us to eat at.

Rafe returned with the cider. "Anything else I can get you?"

"A menu," I said.

He handed us two. "Good luck finding a table."

"Thanks," I said. Grabbing my metallic, sleeveless parka off the back of the high chair, I made my way through the crowd.

A trio of college-aged skiers — tourists — rose as we approached and abandoned their round table.

"You used magic," Lenore said, accusing.

I grabbed a chair and sat, extending my legs. "So? You use it all the time."

She sighed. "Not on people. Jayce, it's—"

"Reckless?"

"Not very nice."

Guilt wormed inside me, and I ignored it. It was only a little magic, maneuvering us into the right place and right time. It wasn't as if the students had needed the table anymore. "I'll send a blessing to everyone in the pub. You won't believe what Rasha just told me."

"Rasha's drunk." She scraped back a chair and sat, pushing empty beer glasses to one side of the table.

"And in vino veritas." I grinned. "I've found the Matt-Phoebe connection."

"I thought they were having an affair."

"It was more than that. Rasha told me Matt used Phoebe as a front to go in as a partner on the wellhouse property."

"Without her knowledge?"

"I didn't get that sense. If he and Phoebe were having a thing, she might have done it willingly, helping him keep his assets away from his wife."

"Why?" Lenore asked.

"To keep his wife's lawyer from finding out about it. He was suing Melanie for half her income and didn't want her to know he had assets of his own."

Lenore frowned. "If he's so broke, how did Matt have enough money to buy into the wellhouse property?"

"Maybe he used his wife's money. Or maybe he earned something off his blackmail. Wynter Swanstrom didn't admit to paying off Matt, but he did say he'd caught Matt snooping through some unimportant documents. But if he was being blackmailed, he wouldn't admit it to me. I have a feeling whatever Matt found bothered Wynter."

She tilted her head, skeptical. "He may have been bothered, but that doesn't mean he paid blackmail."

"No," I said, thinking of Brayden. Matt hadn't asked him for money. He'd only held the knowledge over Brayden's head and demanded favors. My dirty martini turned to dust on my tongue. Would favors be enough to kill over?

"This gives Melanie an even bigger reason to have wanted her husband dead, and Phoebe too," Lenore said. "I'm surprised the police haven't picked her up yet."

"Yes, but..." But what? Melanie seemed the most obvious suspect, but something didn't feel right. I shook it off. "I went to the Historical Association to ask about the wellhouse and their lawsuit against Eric."

"What did you learn?"

A cheer erupted in the corner near the Christmas tree. It wobbled at a drunken angle, its ornaments bobbing and weaving.

"Not much I didn't already know. Doc Toeller is named as, what do you call it? Plaintiff?" Karin was the legal eagle, not me. "The Historical Association can't stand Eric. But even if they'd found out Matt was Eric's secret partner, I can't see them bumping off Matt and Phoebe."

"Neither can I." She frowned. "Though now that I think about it, developing a property from scratch is a big step up from flipping homes. Is this the first time Eric's developed a property from scratch?"

"I don't know." It might not matter, but it was odd. "Did you know the wellhouse has a fairy legend attached to it?"

"What?" Lenore leaned forward in her wooden chair. "That can't be coincidence."

A waitress wove through the crowd to our table. She scooped up the empty beer mugs and wiped it down. "Are you ready to order?"

"I'll take a garden wrap and garlic-bacon-cheese fries," I said.

Lenore made a face at me.

"It's their special," I said, defensive.

She ordered the wild mushroom burger, and the waitress departed.

I crossed my ankles beneath the table. "According to the legend, the man who built the wellhouse was cursed by the fairies and died. But women went to it afterward for the waters, which were supposed to take away their lovesickness."

"And of course the well water always worked, because time heals all wounds."

"Sure," I said, "but it's weird, right?"

"It's weird."

As weird as being at the Bell and Thistle, where my truck had been stolen, and a dead man dumped into its bed, and where there was a fairy connection. As weird as coming to the spot where Eric and his first wife had had their last drink together. As weird as my father dying in a car accident caused by Brayden's mother. A ghost walked across my grave, and I quaked.

"What's wrong?" she asked.

"I was looking into Eric Gertner and found a newspaper article about the crash that killed his first wife all those years ago. They'd been drinking. She was driving. They left from this exact fairy pub and went off the road, hit a tree."

An odd expression crossed Lenore's face. "That's... interesting."

"It's probably a coincidence," I said, trying to convince myself. "We've only got three bars in Doyle. When it comes to picking a place to drink too much and crash your car, your odds are one in three."

"Go to the entryway and take a good look at the framed newspaper article."

"Why?"

"Just go and look."

"I'll look later," I said.

"I think you should look now."

I relaxed in my chair, a strange reluctance stealing through my limbs. My muscles felt heavy, and the wooden chair was so comfortable. "If we go, someone might steal our table."

"I'll stay here. You check the paper."

"I don't want to." I braced my elbow on the chair arm and rubbed my temple.

"What's wrong with you?"

The entryway was twenty feet away. A line had formed inside it, sweaty, annoyed people waiting for a table or a spot at the bar, and I didn't want to be anywhere near them. And I loved being around people. Crowds were what I got my energy from. I extended my aura, feeling for whatever magic was pinning me to my seat.

And got nothing. What was going on with my magic?

"Jayce?" She prompted.

"There's no reason for me not to want to go," I said, my voice thick as cold molasses. "But I don't want to. My body feels like it's welded to this chair. And those people by the door." I shuddered. "I can't go there."

Twin lines appeared between her brows, and her gaze grew distant. "Jayce, I think you're being influenced."

So I'd been right. There was magic keeping me from seeing whatever Lenore had wanted me to see, and I hadn't been able to detect it. Fists clenched, I lurched to my feet. The hell with that. No one turned me into a puppet.

"Wait." Lenore stretched her hand toward me.

"No. Let me do this." I pushed through the crowd. My heel caught in a gap between the wooden floorboards, and I stumbled.

People brushed past me, knocking me backward, and I shuddered with revulsion at each touch. Was this how Lenore felt in crowds?

I saw an opening between two burly men and walked into it. At the same moment, they shifted, closing on me.

"Excuse me," I pushed through, popping from between them like a champagne cork.

They kept talking as if they didn't see me.

Beads of sweat dampened my forehead. I squeezed between two tables.

A woman edged her chair back, and one leg landed on my foot.

I yelped with pain and ripped my boot from beneath her chair.

She didn't turn, didn't notice.

My heartbeat quickened. No one saw me. It was like I didn't exist. I was just a swirl of molecules, and so were they, and nothing mattered.

I ran. Or tried to run. I was in a nightmare, my footsteps preternaturally slowed. Everywhere I turned, someone blocked me. I forced my way past laughing tourists and truckers in holiday sweaters.

A foot tripped me, and I staggered into the white plaster wall. Feeling my way along it, I slithered to the entryway. I pushed through a rowdy bachelorette party to the newspaper article, hanging in its frame.

The article was from nineteen-sixty-six. Its photo looked older, the men in three-piece suits and the women in long skirts and stiff hats. I checked the date — 1920, the year Prohibition began. (I know my drinking history).

Someone bammed into me, flattening me against the wall. I peeled myself free and kept reading.

The article was a gleeful account about how the town boundaries had shifted in 1920. One of Doyle's town fathers had owned the Bell and Thistle, which later became a part of Arcadia township.

But Prohibition had given the owner an incentive to return the Bell and Thistle to Doyle. After intensive negotiations (the author hinted at a payoff), the Bell and Thistle property lines were reincorporated into Doyle, where the police were "more tolerant."

But Doyle hadn't been exempt from Prohibition. The town father in question had connections with the cops, who looked the other way when it came to the Bell and Thistle.

Interesting but unenlightening. Why had Lenore insisted I read it? And why had it been so difficult for me to do so? A draft chilled my flesh.

I studied the article's photo – men and women in clunky shoes and swank hats. If I stared at the faces long enough, I could almost imagine they were people I knew. All except one — one of the women's faces was blurred, obscured by what looked like a burn mark.

I turned away and leaned one shoulder against the wall. My reflection wavered in the glass door, and I took a moment to catch my breath. Dispassionately, I studied my profile. The high heels made my butt look all kinds of awesome, but my ankle ached from my near fall a few minutes ago. There were other aches too. Were the heels worth it?

Cripes. I was turning into Karin.

Shaking my head, I returned to our table. People smiled (or leered) and parted to make way.

Lenore stared at her cider and rubbed her hands.

"I made it back alive," I said.

She looked up as I dropped into my chair. "And?"

"You're right. Something was trying to stop me from seeing that article." I rotated my ankles. Had my shoes gotten tighter in the cold and damp?

"But you got through."

"Yeah, though I don't see what the big deal was. It's just an old article about an old story."

"You didn't notice anything odd about the photo?"

"It was a little damaged, but it's an old article."

Her gaze sharpened. "Not just damaged. A face is burned out, and there's magic on that article."

My stomach cratered. "I didn't feel anything." Why wasn't I feeling the magic? I'd missed someone in Ground – twice – and now this?

"Maybe that's because it's not like our magic. It's… different."

"You think it's unseelie magic?" I sucked in my breath. "So why can you sense it, and I can't?"

"I'm not sure," she said. "Maybe it's because of all the journeying I do. I'm used to encountering different spirits, and they all have their own flavor of magic. But something's here, in this bar, and there's something about that article that's not right. I went to the library to find the original, and—"

The waitress appeared with our food. "One mushroom burger." She slid it in front of Lenore. "And one garden wrap and monster fries." She set the plate in front of me. "Is there anything else I can get for you?"

"I'll have another," I said, nodding to my empty glass and fishing out the last of my olives.

Lenore raised her empty bottle of cider. "One more, please."

The waitress nodded and bustled away, returning a few minutes later with my fresh drink.

"So what did you find at the library?" I asked.

"They keep everything on microfiche now. The microfiche for that page of the paper is damaged. It looks like it's burned, just like that photo. But none of the other microfiches beside it were damaged."

"Which they should have been?"

And then Brayden walked into the bar.

CHAPTER 24

My heart stopped. And then it jackhammered, making up for lost time.

Brayden. His head brushed against a strand of twinkle lights above the entry. They glinted off his unruly black hair. He wore a navy coat unbuttoned over my favorite fisherman's sweater and jeans.

A man walked in behind him — Finn Davidson, one of his fellow paramedics. He'd been at the realty with Brayden after I'd discovered Phoebe's body. Young, red haired, and smiling, he looked around, spotted us, waved.

I couldn't move.

The paramedic said something to Brayden and pointed.

Brayden caught my gaze, and my insides fluttered, turned over. He nodded, and they pushed through the crowd.

"Hi, Jayce, Lenore." Finn wasn't wearing anything beneath his brown, v-neck sweater. Copper strands of hair glistened against his chest. "Can we join you?"

"Why not?" Lenore asked. "But you'll need to find an extra chair."

"That I can manage." Finn plunged into the crowd and returned a minute later with a chair. He clunked it down between Lenore and I. "Don't let your food get cold on our account." He nodded to the wrap and the burger on the table and pointed to Brayden. "The usual?"

"Yeah," Brayden said, leaning across the table and snaking one of my fries. It was a casual, almost intimate gesture, and I felt the warmth of connection between us. Which just goes to show how far gone I was. The guy had been pushing me away, and I get excited because he steals one of my fries? What was wrong with me?

Finn leapt up and pushed through the crowd to the bar.

No one spoke.

Lenore took a bite of her burger and swiped at her mouth with the red paper napkin.

Finally, Brayden said, "I didn't expect to see you two here."

"Is that why you came?" I asked, waspish.

His tanned face flushed. "No. I didn't think you'd be here, but I'd hoped you would."

Lenore scraped back her chair. "Excuse me. I need to find the ladies room."

My mouth twisted. That was subtle.

We watched her make her way through the pub.

"How are you doing?" he asked.

"Better, now that Karin's going to be all right."

We sat in awkward silence.

I gulped my drink and nearly choked on an olive.

"Jayce—"

"Brayden—" I said at the same time.

We smiled briefly.

"There are so many times I wanted to tell you about my parents," he said. "The time never seemed right."

I wrapped my hands around the cool glass, slippery beneath my fingers. "You mean you were afraid I'd react badly." My lips tightened. It wasn't as if I'd been completely honest with him either. I'd never told him the full story of the curse that killed off the Bonheim women in childbirth and their husbands around the same time. I spoke quickly. "I don't blame you for what happened. I'm not even sure I can blame your mother. It was an accident." Or his mother had been a pawn in that centuries-old unseelie curse.

"What's wrong?" he asked.

"Nothing. I'm telling you it's all right. And I know my sisters will think the same."

"No, there's more to it than that. I think I know you well enough to read your expressions."

I rubbed my thumb around the edge of the glass. "The accident might not have been your parents' fault."

"What do you mean?"

"I don't think it was an accident at all."

A vein pulsed in his jaw. "My mother was wrong not to stop, but she didn't do it on purpose."

"I know." I shook my head. "That wasn't what I meant when I said it wasn't an accident."

"Then what did you mean?"

A burly man brushed past me, knocking into my shoulder.

I leaned closer to Brayden, so I wouldn't have to shout. "You know I'm a witch."

He smiled. "You haven't exactly been keeping that under the radar."

"And the Bonheim curse." I doubted anyone but my sisters and Nick knew the details, but the legend was public knowledge — at least among the old timers.

His forehead wrinkled. "Right. Sure."

"There's more to the story than you know. According to legend, one of my ancestresses cast a curse to catch her husband, and it rebounded on her."

He smiled, and dammit, I responded, my lips parting. "Is that what you've done to me?" he asked. "Cast a spell?"

I ignored the warming in my core. "No. The story is wrong."

"Sure it is." His broad shoulders lifted, dropped. "There's no such thing as curses."

I ground my finger into the wooden table. "I mean the story is wrong. My ancestress didn't cast any love spells. The original story is that a fairy became infatuated with my ancestor, Nathaniel. She cast a love spell on him and charmed him into her fairy bower. But his wife was a witch with her own magic, or maybe it was just true love, and he returned to her. The fairy was furious and cursed them both. That's why the Bonheim women die in childbirth, and their husbands die around the same time. And their firstborn — and lastborn —are always girls, so the cycle continues."

He sat quiet for a long moment. "As much as I'd like to blame that car accident on something supernatural, I don't believe in curses. My mom was driving too fast. She panicked. We make our own good or bad luck."

I bounced my foot in frustration. "Not always. Look at Darla."

"Your assistant manager?" He frowned. "What does she have to do with anything?"

"She's unlucky. The fairy's cursed her as well, just like it's woven its spell around all of Doyle."

He shook his head. "We make our own fortune. It's been scientifically proven."

I snorted. As if science could prove something like that! "I've seen Darla's curse. It looks like a butcher knife hanging over her head." My assistant manager's bad luck was more than clumsiness and a defeatist attitude.

"My father was a dirt bag. My mother panicked and ran. And your father died as a result. It was my father's fault, not a fairy's."

"Well, yeah it was his fault. But placing your parents and my dad on that road at just the right moment... Don't you see? This has been going on for over a hundred years. Karin's documented every strange death."

"I'm sorry, Jayce. I can't believe in curses. This is about responsibility. I'm responsible for the results of my actions, and so are you."

My head reared back. "What's that supposed to mean?"

"I know you feel responsible for what happened to Karin—"

"Of course I do. But that has nothing to do with what I'm telling you!"

A shadow of annoyance crossed his face. "The only person responsible is the person who made the choice to shoot at you and hit her instead."

"Yes, the shooter's responsible. But we're somehow being maneuvered..." Defeated, I slumped in my chair. He didn't believe me. How could we ever be together if he didn't understand the risks? "Do you even believe I'm really a witch?"

He blinked. "Why wouldn't I? I've seen you mixing potions and casting your spells."

"But do you believe they work?"

"They seem to work for you."

He was being evasive. I lowered my gaze to hide my hurt. Brayden didn't believe. He'd never believed.

"Jayce, I've read about this stuff. There's science behind it. Look at quantum entanglement, where the parts of a split photon will spin in the same direction regardless of distance. Studies have shown that visualization improves performance. That we make our own luck through the power of our belief. Or take the placebo effect — people believe fake medicine works, and so it does. Or the reverse – the curse effect, where people believe a curse is attacking them and they feel the results."

"Do you really think all my ancestresses died in childbirth because of a reverse placebo effect?" I heard the anger in my voice and bit my bottom lip in dismay. His common sense and logical mind were a big part of what I loved about him.

"In the past, dying in childbirth wasn't that uncommon. Maybe your family has a genetic predisposition—"

"Brayden, you have to believe this."

"Why?"

My fingers twitched. "Because we can't be together unless you understand what you're getting into!"

"Jayce..." He shook his head. "You can't force someone to believe. Isn't it enough that I accept what you believe?"

"Not if it will kill you!"

"The line at the bar was crazy." Finn plunked two beers on the table. Foam slopped over the sides, cascaded down the glass. "Did I miss anything?"

"No," we said in unison.

Finn's blue eyes widened, and he laughed. "If you say so. What happened to Lenore?"

My sister wove through the crowd to our table and glanced at Brayden and me. Understanding flashed across her face. "Are you ready?"

I grabbed my purse and sleeveless parka from the back of my chair. "Right, I forgot." I smiled at Finn. "Sorry, we've got to go."

"Is it something I said?" Finn pressed his freckled hand to his chest, rumpling his sweater.

"We promised Karin we'd stop by the hospital," I lied, "and it's getting late." For the first time in a long time, I was eager to escape a bar. All I wanted was to go to Ground.

Finn's reddish brows pulled downward. "I heard what happened to your sister. Please give her my best."

"Will do," I said cheerily and breezed from the pub. No one hurtled themselves into my path. No magic dragged at my footsteps. In fact, I think I felt a breeze pushing me out.

The front door slammed behind us, and the old bell by the door clanged faintly. I kept walking, my stilettos skidding on the loose earth and stones. My feet felt like they were on fire now, arches aching, toes pinching, skin hot. What was wrong with these shoes?

"What happened?" Lenore zipped up her white parka and jammed her hands in its pockets.

I leaned against my F-150. Paranoia had led me to park beneath a lamp, and I eyed the shadows between the parked cars and the surrounding pine forest. "I told Brayden about our curse. He didn't believe me." My voice broke.

"Oh."

I gestured futilely. "Nick believed. Why can't Brayden?"

"Nick had already come to the conclusion there was something supernatural happening in Doyle. He didn't take much convincing. It takes time to get your head around real magic."

I wondered how much time we had.

In the corner of my eye, one of the shadows moved, and I whipped my head toward it.

Nothing was there.

"Jayce?" Lenore asked.

"Do you sense anything?" I asked.

She closed her eyes and stilled.

I waited, my gaze darting around the darkened lot.

Lenore opened her eyes. "I sense… something. But it's more like a magical background noise, not much different from what I normally feel inside the pub. I don't sense danger."

"I'm not taking any chances. We should go."

She patted the side of my truck. "Drive carefully."

I started at the warning, thinking of Brayden's parents in our father's death. But of course, Lenore didn't know about that.

I stepped into my truck. Waiting for a ramshackle van to pass, I pulled onto the highway.

Brayden didn't believe. I thought he had, but he'd been humoring me all this time. It might not be fair to ask him to share my beliefs, but I couldn't get serious with him if he didn't. It was too dangerous.

The van's taillights vanished and reappeared, playing tag along the road's curves.

I had to give Brayden up.

Grief ripped through me, bringing tears to my eyes. I brushed them away with the back of my hand. All these years of pushing him away, keeping my distance, but I'd always loved him. And now I'd have to keep on keeping my distance. Maybe now, knowing it could never be, I could move on.

And if I couldn't?

I parked in the alley behind Ground. But instead of going inside, I walked around the corner and crossed the street to Antoine's Bar. The hell with fairies and the hell with Brayden. I needed some fun.

I walked through the doors and was greeted with a wave of sound — laughter, chatter, a jukebox. A rock beat sizzled through me, exhilarating. In spite of my anguish, my hips swayed to the rhythm.

"Girl, get over here!" Antoine waved to me from behind the long, western-style bar.

I slid through the crowd.

"You're fourth in line," he said. "What do you want?"

"The usual."

Beside me, a sandy-haired man about my age turned and smiled. He was pleasantly average, so I knew he wasn't from around here. "Come here often?" he asked.

I laughed. "Does that line ever work?"

We chatted easily, and he asked me to dance. I gulped down my dirty martini and joined him on the floor, let the throb and beat of the music take me, driving away the pain in my good-for-nothing heart.

The crowd parted for us. People clapped and cheered as I danced, partner forgotten, Brayden forgotten, the hurt forgotten.

The music turned, a whisper of warning threading beneath the rock beat. I stumbled.

A mutter rippled through the crowd.

A siren wailed outside, and I froze.

The siren grew louder.

I edged from the dance floor.

"Hey, wait," the blond said, grasping my wrist lightly. "Want to get another drink?"

Antoine appeared at my side. He touched my arm, his face creased with concern. "Jayce, there's a problem."

My heart thumped. "What's wrong?" I asked, ignoring my dance partner.

"It's Ground."

The blond's forehead creased. "What's ground?"

I clutched Antoine's arm. "What's wrong?"

"Outside," he said. "There's a fire."

I raced from the bar and scented smoke in the air. More sirens and lights. A black cloud lit with orange billowed upward, blacking out the stars. No, no, no!

Vaguely aware of Antoine behind me, I pounded down Main Street. Fire trucks blockaded the road. Hernandez wound police tape from a wooden beam holding up a balcony and across the street.

I ducked beneath the tape. A wave of heat struck me, made me gasp.

"Jayce!" Hernandez shouted.

I kept running.

A window shattered. Flames roared from Ground. Firemen in thick canvas jackets trained hoses on the blaze. A ladder truck, its ladder extended above the roof of my apartment, doused the roof.

"That's my café!"

Hernandez grabbed my arm. "Jayce! Is anyone in there?"

"No," I said wildly. "Why would someone be in there?"

"We thought you were inside," the deputy said. "Your truck is in the alley. Wait here." He hurried to a cluster of firemen.

I stared at the roaring flames, heat from the blaze striking me in waves.

Ground.

I sank to my knees, my grief crushing, raw, primitive. A suffocating ache tightened my throat.

Ground was gone.

CHAPTER 25

Morning sun glinted through the window of my childhood bedroom. I huddled on the twin bed and fought back tears. My home and business were gone.

My fists clenched in the soft bedspread. The fire hadn't been an accident. Someone had done this to me. My truck had been parked in the alley. Had the arsonist thought I'd been inside?

Something tapped at my window.

Picatrix sat on the sill. She pawed the glass.

I gaped for a moment, wondering how she'd found me. Then I leapt to my feet, the bamboo-colored bedspread slipping to the floor. "You're all right!" I slid open the window and the cat meowed. "You can come in," I said. "Not that an invitation ever stopped you before." She rose to her feet, then suddenly her back arched, her fur spiking. With a hiss, she whipped around and leapt to one of the eaves, and then into the garden.

"Or you can stay outside." Cats. At least Picatrix hadn't been near the blaze. For a moment I watched her, pausing to study the empty birdbath. "You're not going to find a meal there." I tugged down the hem of the over-sized t-shirt Lenore had lent me. All I owned now were my pickup, the clothes I'd worn last night, and the contents of my purse. The firemen had promised they'd secure my small safe, and I hoped it lived up to its hype, protecting the contents from fire. But even that was small comfort. My family photos. My books of spells. My aunt's cauldron. These things could not be replaced.

I stumbled downstairs to the kitchen. Lenore had hung the herbs above her butcher block work island. Though they were dry, I almost thought I could smell them. I beelined for the coffee maker beneath the moss-green cupboards.

Tears threatening, I ran my thumb over the coffee canister, and its Ground label. At least I still had a bit of my own blend.

I set it on the counter. The soft sounds of a door closing, of Lenore's footsteps, drifted down the stairs. I glanced at the wall clock. Ten AM.

Yawning, Lenore stumbled into the kitchen in silky white pajamas. She wrapped her arms around me and said nothing.

"It will be okay," I choked out. That was what she wanted to hear. "I'm alive, and no one was hurt. That's what counts." I tried to feel grateful, but my thoughts overflowed with what I'd lost.

She released me. "I'll make breakfast. Omelettes?"

"I'm not hungry." I opened the fridge and grabbed a carton of OJ, poured.

"I'll make breakfast anyway."

"Coffee's on." I walked upstairs to change. In my bedroom, I stumbled over my discarded heels. Pain lanced my sole, the orange juice slopping onto the sisal carpet.

Wild rage ripped through me, and I hurled the stilettos across the room. I'd been burned out, and my only shoes were these crummy heels?

Breathing ragged, I forced myself to calm. I could buy new shoes. Or borrow something sensible from Karin if worse came to worst. I sniffed last night's turtleneck, draped over a chair. It smelled acrid, of smoke and loss and tears.

I cleaned up the OJ and dressed in last night's clothes. Trudging downstairs, I poured a mug of coffee.

"Why don't we go shopping today?" Lenore asked.

My mouth stretched into a pained smile. "I'll have to. The weekend is my only chance to..." I sucked in my breath. I was still thinking weekends were my only chance to shop, because Ground would be open on Monday. But my business wouldn't open Monday, or possibly ever. Could I even afford to buy new clothing?

The doorbell rang, and we looked at each other, startled.

Lenore ran her hand over her loose hair. "I'd better change. Do you mind getting that?"

"Sure." I walked to the entryway, my bare feet sinking into the blue rag rug.

Three knocks, hard and purposeful.

I looked through the peep hole. A burly, weather-beaten fireman in a blue uniform stood on the porch. Officer Hernandez stood beside him. The deputy carried my small safe beneath one muscular arm. He smoothed his black hair with his free hand.

I yanked open the door and pressed my palms to my heart. "My safe!" Something else of mine had survived the fire.

"Good morning," the fireman said. "I'm Lieutenant Anderson. This is Deputy Hernandez. Are you Ms. Bonheim?"

"Yes, I'm Jayce Bonheim. Come in." Glancing at Hernandez, I stepped away from the door.

They walked inside, Hernandez angling sideways to get the small safe through the entry.

"Thanks for bringing my safe," I said. "I thought I'd have to dig it from the rubble."

"I have some questions for you and didn't want to waste time," the lieutenant said.

"Where can I put this?" Hernandez asked. "It's not exactly lightweight."

I motioned to the living room, painted pale blue. A blue-glass witch ball hung in the bay window.

The deputy set the safe on the wood floor.

Lieutenant Anderson drew a notepad from his breast pocket and studied me. "Where were you at the time the fire started?"

"I guess I was at Antoine's bar," I said. "But I don't know when the fire started. The building looked okay when I parked behind it, but I didn't go inside."

"So the fire just happened to start after you'd left?" the fireman asked. "Do you know how that might be possible?"

I shook my head.

"Run me through your night," he said.

"My sister and I had dinner at the Bell and Thistle." I shifted my weight. "I came home early. Instead of going inside, I parked and walked to Antoine's for a drink."

"What time was this?" the lieutenant asked.

I glanced at Hernandez, who'd remained silent. "Around nine?"

"Did you see anyone loitering around your business?"

"You think it was arson," I said slowly. At least we were on the same page there.

"The investigation is ongoing." The fire lieutenant interrogated me — he was friendly, but there was no other word for it. What had I seen? How did I learn of the fire? Who had keys to the building?

Lenore stopped short inside the living room's wide entry. She'd dressed in white, wool slacks and a sand-colored sweater. "What's going on?"

Hernandez smiled. "A few questions for Jayce. Why don't we leave them to it?"

Hesitant, she looked to me.

I nodded and hoped Lenore could handle entertaining Hernandez on her own. She spoke easily with Karin and me but tended to clam up around outsiders.

"I've got coffee in the kitchen." She pointed down the hall.

"Perfect." The deputy ambled after her.

"Have you got any insurance?" the fire lieutenant asked, suspicion in his voice.

And with a start, I realized I did have insurance. Our Aunt Ellen had insisted, and since she'd funded my café, I'd gone against my poorer judgement and bought a policy. Beads of sweat dampened the skin above my lip. Had I kept up the payments? "It's in my safe. The policy I mean." Hands shaking, I knelt on the floor and turned the old-fashioned dial. Had the contents survived? I spun too far, and had to do the combination over. Finally, I cranked open the safe.

My shoulders sagged. It really was fire proof. My papers were all there. I reached inside and grabbed a stack of file folders. They were warm. "The policy's in here somewhere." I found the insurance folder. Opening it, I scanned the pages and started breathing again. The policy expired next month. I breathed a prayer of gratitude. I was covered.

"Ms. Bonheim?" the fireman asked.

"Oh. Here." I handed the policy to him.

He scanned it, making notes. "Thank you, Ms. Bonheim. Was there any unusual activity around your business prior to the fire?"

"It's not just my business. That was my home." Anguish tightened my throat. "I live in the apartment over Ground. There was a break-in at Ground last Sunday. The police know about it. My sister, Karin, was shot in the alley on Tuesday. She's still in the hospital. And there was a second attempted break-in two nights ago, though I didn't report it. They broke the glass out of the rear, apartment window, but I scared the person off."

His eyes narrowed. "Why didn't you report it?"

"I was getting tired of police interviews." The lieutenant had seemed more surprised by the last break-in than by Karin getting shot. So he'd known the story already — Hernandez must have filled him in, if someone else hadn't.

He asked more questions. Did I own or rent? Had the insurance policy changed recently? What was inside the building? (Oh, so much).

Finally, he closed his notebook. "Thank you, Ms. Bonheim. If I have more questions, I'll be in touch."

I rescued Lenore from Hernandez in the kitchen, and we saw the men to the front door.

We returned to the kitchen.

Lenore leaned one hip against the counter. "They think it's arson. I guess I'm not surprised."

"Hernandez told you?"

Her cheeks pinked. "He wasn't supposed to, but we've known each other a long time. And I can read between the lines. Why else would a fire investigator be here?"

I hunched over the butcher block island, gripping its edges. "Dammit!" I struggled to slow my breath. "We know who's really responsible."

"We do?"

"Belle, the unseelie, or whatever she calls herself." I paced. "My truck was parked in the alley. Whoever set that fire thought I was inside."

"It was a human who set the fire."

"Belle engineered it. She's wrecked the life of every woman in our family since God knows when."

"Jayce—"

"No more. I'm done." I stormed out the back door and into our aunt's garden. Dark clouds massed above the hills. I stalked through a knot garden of low herbs, brown in the winter. Picatrix scuttled from a lavender bush and streaked away, rounding a corner of the house.

Past the bird bath, the ground sloped upward, the property line ending in a line of oaks. Behind them, slightly up the hill and beyond the property boundary, stood a trio of pines.

I stared sightlessly. Darla wasn't the unlucky one. I was. No matter what I did, disaster found me, and now Ground was gone. It was only thanks to our aunt I had insurance. I couldn't remember how much it covered, but I had something.

A crow squawked at me, and I blinked, returning to reality.

The bottom branches of the three pines were bare, and I frowned. The trees' upper branches had faded to yellow. Dry needles lay thick on the ground beneath them.

I stooped and ran my fingers through the prickly needles. A chill ran up my arm. The blight.

I scanned the treeline. Other trees were dying as well — none on Ellen's property, but... Didn't blights usually keep to one species of tree? This had hopped from redwood to pine, another sign that magic was at work.

Red heat blazed in my mind, my rage mounting. The unseelie. It wasn't enough for her to burn me out of house and business, she had to blast the entire mountain with her curse. Something hard and ugly stirred inside my chest.

The unseelie had woven a powerful curse — maybe more than one — but witches could curse as well.

I picked up a handful of needles, their ends pricking my palm. All the better. The blight had to be the unseelie's work, so the dead needles were connected to her. "You think there are no consequences?" I shouted.

A breeze soughed in the pines.

"Right back at you, Belle!" I imagined the unseelie, saw her stiffening to granite, unable to attack me or anyone else. I imagined the roots of my power sinking into the earth and branching into the sky, and I felt the power flow through the roots, into me. It was time to fight back.

CHAPTER 26

Cold wind whipped my hair and tossed dirt into my eyes. The dying pines bent, branches snapping.

I was done being a victim. It was time to return the favor in a language the unseelie understood. "I cur—"

"Jayce?"

I started and turned.

Karin stood on our aunt's back porch. She leaned one hand on the wooden railing. Nick's arm coiled around her waist.

I stared.

"What are you doing?" Her hazel eyes flashed, and her hand gripped the rail a little too hard, the whites of her knuckles showing.

The breeze died. I relaxed my hands, and the dry needles cascaded to the ground.

"Karin! You're out of the hospital." Stunned, I walked down the path to them.

"Is everything all right?" Nick looked to Karin, his expression uncertain.

My sister's jaw clenched. "Yes."

Shame cascaded through my veins. "Karin, I didn't—"

"Nick," she said, "can we have a minute alone?"

"If you're sure you're steady enough," he said.

She nodded, and he retreated inside our aunt's house.

"It's not what you think," I said.

"That you were casting a curse?" Wearily, she lowered herself to a deck chair missing its cushions. Lenore had packed them up and stored them inside for winter.

"All right," I said, "it was what it looked like. But not a curse against a person, against Belle."

She rubbed her face. "I worked dark magic once. I had all sorts of justifications for it too. But I knew it was wrong. And someone I cared about paid the price."

My legs folded abruptly. I sat beside her, the wooden chair creaking beneath our combined weight. I knew what she'd done. It hadn't been easy to forgive, but a part of me had understood. Karin never had forgiven herself.

"I'm not sure it's the same," I said in a low voice. "The unseelie keeps coming after us. It's time we fought fire with fire."

"Is it?"

Unseeing, I stared at the hillside and the dying pines. A crow rose from behind a tuft of tall, brown grass and flapped away. "The blight is spreading."

"Curses don't belong in this world," Karin said. "Their effects ripple outward like waves on a pond. We can't predict who they'll harm."

My cheeks burned, and I angled away from her on the chair. Karin was right. I'd been reckless. As usual, I'd been avoiding my real problems — Brayden's lack of belief and the murderer who'd tried to burn me like a witch.

And I'd always been that way. I'd slam headfirst into something I didn't want to face, so I'd spin off in another direction. A college test I hadn't studied for — skip it! A guy I liked but wasn't ready to unveil myself to — find someone I didn't care about and go too far. The only part of my life where I'd taken the roll-up-your-sleeves, responsible path had been Ground. And now that was gone. My throat swelled, choking.

"I'm sorry about Ground," she said.

I glanced at her, startled, and wondered again if Karin had picked up some of Lenore's talents. "Thanks."

"What are you going to do?"

I forced away my hurt. Ground had been my talisman, my guiding star. I'd always known what to do there, even when what needed doing was difficult.

The building was gone, but I couldn't give up on Ground yet. "I have insurance," I said. "Ellen insisted. I need to call the agency and let them know what happened. And then there's the company that manages the property." I spoke more rapidly. "The police have probably contacted them, but I need to ask about rebuilding. Once I know their plan and the details of the insurance, I can decide what to do. What are you doing out of the hospital?"

"There was no reason to keep me there anymore." She nudged my shoulder with her own. "Being a witch isn't all bad. That miracle tea of yours and whatever Lenore's been doing got me on my feet faster than the doctors can explain. The surgeon said he wants to do a paper on me. I think he was joking, but my fast recovery may have made him suspicious."

"Maybe you should have taken it easy on that tea," I joked.

"That would have been the smart thing," she said. "But we can't always do what's smart, can we?" She smiled, and I knew she was talking about my attempted curse.

The deck lightened, and I glanced up. A break appeared in the gloomy clouds. "I'll be okay." I laid my hand on Karin's knee. "No more crazy curses."

"Are you sure?"

I nodded. "I know what I need to do."

CHAPTER 27

The clouds pressed Saturday's sun into a hard, white disk. Alone, I stood in the weak afternoon light and stared at the fractured shell that had once been my home and business. Heat from the fire had shattered the windows. Shards of glass lay in piles behind yellow police tape. The bricks were blackened, the exterior stairs gone.

It was a miracle the firemen had kept the fire from spreading beyond my coffee shop and apartment. The buildings next door were singed, but otherwise unharmed. I had been the only loser.

Something snapped inside me, the crack echoing in the empty alley, and I gasped. Last night my clothes, my talismans, my work had burned, vanished in smoke, floated to the sky. Now, my tiny, fearful self rose up to join them.

I'd lost everything.

A gust of chill wind tossed ashes into the air. They spiraled above me, and then descended like flutters of doves' wings. They landed, feather-light on my upturned face, and stillness descended. Maybe like snowflakes, no two ashes are the same, but in that moment, I could see every wrinkle and jagged edge. And they were beautiful.

I was okay.

I had everything I needed and more — my sisters, a good bed in my aunt's house, a future. A peace I'd never felt before flooded my cells.

I was still standing, and I'd survive.

Ducking beneath the police tape, I walked inside the ruins. A blackened curve of wire stuck out from a pile of rubble. I reached for it, pulling the bits of broken wood and crumbled brick away.

My aunt's cauldron.

I sat back on my heels. The cauldron had survived.

I glanced up. The ceiling here seemed intact. How had the cauldron gotten from my apartment to the coffee shop? I picked it up, unheeding of the soot darkening my palms. Not everything had been destroyed.

I searched the rubble and picked up a coffee mug, shockingly white and undamaged. I set it inside the cauldron.

There, a butter knife.

I moved into the seating area. One-handed, I lifted a table, weirdly unscathed, and tilted it upright. I had a table! I ran my hand along its top. How had it survived?

Above me, the ceiling sagged, black and ragged, curtains of singed insulation hanging through gaps in the wood. Melted cables of twinkle lights, each bulb burst into a jagged flower, dangled alongside them. I climbed over the detritus, loose boards and unidentifiable bits of wood skidding beneath my feet.

I stopped at the base of the blackened stairway leading to my apartment. The door above was closed. I wasn't supposed to even be in the coffee shop. Did I dare go upstairs and try my key?

No, I didn't need to risk my life for things. I carried the small items I'd gathered to my F-150, parked in the alley and laid them in the cab. Returning to Ground, I picked up the undamaged table and lugged it outside, hefted it into my truck bed.

"So it's true," a woman said.

I whipped around.

Melanie stared at the wrecked building. Her red hair was wild, and for a moment I saw her as a forest witch, crouching, primitive, leaves tangled in her hair. Then the image cleared, and it was only Melanie.

Melanie, the woman with the most to gain by Matt and Phoebe's deaths. Melanie, the wronged wife. Melanie, smelling faintly of stale alcohol and cigarettes. And we were alone.

I stepped away, my butt hitting the lowered tailgate. "What are you doing here?" My voice cracked, the moment of zen gone.

"I heard about the fire and came to see for myself," she said without tearing her gaze from the building. She rubbed the arms of her brown sweater, its loose hem curling over the top of her rumpled jeans. "Someone really hates you."

"Oh?" Is it you?

She glanced at me and one corner of her mouth curled. "Don't worry. You're in good company."

"What do you mean?"

"Someone hates me too. I expect the cops will arrest me any day now. I'm only surprised it hasn't happened yet. But they will. I don't have an alibi for this either." She motioned toward the ruin. "Amazing you weren't killed."

"I wasn't home."

She nodded. "The killer won't make that mistake again. But who knows? Maybe you'll get lucky, and I'll be arrested first. Then whoever bashed Matt's head in won't need to kill you."

I edged around the side of the pickup. "Why do you think you'll be arrested?"

"All signs point to me. It's why I'm here. You've been asking questions, poking around." Her smile turned bitter. "All things I should have been doing, but I was too busy feeling sorry for myself."

"Your husband was murdered. You were in shock."

"I was wallowing in self-pity. And now I'm afraid it's too late. Did you learn anything?"

My hands gripped the tailgate. "I heard that Matt enjoyed holding things over people."

"He did." She nodded. "Maybe this is my punishment for not speaking up, stopping him. But I thought he was clever, and this town was full of hypocrites who deserved what they got."

"Who was he blackmailing?"

"Lately? I don't know. He stopped confiding in me the way he used to. Now I know why." Her voice hardened. "He had someone else."

"Phoebe."

"The police have it wrong though. He wasn't using Phoebe as a blind to keep me from knowing he'd bought into the wellhouse property."

"Oh?"

"I knew. He never made much money. I supported him in everything. I paid rent for the storage space where he kept his equipment. I paid for his office. I paid for the food, his clothes, his debts, everything."

"His debts?" I asked, confused by the conversational leaps. Everything about Melanie seemed disjointed. Her jerky movements. The band of flesh that broke the line between her sweater and faded jeans. Her scurrying gaze.

"You should see the stack I'm dealing with now. Even if I do get my share of the wellhouse land, I'm not sure I'll be able to pay them all."

"Who did he owe?"

She arched a brow. "You think one of the people he owed money to killed him? That's not likely. It would only lower the odds of Matt ever repaying. My point is, he couldn't have bought into that property."

"But he was working as a handyman. He must have earned something."

She snorted. "And spent it just as fast. He had nothing."

"Could he have blackmailed Eric into letting him in on the partnership?"

She canted her head. "Maybe. He never took money from his victims, but..."

"But what?"

"But he did take favors. He's done a lot of work for Eric, even pointed him towards properties that were ripe for flipping. Matt had a knack for finding deals. And he believed Eric owed him. If my husband had something over Eric, he might have used it to pressure him into giving him a share in the wellhouse property. Matt wouldn't have seen that as wrong."

"But Matt's name wasn't on the deed," I said.

"No, Phoebe's was."

"So either Phoebe invested her own money, or Matt used some sort of leverage to get into the deal and used Phoebe's name to hide his ownership from you?" But what sort of leverage might he have had over Eric? Was there something about the car accident that had killed Eric's first wife worthy of blackmail? Something only Matt and Eric had known?

"We'll never prove it," she said. "Not unless Eric talks. And why should he?"

"Did Matt ever say anything to you about what he might have had over Eric?" I didn't trust the new, helpful Melanie, but why not ask?

She arched a brow. "No. But he wouldn't. He knew Rasha and I were good friends." She moved toward me, and I stepped away.

She stopped short, her lips compressing. "Scared to be alone with me?"

"Jayce!" Darla raced down the alley. She stumbled, panting, to a halt behind Ground and pressed her hand to her mouth. "Oh, no. Oh, my God. Jayce!" Turning, she flung her arms around me, pulling me into a long hug. "Thank God you're okay. What can I do? How can I help?"

"Thanks Darla." I pulled away. "But I'm not sure yet what needs doing."

"What about insurance?" Her brown eyes were wide, anxious.

Wordless, Melanie walked away. Her slim frame hunched, fragile.

"I've got insurance," I said, dragging my gaze back to Darla. "The company's waiting on the results of the investigation."

"Investigation?" Darla asked. "What's to investigate?"

"It might have been arson." My throat tightened. "I guess they want to make sure I wasn't the person who set the fire."

"Of course you wouldn't do that." She spun on her heel and motioned toward the wreckage. "But... everything's gone! What are we going to do?"

"Not everything." I reached into the truck bed and patted the table. "We'll be okay."

"You went inside? Is it okay to go inside?"

"Probably not, but I couldn't help myself. Look, I'll call you when I figure out the next step. Hopefully, I'll have some news from the insurance company soon."

I trudged to the gash in the brick where the back door used to be. Ducking beneath the police tape, I walked inside.

"Wait!" Darla hurried beneath the tape after me. Her shoe crunched on something, and she winced. "I'll help."

"No," I said. "I shouldn't even be in here. The police tape is up for a reason."

Her jaw set, mulish. "Then they can arrest us both."

"Darla, that's an order."

"Oh, are you paying me now? Because the way it looks to me, you're out of business, and I no longer work for you."

"Darla—"

She braced her fists on her hips. "I'm helping whether you like it or not. Helping. You're not paying me for this."

I scraped my hand through my hair. If she stayed because of me, I'd be putting her in danger. The hell with my impulses, it was time to grow up. "Thanks, but there's no need. I just wanted one last look around. I'm leaving now." I clambered to the exit and scooted beneath the police tape, hoping she'd follow.

She didn't.

I stood outside, tapping my foot. "Darla, let's go."

"Do what you want. I'm staying." A drawer scraped. "Look! The stuff in the junk drawer survived."

I crossed my arms, exasperated. "Just what we need. Junk. Come on."

Grinning, she hurried outside, the drawer in her arms. She loaded it into the back of my truck.

"Thanks. I think that's everything." I jingled my keys, walking toward the F-150.

But she bustled past me into Ground.

I groaned. "Oh, come on." The universe was conspiring to keep me from doing the right thing.

Shaking my head, I followed her inside and paused to gaze again at the burnt-out stairs to my apartment. If things had survived in the café, something must have survived in my apartment.

Footsteps crunched behind me.

"Don't go upstairs," I said. "It's too dangerous."

"It's all too dangerous," a man's voice graveled.

I turned.

Antoine stood in the doorframe, his arms crossed over his broad chest. His gray hair was flattened on one side, like he'd just rolled out of bed.

"Are you going to tell on me?" I asked.

"The way I see it, the fastest way to get you out of here, is to help. I'll see if there's anything salvageable in the front." The older man moved past me into the coffee shop.

More people arrived. I told each to stay away, it was dangerous, we needed to leave. Each ignored my pleading, walking past me and into the wrecked café.

Lenore appeared, and then Karin and Nick. Soon a chain stretched from inside the building to my truck, each person passing some small thing to another. A chair, a metal trash bin, a plate. They were endangering themselves for my stuff, and my stuff wasn't worth their lives.

"I appreciate this, everyone," I shouted, setting a drawer full of utensils in my truck bed. "But it's enough. We're not supposed to be here. You can all go."

A siren bleeped, and muttering flowed down the line. A black-and-white SUV cruised to a halt in the alley. Glowering, Officer Hernandez stepped out. "Don't you people know what police tape means?" he roared. "The building hasn't been cleared for safety! Get the hell out of here, everyone." He turned on me. "Have you any idea how reckless this is?"

I hung my head. Even if I had tried to stop them, this was on me. "You're right. I'm sorry."

Nick laid a hand on my shoulder. "My client didn't have much choice in the matter. She told us to get out, and we all ignored her. What else could she do?"

Hernandez braced his fists on his hips. "I don't know, call the police?"

Lenore clambered over a pile of blackened rubble and smiled. "What are the odds of that happening?"

Hernandez whipped off his hat and rubbed the back of his neck. "I thought you had more sense, Lenore."

"I think we're done here anyway," I said in a loud voice. "Everyone can go."

The crowd disbursed, stopping to shake my hand, clap me on the back. Beneath Hernandez's glare, I meekly returned to my F-150. The truck bed was piled high with tables and chairs. Someone had found a rope, stacking and lashing the furniture together.

Karin sat on the driver's side, her legs dangling through the open door. "Sorry," she said. "I'm not much help."

Nick hurried to help her down. Gently, he guided her to his SUV and handed her inside.

"I should report this," Hernandez said.

"Do you have to?" Lenore asked.

He blew out his breath. "The arson investigators said they were done with the site, so at least you haven't messed up a crime scene. But please tell me you didn't go upstairs."

"You mean they're still investigating the upstairs?" I asked.

"It's unstable," the deputy bellowed.

"No, we didn't go upstairs," I said.

"Go ho—" He grimaced, about to say: go home. But my home was gone. "Get out of here."

Lenore followed me to my truck. "Are you going to be all right?" She asked, her expression anxious.

"Yeah." And to my surprise, it was the truth.

CHAPTER 28

Inside the window seat, our aunt's witch ball gleamed blue, turning slowly in the moonlight. A veggie pizza, still in its open box, steamed on the dining room table.

Movements stiff, Karin reached for a slice. Even with her new, unnatural paleness, that strange perfection to her skin remained.

I glanced at Lenore. She faced away from the window, blackened by night. Her skin had that same, plastic look too. Beautiful or not, it had to be part of the fairy magic, and it was creeping me out.

"Melanie paid a visit to Ground before you got there," I said. "Or to what was left of it."

"Matt's widow?" Karin's eyes narrowed. "You think she was returning to the scene of the crime?"

"I'm not sure," I said. "She told me she thought she was going to be arrested soon. She was digging for what I'd learned."

"Which is exactly what the killer might do." Making a face, Lenore picked a strand of her long, blond hair out of her pizza.

"Melanie hinted at blackmail," I said. "It might have been why her husband partnered with Eric in that wellhouse property."

"Matt used the blackmail money he'd collected to buy in?" Karin asked.

"No," I said, "she told me Matt didn't blackmail people for money. He did it for leverage, for favors." I thought of Brayden, and tendrils wound around my heart, squeezing. He still hadn't told my sisters the truth. I wasn't sure I wanted him to.

"Which gives Eric a motive," Karin said. "But what did he have over Eric?"

"I'm not sure," I said. "I did some research—"

Karin raised her brows.

"Yes, I can do research," I said tartly. "I was telling Lenore earlier about Eric's first wife. She was killed in a drunk driving accident. They were in the car together, and his first wife was driving. He survived, she didn't."

Karin picked a mushroom off the pizza. "Usually it's the drunk driver who survives and the passenger who dies. I'm not talking statistically — I've no idea what the statistics are. But doesn't it always seem that way from the news reports?"

It did. Troubled, I shifted in my chair. something else seemed odd about that accident, but what?

Karin shook her head. "Convenient that Melanie tells you this just before she's about to be arrested. Did she throw any other suspects under the bus?"

"No. But I think Matt was blackmailing Wynter Swanstrom — I'm not sure over what. And the wellhouse development is being sued by the Historical Association and Doc Toeller. I wonder if the Doc knew Matt was the real partner behind Phoebe?"

"You think Matt and Phoebe were killed over the lawsuit?" Karin asked.

"Does it matter?" Lenore asked. "The fai—"

Karin shot her a look.

"The unseelie is behind everything that's happening," Lenore said. "We should be concentrating on her, not lawsuits. Our problem is supernatural."

Karin folded her arms over her chest and winced. "It matters if one of us is dead or in jail."

"The police aren't focused on Jayce," Lenore said. "Once they make an arrest, the killer either won't be able to attack her or will have no motive to."

"Will have no motive to?" Karin's forehead wrinkled. "So it's okay for an innocent person to go to jail as long as it's not Jayce?"

Lenore flushed. "Of course not. But we're attacking the symptoms, not the root of the problem."

"If we knew how to attack the root of the problem," Karin said, "I'd be all for it. But we don't."

"And we never will unless we start exploring how." Lenore dug her forefinger into the blue tablecloth.

I half-listened to them argue. Something was off. Something I should have paid attention to before, but I'd been too wrapped up in my own dramas. I stared at my plate, at the denuded pizza crusts. "You're not telling us the truth," I muttered.

The two fell silent.

"I haven't lied about a thing," Karin asked.

"Not you." I turned to Lenore. "I didn't question your obsession with the fairy."

"She's trying to kill us," Lenore said. "Of course I'm obsessed."

"We die in childbirth," I said, "and that's a long way off for us all. The murders, the arson, are happening now. Why are you so focused on the fairy?" I knew Lenore. We were the closest of the three sisters, which wasn't fair to Karin, but it's the way it was. And she hadn't been honest with me.

"Because people are dropping dead," Lenore said.

"You know something," I said. "Or you've seen something, and you're not telling us."

"You're imagining things," Lenore said, her voice cool.

"No," I said, "I'm not. You've been pushing me to help you with the magic but not Karin. Why?"

She looked away. "Karin's been in the hospital."

"Wait." Karin's gaze ping-ponged between us. "What magic? What did you two do?"

My fists clenched. "I can't believe you're lying to me!"

"I'm not." A vein pulsed in Lenore's jaw. "I'm just not telling you everything."

"What the hell's going on?" Karin asked.

Lenore shoved aside her plate and braced her head in her hands. "I've been having strange dreams," she muttered.

Karin made a muffled sound. "What kind of dreams?"

She looked up. "Visions of another world, and someone who's a prisoner, or was a prisoner for a long time. I think it's the Rose Rabbit."

"I knew it," I said, torn between triumph and disappointment. I was finally figuring things out, but Lenore hadn't been honest with me.

"Tell us about the visions," Karin said.

"It's another world," Lenore said, "the unseelie world, I think. And it's falling apart. There's a blight—"

"Like the one here?" I asked.

She nodded. "Yes, but worse. I think the rabbit — who really isn't a rabbit, I think it's a title — was imprisoned, but he managed to break free, and now..."

"Now what?" Karin asked.

She looked at me. "Now he's here."

My nails bit into my palms.

"Is he working with the unseelie?" Karin asked.

"No," she said. "I don't think so. I think he could be our ally."

"Why didn't you tell us this before?" I asked, stung.

"Because I wasn't sure how to interpret any of it. I'm still not sure. I just have this feeling that if we find him, we may be able to get rid of our unseelie problems."

"Then we'll find him," Karin said. "But we need to deal with the immediate problem first — the murders, and whoever burned out Jayce and shot at me."

We fell into a grim silence. None of us had any idea how.

CHAPTER 29

I stewed, twisting in my sheets, watching lines of moonlight shift across the floor. Lenore had held out on us for so long. Why hadn't she said anything sooner?

Late the next morning, I was still kind of pissed at my sister. But she'd been dealing with weird visions she didn't understand. Lenore lived and breathed visions from the Lower and Upper Worlds. Not understanding this one must have driven her crazy.

Besides, I had to forgive Lenore. She was my sister. She'd also lent me her favorite white, quilted jacket. I zipped it to my chin. She loved this jacket, and I knew she didn't trust me not to spill wine or drip nacho sauce onto it.

I walked down Main Street in my brand new jeans. The sky was cloudless, a snap in the air parching my lips. Last night's discussion had given me some nebulous ideas. But I could be strategic. Instead of chasing these new leads, I gave my mind more time to work through my thoughts. And without Ground or my apartment to work in, I needed something to keep me busy while my brain's gears processed the problem.

A church bell tolled. Would Karin and Nick get married in our little wooden church? I lengthened my stride, a pleased glow warming my blood.

I walked to the newspaper office and up its brick steps. Inside the wood-paneled entry, I hesitated at the base of a wooden staircase.

The newspaper had published an article on the Ground fire. The reporter might know more he hadn't printed. And I was curious about that old article framed in the Bell and Thistle. One person's face had been obscured by a burn mark. Who had it been? The original photo might still exist. Uncertain who to ask, I gnawed the inside of my cheek.

A broad shouldered young man emerged from a room to my left. His head bent over a stack of papers.

I smiled, recognizing Doyle's ex-star high school football player. "Hi, Tom."

He looked up, and his blue eyes lighted with interest. "Jayce! What are you doing here?" He sobered. "Your coffee shop, your house... Is there any news on what caused the fire?"

"Is this for an article?" Because I wasn't sure how I felt about that.

He grimaced. "I'm planning a follow-up to the article I wrote Saturday."

"You probably know more than I do about the investigation." Would he drop some breadcrumbs for me to follow?

He shifted the papers beneath one arm. "I talked to some of the firefighters. Word is, the blaze started in several places at once, and it moved unnaturally fast."

"Arson." Even though I'd already known, my stomach swooped, sickening.

"You're lucky you weren't inside." He glanced around the entryway, but we were alone. "Something else I wasn't able to print, because I'm not supposed to know it," he said in a low voice. "The doors to your apartment were blocked. Someone had wedged triangles of wood beneath them — you know, like door stoppers?"

I sucked in a breath. Someone had tried to kill me. They'd really tried to kill me. I'd guessed that as well, but hearing it and guessing it were two different things.

"Hey, are you okay?"

"Yeah. I'm fine."

But he grasped my elbow and led me inside a room packed with desks. Tom sat me behind a battered wooden desk stacked unevenly with documents. The Doyle newspaper was not a paperless office — something I was counting on.

"So you hadn't heard about the door." His hand lingered on my arm, then he lowered himself into a rolling, wooden chair across from me.

I shook my head. "No, and I won't tell anyone you told me. I wish I could give you a scoop in repayment, but I don't have one. I came here looking for information."

"About the arson?"

"That, and the Bell and Thistle." The fairy might not be my immediate problem, but I needed to do something while my brain set the puzzle pieces into place.

"The Bell and Thistle?" His dark brows rose, and he braced his elbows on his knees.

"Your newspaper wrote an article about it on May 21, 1966. It was sort of a retrospective. There was a photo in the article from the 1920s. But the microfiche in the library is damaged, so I couldn't get a good look at the picture. Do you think the paper might still have a copy?"

He gazed at the battered file cabinets, the paper files piled high on desks, and laughed. "Are you kidding? The publisher won't let us throw anything away. And he doesn't believe in computer files — says one good electromagnetic pulse will wipe 'em out. One good fire will do the same to paper. Wait here."

Rising, he ambled to a collection of file cabinets against the rough, brick wall.

I rubbed my damp palms on my jeans. Would he have a decent photo? Would it matter if he did?

He stooped, and a metal drawer screeched. A few minutes later, he returned to me with a manila folder. "Here. We've got the original background materials, but not the printed article."

I took the folder from him and looked inside. A typed copy of the original article. Clippings from past articles about the Bell and Thistle. The reporter's notes, scrawled in pencil. And a curled photo.

Holding my breath, I flipped it over. Six people in a row. They wore 1920s era clothing, hats and coats and wide-heeled shoes. I scanned the faces and frowned. "Do you have a magnifying glass?"

"I think one of our old-timers does. Just a sec." He strode to another desk and rummaged through a drawer. "Eureka!" He brandished a rectangular magnifying glass and handed it to me.

"Thanks." I looked through it at the photo, and an icicle pierced my core. My fist tightened on the glass's plastic handle.

"What's wrong?"

I swallowed. "Nothing." Everything. The woman in the photo in the chic dress and flowered hat was Doc Toeller. The woman who'd delivered us. The woman who would have let Lenore die inside our mother, had it not been for a nurse... Acid burned my throat.

"Hey, let me see."

Reluctant, I handed him the photo and glass.

He squinted at the picture. "It kind of looks like old Doc Toeller. Must be a relative." He flipped the photo over and frowned. "Usually they write names on the back of the photos, but this is blank. Huh. Think Doc Toeller would like a copy of this?"

Oh, God no. And short of casting a forgetfullness spell on him — which would be unethical — I didn't know how to stop him from blabbing. "She doesn't strike me as the sort who's interested in the past," I said quickly.

"She's in the Historical Association."

Hell. But even if he did show her the photo, he assumed it was a relative. Tom shouldn't be in danger. But if he told her I'd found the picture... Well, Belle/Doc Toeller/whatever was already after us. This couldn't make the problem worse, could it? "Anyway, I'd like a copy. Can I get one?"

"Sure."

I followed him to a photocopy machine, its plastic edges gray with dirt. It hummed and rattled and spat out a paper. I snatched it from the tray, the paper warm from the machine. "Thanks."

"If you need anything, anything at all, let me know." His jaw tightened. "I already miss Ground. We've got to get you back in business." He snapped his fingers. "Hey, what about a fundraiser?"

"Let's see what the insurance company says first. They're still processing the claim."

"Has the building owner said anything to you about reconstruction?"

I nodded. I'd called the man yesterday. "He has insurance, so he's ready to rebuild. It's just a matter of getting permits and organizing the construction."

"The permits won't be a problem. Doyle's not going to go without its coffee fix."

"I hope you're right."

He grinned. "You've got the power of the press behind you. Of course I'm right."

I thought of all the people who'd helped me salvage things from Ground, and my eyes warmed. Doyle might be fairy cursed and its people not quite human, but they were good people. I was lucky.

Folding the paper, I stuffed it in the pocket of my borrowed jacket. "Thanks."

I hurried outside and walked down Main. The Sunday tourists were out in full force, their noses red from a Saturday on the slopes, wine tasting, or both. A couple walking a blue-eyed husky passed me and smiled. Automatically, I smiled back and kept smiling until I saw the cluster of gawkers outside Ground.

Veering right, I turned into the alley and approached my coffee shop from the rear. I couldn't blame the town for gawking, but I wanted to be alone with Ground and my thoughts.

In the alley, a man in a bulky jacket stood staring at the wreckage. My heart skipped a beat. Brayden.

He turned at the soft echo of my footsteps, his bronzed face worried. "Jayce." Wordlessly, he pulled me into a hug.

I rested my head against his chest.

"I'm so sorry," he said. "I tried calling you."

I didn't answer. My charger had been in my apartment. My phone was DOA – buying a new charger was just another thing I'd have to deal with.

"This was intentional," he growled. "I read the article. It said the investigation was ongoing."

"It will be all right." The sound of his heartbeat was a comforting thump.

"I should have been here," he said.

"You couldn't have known—"

"No." He stepped away from me and laid his broad hands on my shoulders. "I should have been here, with you. It's always been you, and I'm sick of guilt and fear keeping me from the one person I want to be with, the one person I should be supporting. I love you, Jayce."

My eyes burned. "I love you too." And I gave in to reckless Jayce, the Jayce who didn't care about consequences. I kissed him, indulged in the hardness of his lips, in the joy spiraling through me, in the fire burning my mouth.

Unbidden, magic rose inside me. I could feel the turn of the earth, the wheel of the stars, invisible above us. Everything dropped away, and there was nothing but Brayden. And then I remembered.

We broke apart, gasping.

"We shouldn't," I said. I'd promised myself this was the end.

"Why?"

"You can't believe in the curse, and I won't lose you. Not that way."

"Jayce, it doesn't matter," he said, his green eyes serious. "Don't you understand? Even if I knew being with you meant I'd be dead in a year, I'd do it."

"But if you really believed that—"

He pulled me into his arms again, his kisses slow, determined.

"Brayden," I murmured. He knew, he believed, and he didn't care. "We can't. It's dangerous."

"You asked me to trust you," he said into my ear. "I do. Now trust I know what I want, and I know what I'm doing."

Heat blossomed in my chest. I loved him because of his strength and determination. How could I deny him now? "Are you sure?"

"Never more so." His lips brushed mine, and my knees trembled. "What are you going to do about this?" He nodded toward the ruined building.

"I think... it's time we end this." It was time to face Melanie and this time on my terms.

He looped an arm over my shoulder and kissed my forehead. "Thanks."

"For what?"

"For saying 'we.'"

CHAPTER 30

Brayden curbed his Jeep's wheels on the steep street, dusted with snow.

Stepping from the car, I slipped on a patch of ice and grabbed the open door for balance.

"Careful." Brayden walked around the Jeep, and I tucked my arm in his, tried not to notice the hard planes of his muscles, his cedar smell.

The gate to the Zana house stood open, and we walked into the garden. The lavender bushes were powdered white spikes.

I gripped his arm. We weren't alone.

Her back to us, Rasha stood on the front porch. She pounded on the door. "Melanie?" The gray wool slacks and black turtleneck she wore accentuated her tall, slim figure. Her dark hair, up in a loose bun, added to her height. A red, wool scarf draped over her shoulders.

"She's not home?" I asked, climbing the steps to join her.

Rasha turned to us. "She should be. We were supposed to meet for lunch. But she's not answering her phone. She's been so depressed after Matt's... death. You don't think something's happened to her?"

A chill breeze set the white-dusted lavender swaying, and a cold sliver of worry slipped between my ribs.

Brayden peered through a window. "I'll check around back." He hurried down the three steps and around the corner of the house.

"What are you doing here?" Rasha asked me.

"We came to check on Melanie," I said. "She stopped by Ground yesterday."

She lowered her head and studied me. "Did she? Why?"

"Curiosity, I think. The whole town seems to have come to check out the damage."

Her mouth crimped. "That fire. Awful. What will you do now?"

"I'll know by the end of the week." I tried to peer through a gap in the curtains, but all I saw was an empty lounge chair in the green-carpeted living room. A plaid scarf had been thrown across the chair's arm. I straightened from the window. "The property owner has hired a contractor to take a look at the building. He's planning on rebuilding, but we don't know how long it will take."

"Jayce!" Brayden shouted.

Glass shattered, and I started.

Rasha and I raced down the steps and around the corner of the house. We bumped shoulders in a narrow side yard stacked with garden tools, and ran into a grim backyard. A thin layer of snow covered the lawn. Broken glass glittered on the brick patio. One of the tall, sliding glass doors had been broken out.

Inside the house, Brayden knelt beside Melanie, sprawled on a beige-colored carpet. He pressed two fingers to her neck.

"Oh, my God," Rasha said. "Is she okay?"

"Call nine-one-one," Brayden said brusquely.

She turned away and dug in her shiny red purse for a phone.

I clutched the straps of my own purse. Melanie's skin was pink, so she was still alive. An empty glass lay on the carpet beside her.

Stomach roiling, I stepped through the broken, glass door, but he shook his head.

Brayden rose and walked to me. "I think we should wait outside."

"But..." Mouth slack, I stared, confused. He was a paramedic. Paramedics didn't walk away from injured people.

"She's gone." He put an arm on my elbow and guided me into the backyard.

"What? That's not possible. She..." Numb, I motioned toward Melanie. Matt's wife stared, blank, at the ceiling. "But she looks so alive."

"Her breath smells like almonds. The flushed skin... I read about this in med school. I think she might have taken poison. Cyanide."

"Where would she get cyanide?" I asked, sickened and disbelieving.

"Apple seeds maybe? I don't know."

A siren wailed in the distance.

Another death. If I'd been faster, more determined, Melanie might not have died.

"They'll be here right away." Rasha tucked the phone into her purse. "How is she? Why aren't you working on her?" she demanded.

"I'm sorry," he said. "She's gone."

Sheriff McCourt and two uniformed deputies — Hernandez and Owen — rounded the corner.

"Where is she?" the sheriff asked.

I blinked. Even for a small town like Doyle, the appearance of the cops had been suspiciously quick.

Brayden pointed to the house, and the sheriff walked inside, her boots crunching on the broken glass.

"Who broke the sliding door?" she barked.

"I did." Brayden gestured toward the ragged shards of glass, still clinging to the door's metal frame. "I thought she might be alive."

"You got here quick," I muttered to Hernandez.

He shook his head. "We were already on our way," he said in a low voice.

"How?" I whispered.

"We were coming to bring her in."

CHAPTER 31

Rasha reeled away from us and buried her head in her hands. "Mel knew you were coming to arrest her. That's why she did it!" Her shoulders quaked.

Uneasy, I rubbed her back. Melanie must have had had the answers all along. If I'd only pressed her, followed up more quickly...

"You two." The sheriff nodded to the deputies. "Take the ladies' statements. I'll speak with Mr. Duarte."

The deputies separated us, taking Rasha and I to opposite corners of the yard. Staring at the tracks we'd left in the thin snow, I told Hernandez what I'd seen.

"Why did you come here at all?" he asked.

I hesitated. "I didn't feel Melanie was guilty, but I suspected she might know something."

He grunted. "Looks like your feelings were off."

But had they been? "The sheriff thinks it's suicide, doesn't she?"

On the brick patio, the sheriff spoke with Brayden. He shook his head violently.

"We can't jump to conclusions," the deputy said. "That's why we have autopsies. Come on." He led me to the patio, where Rasha stood shivering. Brayden removed his thick jacket and draped it over her shoulders.

Had my feelings been off? My sense of wrongness intensified. "This isn't right," I muttered.

The deputy's expression shifted. "What do you mean?"

I struggled for words. Feelings weren't worth a lot to a cop or to a court. I needed to find my inner Karin and apply some logic. "Matt was a blackmailer — not for money, for favors and a sense of superiority. He had no money. The only way he could have become a partner with Eric was if he'd blackmailed his way into it."

"That's not true," Rasha said.

"Which part?" I asked. "You told me yourself Matt was flat busted. He was up for a big divorce settlement."

"That was just one of the reasons why Mel was depressed," Rasha said.

"Melanie struck me as more angry than depressed." I gazed at the broken glass scattered across the brick patio. A barbeque covered in dust, its lid askew, stood beside a half-dead, potted fern.

"Which would explain why she killed her husband and his lover," Hernandez said.

I shook my head. "But she wasn't the only one with a motive. Matt was blackmailing Eric."

Rasha hissed an indrawn breath. "He wasn't!"

"I'm sorry," I said, "but he was, though I couldn't figure out why. The only dark moment I could find in Eric's past was that old drunk driving accident that killed his first wife."

Rasha raised her chin. "That wasn't his fault."

"I looked into that." Hernandez nodded. "But Eric's wife had been driving, and it was old news. Literally."

"Don't you think that's a little strange though?" I asked. "That his wife was driving? Does Eric strike you as the sort to give up the wheel of a Porsche? What if Eric had been driving? What if he moved his dead wife into the driver's seat?"

"Speculation," Hernandez said. "There's no evidence of that."

"Have you checked?" I asked. The cold seeped through the soles of my new, almost-sensible shoes.

"I have," the sheriff said.

We turned toward her.

"One of the officers on the scene believed there was more to the accident than there appeared." She removed her wide-brimmed hat and ran a hand through her hair. "But he never had enough evidence to prove it. His suspicions remained a note in the file." She replaced the hat.

"Matt was on the scene," I said. "He found Eric on the road that night after the crash. Maybe he saw what Eric had done. Maybe he helped, or even suggested moving Eric's wife behind the wheel."

"My husband wouldn't do that," Rasha snapped.

"Does he ever let you drive?" the sheriff asked.

She opened her mouth, closed it. "Of course."

"His sportscar?" McCourt asked.

"Well, that's his."

"I keep coming back to the old wellhouse property," I said. "There was so much controversy over it. The Historical Association was suing Eric to keep him from developing the property. Phoebe was on the deed only as a blind for Matt. She told me she thought she was in danger of being arrested because her name was on the deed. What she didn't know was she was in danger of being killed."

"My husband has lots of properties." A vein pulsed in Rasha's elegant jaw. "As a realtor, Phoebe was useful to him. He had no reason to kill her."

"No," I said. "But you might have."

Rasha blanched. "What? That's ridiculous."

"Is it?" I asked. "Phoebe told me Matt knew too many things. He'd told her everything, including the truth about Eric's long ago car accident." I wasn't sure about this, but Phoebe had told me Matt knew a lot. "So you killed them both to get them out of your lives. And then, when it looked like the cops might come for Eric — he's an obvious suspect — you pushed me and everyone else toward Melanie. You fed me all that information about the divorce, and Melanie's fury at Matt. And here you are now, at the scene of her death. You hadn't just arrived, had you? You were leaving after you'd poisoned Melanie. Then you saw us on the sidewalk, and you turned right around and knocked on Melanie's door."

"Of course not." Rasha's dark eyes turned flinty.

Head cocked, Sheriff McCourt rested her hand on the butt of her gun.

"Is it?" I asked. "As ridiculous as you giving your husband an alibi for Matt's murder? You told me he was with you that night. Later, Eric admitted he wasn't. At first I thought you were trying to protect him. But you were giving yourself an alibi as well, weren't you? You are protective of Eric. That's why you killed Matt, and it's why you killed Phoebe, and it's why you killed Melanie and tried to make it look like a suicide."

"You're crazy," she said.

"Matt had called Eric to the Bell and Thistle for another bout of blackmail, hadn't he?" I asked. "But you got there early, saw an opportunity to rid yourself of an irritant, and took the tire iron from my truck bed and killed him. Then you took off with the body before Eric arrived, thinking you'd give him an alibi. But Eric messed up your plans. He never showed at the Bell and Thistle. Instead, he drove around and then went home."

"Leave Eric out of this." Her voice rose. "Melanie killed them. She killed them all!"

"No," the sheriff said. "Mrs. Zana had an alibi for Ms. England's murder. She was in an interrogation room. With me."

"But..." Rasha looked around the patio wildly. "You said you were coming to arrest her."

"We were coming to take Mrs. Zana into protective custody," the sheriff said. "Where were you the night of Matt Zana's death?"

"This is absurd," Rasha said. "If you're going to interrogate me, I want a lawyer."

"My only question is the car," I said. "It's a long walk between your house and the Bell and Thistle, and I didn't see your car in the lot. There's a turnout about a hundred yards from the pub. You could have parked there. It was a damp night. I'll bet there are still tire tracks."

"You witch!" She lunged for me.

Brayden and Hernandez leapt between us. Hernandez pulled her away, struggling and snarling. Her scarf slipped to the patio, puddling in a crimson pool.

"Rasha Gertner," the sheriff said, "you're under arrest for attempted assault.

We may have more charges once we investigate that turnout."

Hernandez cuffed the woman, and she went limp.

"But..." Brayden's brow creased. "That doesn't make sense."

"Oh?" the sheriff asked.

"If Rasha parked in the turnout," he said, "then it was premeditated. She was trying to hide her car, and then she laid in wait. But she used Jayce's tire iron. She couldn't have known it would be there."

"She's tall enough to easily see inside that bed," I said. "Maybe she brought a different weapon, but she saw an opportunity to shift the blame onto someone else by using my tire iron." Karin wasn't the only logical sister in our trinity. Even though it was wrong, I felt a twist of angry triumph. I'd beaten a killer.

"This isn't over," Rasha screeched. "You're not safe. You'll never be safe!"

Hernandez shook his head. "You should never make threats in front of cops."

But it wasn't an empty threat, and a tide of fear swept my skin. The curse wasn't done with us.

CHAPTER 32

"Doctor Toeller is the unseelie?" The blood drained from Karin's face. Abruptly, she dropped onto our aunt's ivory sofa and gasped, pressing a hand to her side. The photocopy fell limp from her hand.

"Karin!" I leapt to the sofa, but she waved me off.

"I'm okay." She panted. "I just moved too fast."

"You're not okay," Lenore said. "You're recovering from a gunshot wound."

Karin rubbed the back of her neck and shivered, then looked up, her eyes haunted. "The doctor was in our house. She treated Aunt Ellen! Did she...?" She looked away.

"Ellen had cancer," Lenore sat beside her and took her hand. "We can't blame anyone for that."

"Can't we?" Karin asked bitterly.

"At least we know now," I flopped into an arm chair and crossed my denim-clad legs. We'd been lucky Toeller hadn't been at the hospital when Karin had been brought in. My stomach tightened. If Toeller had been involved in the surgery, would Karin have recovered?

"A celebration's in order," I said, not really feeling it, but this was a win. It needed to be recognized. "Rasha's been caught." It had only been by luck or magic she hadn't killed Karin. And poor Phoebe – her parents, stunned and pale, had come to collect her body yesterday. How many other people would she have hurt to protect her husband? "And now we know to watch our backs around Toeller."

"And we will," Lenore said, dour.

Karin smiled. "Drinks are definitely in order, especially now that I'm free of the hospital."

"An even better reason to celebrate," I said.

"Where to?" Karin asked.

"The Bell and Thistle." I tugged on the collar of my new, emerald turtleneck. The fabric was soft, but the room was a little too warm.

"I don't know." Lenore rubbed the thighs of her white slacks. "That pub's connected to her, somehow. Maybe we should leave it be."

"The Bell and Thistle is a part of Doyle," I said. "And I'm not going to let Toeller scare us away from one of the only three bars in town."

"How would we survive with only two?" Karin laughed and lumbered to her feet. "I'll drive."

"No way," Lenore said. "Your car is too small. I'll drive."

Karin smirked. "That's makes you designated driver."

"I don't feel like drinking anyway." Lenore raised her nose, haughty and totally lying.

We strolled outside, Karin leaning on Lenore, and piled into the Volvo. The moon had not yet risen, and stars blazed in the crystalline sky.

Lenore buckled up, started the car. "I know there's a connection between the unseelie and the Bell and Thistle – that photo you found proves it. But why would Doc Toeller care about keeping the Bell and Thistle a part of Doyle?"

"I wonder if it has to do with boundaries?" Karin asked from the backseat.

Lenore drove onto the highway. Tall pines flashed past in the headlights.

"She can't operate outside Doyle." And the more I thought about it, the stranger that seemed. "Why is that?"

"I've been researching fairies," Karin said.

"You mean unseelies?" I raised a brow, needling.

"Most of the lore comes from England," she continued, ignoring me. "But there's a belief that the old Roman roads disrupted the fairies somehow. They were the first sign of human civilization, and somehow, the boundaries of fairyland and our boundaries are linked. According to the literature," she added.

"Okay," Lenore said, "We know what we're dealing with, and we know who it is. Now what? Did your literature tell you how to get rid of a fairy?" Lenore adjusted her long, off-white knit duster, pulling it closed.

Karin barked a laugh. "Sure. Set them on fire, force nasty potions down their throats. We can't do that to the doctor. We're not killers, and she's..." she waved her hands. "She's the doctor."

I pondered that, feeling slightly sick.

"And she told me..." Karin trailed off.

"Told you what?" I asked sharply. "You spoke with Toeller? When?"

"In the hospital. She checked in on me."

I swore. The doctor had been so close at our most vulnerable moments.

"What did she tell you?" Lenore asked.

"I'm pregnant."

Elation and horror tangled inside me. "Pregnant." No wonder Toeller hadn't tried anything in the hospital. She didn't have to. For our family, pregnancy was a death sentence. And then anger came, even though I knew it was wrong. How could Karin have been so reckless? I grimaced. How many times had she said exactly those words to me?

"I don't know how it happened," Karin said into our silence. "We were so careful. You don't think the unseelie... She couldn't have, could she?"

"Of course not," Lenore said quickly. "Accidents happen, and this is a wonderful one." Lenore reached an arm over the seat and grasped Karin's hand. "Congratulations. Does Nick know?"

It was a better response than mine, and I hunched, fiddling with the radio until I reached a rock station. I watched my sister in the rearview mirror.

"Thanks. Nick knows." Karin touched her stomach. Joy threaded her voice, but there was fear too. "We've decided on a June wedding to keep this baby legit."

"That's wonderful," I said, my throat tight. A baby.

"Doctor Toeller's expecting to deliver the baby," Karin said, her voice choking.

"You can't let her!" I said. "For all we know, the doctor is the real reason every Bonheim woman has died in childbirth."

"I know," Karin said. "And I'm worried about Nick. If anything happens—"

"Nothing will happen." I forced confidence into my voice. "And if it's true Toeller's got no mojo outside of Doyle, you can leave. Just leave Doyle." It was such an easy answer. Why hadn't we considered it before?

A truck barreled toward us on the opposite side of the highway, its lights blinding. Wincing, Lenore pulled down the visor. The truck roared past.

"How far along are you?" I asked Karin.

"Only a month."

So we had a deadline. "We know who the problem is now," I said. "We'll fix this. And if you have your baby outside—"

"I'm not sure the curse will be that easy to break," Karin said.

"I thought learning who the unseelie was would make things clearer," Lenore said. "It hasn't."

"I wonder what her interest in the wellhouse property is?" Karin asked, changing the subject.

"At least we know she has an interest in it," I said. Maybe we knew more about old Doc Toeller than we thought. "Now I really could use a drink."

One corner of Karin's mouth slanted upward. "As thrilled as I am that you're no longer a murder suspect and the woman who shot me is in jail..." She frowned. "Rasha did burn down Ground, didn't she?"

"Yes, she confessed," I said. "She was trying to kill me. As a handyman, Matt had access to keys, and he made copies of them whenever he could. After Rasha killed Matt, she took the keys from his pocket. Ground's was on the ring. That's how she got inside to plant the tire iron and later, to splash gasoline around and set the building on fire."

"She did all that for her husband?" Lenore shivered. "Love made her a monster."

"She made herself a monster," I said. "Don't blame love."

"But how did Rasha get Matt's body inside your truck?" Lenore asked.

"She had practice," I said. "She mentioned that she'd taken care of her dying mother. She learned how to move dead weight then."

"But how'd she get into your pickup?" Karin asked.

"When she was a minor," Lenore said, "she and her boyfriend got into some trouble with the law. He was a car thief. Her records are sealed, but I'm guessing she learned a thing or two."

Karin and I stared at her.

"What?" she asked.

"Where did you hear that?" I asked.

"From Deputy Hernandez. I told you, he likes to read. Urban fantasy, mostly."

"I still don't understand this rose rabbit business," Karin said from the backseat.

I twisted to face her, the seatbelt pinching my chest. "Neither do I, but whatever he or it is, the rose rabbit exists, and it's a part of this."

"He needs our help," Lenore muttered.

Karin darted a worried look at me. "What?" she asked.

"We'll find him," Lenore said.

"That wasn't what you said," Karin said.

We flashed past the welcoming sign to Arcadia.

"It's just a sense I have," Lenore said. "That he can help us, if we help him." She glanced at me. "Brayden told us about his mother's car accident."

My pulse grew loud in my ears. "Oh."

"It must have been a terrible burden for a small boy," she said. "No wonder he had trouble dealing with it as an adult."

I sucked in my cheeks. "None of it was his fault."

"None of it was his mother's fault either," Lenore brushed her blond hair behind one ear. "She was being manipulated, influenced, just like everyone else who enters Doyle."

"I can forgive his mother," Karin said. "It was an accident. But I'm not sure how I feel about absolving everyone just because of the fairy. We all have free will. Ultimately, we're responsible for our actions."

"It's more than that," I said. "The coincidence of her being on that road the same moment our father was… It's too much. Was it coincidence that Rasha murdered Matt beside my truck, using my tire iron? That I became a suspect in Doyle's second murder investigation in a year? That a town the size of Doyle even had so many murders within the space of a year?"

"No." Karin's voice was tired, flat.

"The people who were murdered," I said, "don't you see how convenient their deaths were for the doctor? Matt and Phoebe were opposing her on the wellhouse project, and they're dead."

"Eric was the lead on that project, and he's all right," Karin pointed out.

"He is now," I said, "but he could have easily taken the fall for the murders. And the deaths earlier in the year — Brayden's wife. She was writing an article on Doc Toeller before she was killed. She even was developing a geneology. Toeller couldn't have liked that. I'll bet Toeller was helping Rasha out on the sly too, masking Rasha's presence at Ground with her magic." It was the only explanation I could come up with. I'd tested myself over and over, and I hadn't lost my mojo. It had only failed when it came to Rasha.

"All right," Karin said hotly. "Maybe the killers were influenced or nudged. Maybe even manipulated. But Rasha still had free will. She was responsible for what she did, and I'm glad she's behind bars where she can't hurt anyone else."

Lenore came to the trailhead and slowed. In its parking lot, a red car glinted through the trees. We rounded the bend. Lenore swerved, sped up.

"What are you...?" I trailed off. Where the Bell and Thistle should have stood was a clearing surrounded by pines. And nothing more.

I frowned, confused. We'd somehow missed the pub.

"Did I space out and drive past?" Lenore asked.

"What's wrong?" Karin asked.

"The Bell and Thistle," Lenore said. "I swear that was the Redwood trailhead, right before the pub."

"It was," I said, too loudly. "Stop here." Breath quick and shallow, I unbuckled my seatbelt.

She bumped to a halt, and I leapt from the Volvo.

"Jayce, wait!" Karin shouted.

A bell tolled faintly, as if from a distance.

My eyes adjusted to the darkness. I found the narrow trail that cut over to the Bell and Thistle and plunged through the pines.

Lenore shouted something, but I kept going, fear driving me onward. The Bell and Thistle had to be here. Maybe its power had gone out, and that's why it had seemed invisible.

The trees thinned, and I plunged into a clearing filled with dried thistles. The cold air turned colder, murky. The prickly weeds clawed at my jeans, and I slowed, as if stumbling through tar.

The Bell and Thistle was gone.

Hair lifting on the back of my neck, I turned in the center of the weed patch. There, by that twisted pine, was where the pub entrance had been with its old, brass bell. And here, where I stood, had been the parking lot.

The pub was gone, a crater cracking the earth where it had stood.

If you enjoyed the book (and even if you didn't) please leave an honest review! A few sentences about what you did or didn't enjoy is all it takes. Other readers want to hear what you think. P.S. You needn't have purchased the book on Amazon to leave a review there.

Sign up for a free exclusive content, and author updates at kirstenweiss.com

Spell for Home Protection

Do a house cleaning, washing any windows in a clockwise direction and while working, meditate on the following mantra: I remove negativity from my home in my greatest and highest good.

When finished, take a shower, then sit in the center of your home and imagine a ball of white light inside your chest, expanding outward, outside your house, and pushing any remaining negative energy into a violet flame.

SPELLED BATH SALTS

You'll need:
1 C baking soda
2 C citric acid
1 C Epson salt
20 drops essential oil of your choice
3 T base oil like almond oil or coconut oil
4 T dried, crushed rose petals
2 T dried lavender petals
2, 5x7 muslin bags (optional)
A container with a lid

Stirring clockwise and meditating on your intentions (e.g. more self-confidence, grace and lovingkindness, or to radiate your inner beauty), mix the dry ingredients and make sure there are no chunks.

Add the oils a couple drops at a time, preferably using a dropper, or you'll activate the citric acid. Mix.

Put the mix into the container. Tuck the two muslin bags on top.

When getting ready for a bath, add half the mix to one of the muslin bags, tie it off, and set it in the water. The bags will keep the flower petals from getting all over the place, making for easier cleanup.

Bath salts are **for external use only.**

GET GROUNDED

Go outside on a warm summer day (do NOT do this on snow or ice). Take off your shoes and step onto earth or grass. Visualize your own roots sinking from your core, down through legs, through your feet, and into the soil. Take a deep breath. Feel yourself being grounded.

BOOKS BY KIRSTEN WEISS

The Witches of Doyle Series
Bound | Ground | Down | Witch | Fey |

Doyle Witch Supplements
Spirit on Fire | Shaman's Bane | Lone Wolf | Tales of the Rose Rabbit

Doyle Cozy Mysteries
At Wits' End | Planet of the Grapes

The Perfectly Proper Paranormal Museum Cozy Mysteries
The Perfectly Proper Paranormal Museum | Pressed to Death | Deja
Moo

The Riga Hayworth Paranormal Mystery Novels
The Metaphysical Detective | The Alchemical Detective | The Shamanic
Detective | The Infernal Detective | The Elemental Detective | The
Hoodoo Detective | The Hermetic Detective

The Mannequin Offensive

Pie Town Cozy Mysteries
The Quiche and the Dead | Bleeding Tarts

Sensibility Grey Steampunk Suspense
Steam and Sensibility | Of Mice and Mechanicals | A Midsummer Night's
Mechanical

ABOUT THE AUTHOR

Kirsten Weiss authors genre-bending stories of mystery, suspense, and enchantment.

She worked overseas for over fourteen years, in the fringes of the former USSR and deep in the Afghan war zone. Her experiences abroad not only gave her glimpses into the darker side of human nature, but also sparked an interest in the effects of mysticism and mythology, and how both are woven into our daily lives.

Now based in San Mateo, CA, she writes paranormal mysteries, blending her experiences and imagination to create a vivid world of magic and mayhem.

Kirsten has never met a dessert she didn't like, and her guilty pleasures are watching Ghost Whisperer reruns and drinking good wine.

You can connect with Kirsten through the social media sites below, and if the mood strikes you, send her an e-mail at kweiss2001@kirstenweiss.com.

Follow her on Twitter: @KirstenWeiss

Check out her story world boards on Pinterest: www.pinterest.com/kirstenweiss/

Sign up for her newsletter for cool free stuff and book updates at: kirstenweiss.com

Made in the USA
Coppell, TX
04 February 2021

49566648R00115